There's Something About Vegas

EMBER-RAINE WINTERS

ACKNOWLEDGMENTS

I have the best family in the world! They put up with my crap and are super supportive. Especially, my mom and sister. They are the best!
The best Goodreads group ever! Particularly authors Annie Arcane and Jane Blythe. You ladies have helped me so much in the last few months! Thank youuuu!! Mwah!
Last, but not least my editor, Randie Creamer. editorrjc@gmail.com I couldn't do this without you! Thank you so much!

Dedication

To my parents, thank you for never letting me get in a situation like this one!

Table of Contents

Acknowledgements

Dedication

Prologue: _____ 1

1. _____ 6

2: _____ 11

3: _____ 14

4: _____ 18

5: _____ 22

6: _____ 27

7: _____ 31

8: _____ 40

9: _____ 44

10: _____ 50

11: _____ 55

12: _____ 60

13: _____ 64

14: _____ 69

15: _____ 72

16: _____ 76

17: _____ 79

18: _____ 87

19: _____ 90

20: _____ 95

21: _____ 104

22: _____ 114

23: _____ 120

24: _____ 132

25: _____ 135

26: _____ 142

27: _____ 147

28: _____ 151

29: _____ 158

30: _____ 164

31: _____ 170

32:	177
33:	182
34:	185
35:	193
36:	198
37:	202
38:	210
39:	213
40:	219
41	223
42	231
43	235
44	239
45	238
46	249
47	253
48	257
Epilogue:	260

More Books By Ember-Raine Winters
Author Note
Are you stalking me?

Prologue

RISSA

Groaning at the injustice of the light pouring in through the blinds, I blinked rapidly. The opulent room was not one that I was familiar with. The bedroom of the suite alone was bigger than my apartment, and I had no memory of how I got there.

I left LA on a whim and drove to Vegas. Well, it wasn't a whim exactly, more like a poorly executed escape plan. I remembered checking into the crappy hotel room off the strip before hitting the club at the beginning of the night. Everything beyond that was a hazy bunch of nothing.

A groan that wasn't mine rent the room, but that wasn't all that startled me. A very male and very well-muscled forearm snaked out over my stomach. My mortification was swift—I never did stuff like that. I took a peak under the soft white comforter and blanched. *Oh no! What have I done?* Scooting out of the bed carefully, I was able to get out from under the arm without waking the male attached to it.

Searching the room, I found my clothes scattered across the

bedroom floor. I'm not too proud to say that I ran terrified into the guest bathroom and put my clothes back on, and I'm not even ashamed to admit that I left that hotel without a word or a backward glance.

I took the walk of shame back to my grungy hotel room on the exact opposite side of Vegas from where I woke up. Is it really a walk of shame in Vegas though? Plenty of people were walking the streets in their club outfits, but I was too exhausted and hung over to delve any deeper into that thought process. The only thing I was thinking the entire way to the hotel was, who the heck was mister well-muscled arm and what on earth happened the night before?

I was packed up within minutes of arriving back to reality. My phone was on the night stand and I cursed the number of missed calls I had from Wes—what an absolute jerk. How dare he call me repeatedly asking for forgiveness after what he did? We had been together for two years, and I had a feeling he was trying to use my connections to get ahead. If I never used my own connections to get ahead, why would I let him?

I hadn't brought much into the room with me. Everything I owned was in the back seat of my beat up old Chevy pick-up truck. Fleeing the scene of whatever happened the night before was the only thing on my mind as I threw my phone in my purse and headed out the door.

I was almost back to LA when the glare of the California sun captured my attention, light refracting off of something shiny. Looking around for the offending object, I noticed something suspicious on my left hand; the bottom dropped out of my stomach. I had to pull the car over on the freeway to keep from running my car off the road. The ring was probably two carats and flawless. I gawked at it as if it were a snake that was about to bite me. Some pretty colorful swear words came to my mind but I kept them to myself.

"Come on, you stupid phone, where are you?" I cursed my lack of organization as I rummaged through the thousand receipts looking for the phone I had literally just thrown in there hours before.

I was mortified by the idea that I had just escaped a horrible idea of marriage with a womanizer only to jump into it drunk in Vegas with a complete stranger. *What in the actual crap is wrong with me?* I was still berating myself for my monumentally stupid decision when my phone rang and I cringed. The only good that came from another call from Wes was that I found my phone. Cancelling the call, I dialed the only person that I could share my idiocy with.

"Rissa? Where the hell have you been? Wes has been blowing my phone up since like noon yesterday."

"Oh my God Cassie. I think I have done something really, really bad," I shrieked, completely ignoring any reference to Wes the weasel.

"Do I need to bring a shovel to your place? I'm telling you that douche nugget completely deserves it, and I will totally help you hide his body."

I laughed then. I couldn't help it. I knew there was a reason I called her my BFF. She always helped me put things in perspective. Plus, I loved her colorful use of the urban dictionary.

"No, no shovels are needed. The douche nugget is very much alive."

"Damn, I was hoping I would have a reason to use the wood chipper I rented after you called me yesterday," she sighed dramatically.

"Nope, what I did may just be worse than killing that cheating butthead."

She laughed at that. "Babe, we need to work on your language skills, or lack of them."

"Cassie. I am sitting on the side of the freeway having a panic attack. Can you focus? Please?"

"Wait, what? Why are you sitting on the side of the highway?

3

Where are you going?"

"It's not where I am going—it's where I have been…" I groaned as images of that arm—sexy as it was—snaking around my waist came back to the forefront of my mind. "I went to Vegas yesterday."

"And? What happened in Vegas?" she asked tentatively.

"Let's just say that in this case what happened in Vegas isn't likely to stay there."

"No, you did not pull a Carrie, did you?" She gasped into the phone so loudly, I had to pull it away from my ear.

"Yup, I absolutely did. At least I think so. There is a huge rock on my hand, and I woke up next to an insanely hot forearm. I couldn't tell you for the life of me how the rock or the forearm got there."

"You woke up next to a forearm? You didn't even look at the guy's face?"

"Nope, I was so freaked out I just bolted."

"*What?* So you have no idea who you are married to?"

"I didn't even see the ring until right before I called you," I yelled, exasperated.

"You don't just wake up naked next to an insanely hot forearm and not look at the face attached to it!"

"I was freaked out okay?"

"Well, now you can tell that asshat Wes to take a hike, that you obviously can't marry him because you are already married."
Bitch was enjoying this!

"No. No one is ever to find out about this. It will ruin my career before it ever starts. Swear to me. Not a soul," I warned.

"Honey, you know I'm just messing with you. Do you need a place to stay? I'm assuming you're not staying with the ass clown anymore?"

I giggled again at the use of her Wes descriptions and shook my head. "No, we are done. I don't want to put you out though. I might go stay with mom for a bit."

She sucked in a sharp breath. "No, I'm not subjecting you to all that. Come to my house. No arguments," she said and hung up. Knowing who my over-the-top mom was and how I loved her, yet she could rule all the Western hemisphere with her eyes closed, I was totally taking Cassie up on her offer. Besides, if anyone could figure out I was hiding something it would be the ruling queen of Hollywood.

Despite the shock of not even knowing my new last name, I felt good about my future. Life was going to be going my way from that moment on. I just knew it.

RISSA

5 years later...

I woke up alone in bed soaked in sweat and completely turned on. I never could see the man's face, but his dark hair and chiseled body were that of the Greek Gods, and I always woke up with my hand in my panties after a dream like that.

I didn't know why I kept having that same dream night after night, and had no idea where it came from, but it was the hottest dream ever. I circled my clit remembering the muscled chest and abs hovering over me. The full head of dark hair I was tugging with my hands, keeping his mouth from leaving my nipple that he was sucking into his mouth with the most delicious intensity. I felt him smile against my skin as he let go of it with a pop and traveled lower. He ran his tongue down my belly and I squirmed beneath him, nearly coming on the spot just from the graze of his teeth over the sensitive nub.

My phone rang, interrupting my leading man, and I leaned over to the edge of the bed and saw it was Joanie, my publicist.

"Joanie? Why are you calling me this early?" I grumbled groggily. "Darling, it is ten in the morning on a Tuesday. Why else would I be calling?"

"Dang it. My alarm didn't go off." I panicked and bolted upright, regretting the motion immediately when my head began to swim.

"Honey, you are the star of the show. They all know you were out at your engagement party last night. It's all over TMZ. Don't worry, I had your call time switched to noon. Take your time and get there by then. Bye, darling."

Flopping back on the bed, I rolled over wondering where Jake was. I was pretty sure my fiancé had gone to bed with me the night before, being it was our engagement party after all. Searching everywhere I could without actually moving because I wasn't ready to get out of bed yet, I noticed a small piece of my stationary propped on his pillow.

Honey,
Had to go to the studio early. See ya tonight.
Love ya,
Jake

Well that solved the mystery of the missing fiancé, I thought briefly before looking down at the huge ring on my left hand. It was a bit ostentatious, and I wasn't a fan of the way Jake operated—he knew I hated flashy things. Yet one more "mom memory" I just didn't need. The "literal" rock was way more diamond than anyone should wear on one finger. Jake was a rock star though, and he didn't listen when I told him I just wanted to be with him, but extravagant gifts were how he showed that he loved me, so I let him get away with it… sometimes.

The ring was nothing like the gorgeous two-carat beauty I got from the mysterious forearm… I gasped out loud. *Oh my God, I'm in so much trouble.*

Thankfully, Jake was gone and wasn't there to witness my immediate shock. I had a very big and very real problem that I needed to solve—like five years ago.

As I laid there wondering how I was going to get myself out of this mess, my phone started ringing. "Um… Cassie? I am in some deep dookey," I blurted into the phone.

"Rissa, babe?" She was laughing at me. "It's all right to curse sometimes. Especially when you realize you're already married. I was wondering how long it was going to take you."

She continued laughing and I literally growled into the phone. I mean, that was acceptable, right? It was barely ten in the morning. "You are being supremely unhelpful, Cass."

"I know, I'm sorry. It's just that you never get yourself in messes like this, oh well, except for the five-year-forearm." I'm pretty sure she was cackling by this point. "I wanted to enjoy it a while longer before we try to figure out how to get you out of this whole thing."

I rolled my eyes and huffed in exasperation. This was a serious problem and my best friend was making fun of me.

"I know you wanna curse at me," she taunted.

"No, I really don't."

"Not even a little?"

She loved it when I cursed, which was probably twice in our whole lives. My lack of colorful vocabulary was a pet peeve that she was constantly on my case about; however, she did not grow up with the queen of Hollywood like I did. Cursing wasn't allowed, and well, feelings were also high on my mom's list of "things to avoid."

"Nope," I lied. I really wanted to show her that I could actually curse, but it would just encourage her and her shenanigans.

"Damn, well one day you will curse at me, and I am going to video tape it and put it on YouTube." She laughed like a hyena. *How was this woman my best friend?*

"I will not and you will not. Can you focus please? I need ideas on how to find the forearm and get a quiet divorce, so Jake never finds out."

"Ugh, I still don't know why you agreed to marry that

ostentatious jerk."

"Stop, I know how you feel already."

"You do realize that last time I was right about the idiot you were with, right?" Okay, so her pet peeve may be my lack of extensive vocabulary, but my pet peeve was her damn smug tone. See? I can curse… just not out loud.

"Yes, yes I know. You were right about Wes, but can we *please* get back on track?"

"Fine. But, just so you know, when Jake shows his stripes I won't tell you I told you so only because I already did." *I'm telling you, smug!* "So," she continued, "how are we going to find the forearm?"

"I don't know," I sighed. "A couple years ago I hired a private investigator but he couldn't find anything."

"Why didn't you go down to Vegas then and find out for yourself?"

"I tried remember? But all my current identification says Honey Davies now. They won't believe that I am really Rissa Taylor, especially once the look at me."

"Oh, yeah I can see that," she replied quietly. The phone was silent for a minute. "What are you going to do?"

"I don't know."

"Do you have a copy of your birth certificate?"

"Somewhere? Maybe? Why?"

"Riss… I thought you were the smart one. Take all your paperwork down there with your ID and make them show you the marriage certificate."

"But then, they will know who I am, and the tabloids will have it all over the front page. Cass, I am Hollywood's good girl. I can't let them tarnish my reputation over something stupid I did when I was twenty-two. I finally got my career on track, all without my mother's name. Plus, Jake will find out."

"Shit, I guess I'm still thinking like a normal person, not Hollywood's newest starlet."

9

"Ugh, I have a call time in an hour that I have to get ready for. Call me when you decide you have something helpful to contribute." I know I shouldn't be annoyed with her, since my impending doom was my own fault, but Cass was the only person on the planet that knew what I'd done.

"I'm sorry Riss, I didn't call to harass you, I swear. I just wanted to make sure that you're gonna be at my opening tonight?"

"Of course, it's already on my schedule. I will see you at seven."

"Is Jake the jerk coming?"

"No, and don't call him that. He is recording all day; it will probably run late," I murmured, not wanting to give her any more ammunition against my fiancé. "Talk to you later Cass."

"Bye, Chica."

CHAPTER 2

COLE

She haunted my dreams every day for the last five years.
Hovering over her I watched as she tilted her head back in
complete ecstasy. Her blonde hair was fanned out across the white
silk pillowcase. I couldn't help but reach down and draw one of
her perky nipples into my mouth, her hand gripping my longish
black hair. I smiled against her milky white skin and released her
nipple with a pop. She moaned as I kissed my way down her belly
and sucked her clit into my mouth. I groaned, never having tasted
anything so good in my entire life. I was addicted. Call me a
junkie. I'd gladly accept that title if it meant I got to taste her every
day for the rest of my life.

Then she was gone. She bolted sometime before I woke up and
I never saw her again. How do you have the best night of your life
and then everything comes crashing around your feet the next
morning when you wake up with a wedding band on your finger in
an empty hotel room?

It was as if my wife didn't even exist. I hired private investigators to look for her but she was nowhere. All I was left with were erotic dreams and sexual frustration for five years. No one held a candle to my Rissa—the idea of being with anyone else completely repulsed me. I knew I would find her, eventually. Rubbing the last dregs of sleep from my eyes, I heard my phone ringing from my night stand. "It is way too early for you to be calling me, dickhead."

"Morning to you too, brother." Jake laughed.

"What do you want?"

"Just making sure you're coming for the party on Friday. Honey is excited to meet you."

"I don't know, I'll try. Dad is having some investors coming in this weekend that I'm supposed to show a good time." I was not looking forward to meeting *Honey the fiancé.* Who named their kid Honey anyway? It sounded like a stripper name. And knowing my brother's taste, she was probably a porn star or something.

"Dude, tell dad that you already have plans and get one of your assistants to show them a good time. I'm getting married, and I want you to meet my fiancé."

"I'll talk to him about it," I lied.

"Good, I gotta go. I have a recording session."

"All right talk to you later, little brother."

After hanging up the phone, I got up from the bed with a raging hard-on that wasn't even lessened in the least from my chat with my brother. I swore to myself when I found that pretty little wife of mine we weren't leaving my suite for at least a week, maybe longer.

I went through my morning routine and put on the stupid suit that I hated. I hated wearing the damn things, but running the hot new Vegas hotel meant that I had to look the part. When I was young, the idea of running a five-star hotel and living in the penthouse was exciting. Wearing a suit every day seemed like a small price to pay for the amount of money and women that would line my pockets and grace my bed. Plus, I was good at it. But, as I got older the idea was less appealing. I wanted to settle down and the idea of wearing the damn suits every day for the rest of my life was cringe-worthy.

I dialed Mark, the private investigator that I hired five years ago, and he answered on the second ring.

"Cole, how's it going?" "I would be better if you had information for me."

"I'm sorry, Cole. She's a ghost. There is no information on her anywhere. It's like she disappeared off the face of the earth."

"What am I paying you for?" I growled into the phone.

"You're paying me because I'm the best. I always find my mark."

The word mark got my hackles up. Before running one of the family hotels, I was a Marine and a *mark* was someone you were looking to kill more often than not.

"She is not a *mark*." Angry flashes from my time in the military whipped across my mind.

"Shit, sorry Cole. I forgot."

"It's fine. Just find her. My brother just got engaged, and I want my *wife* found before the wedding."

Rissa Taylor, where are you?

RISSA

I was dragging and everyone noticed. Having an off day was the worst, and by lunch I was dead on my feet and there were still three hours left of filming yet to be done.

"Honey, darling. I had Vincenzo bring over my hangover cure for you. It works every time." Maria, my gorgeous Latina co-star, announced after the last scene.

"Thanks, but I don't have a hangover," I replied yawning as I stared down at my plate of unappetizing food.

"Oh, I see. Your stud of a fiancé kept you up all night?" She wiggled her eyebrows and fanned herself.

"What do you know about Jake?" I knew it was a stupid question. Jake had been a playboy before meeting me. His father was a big-time hotel owner—the likes of the Hilton's—and he grew up semi-famous before becoming a rock star.

"Let's just say you are a very lucky girl to lock that down." The way in which she tossed that comment at me as she handed me the Styrofoam container of whatever concoction she made gave me pause.

"Don't listen to her," Chris, one of the producers, said from behind me as I watched Maria saunter off. He plopped himself down on the bench next to me and started picking off my to-go container. "She's just jealous. She tried to lock Jake Moore down forever, and he didn't want anything more than a good lay from her."

"What?" I asked in shock. "He slept with her? *They slept* together?"

"Shit, I thought you knew." He paused before putting a pretzel in his mouth and looked uncomfortable. "Everyone knows. It was all over the rags. Honey, I tell you all the time to at least *Google* yourself once in awhile." He shook his head in dismay at my obvious ignorance.

"People are mean," I replied defensively. "And, most of the rags spout nothing but lies anyway."

"Whatever you say, Honey-bun."

"I don't think I'm going to eat this now." I pointed down to my food that Chris was slowly consuming. "If you're right about her, it could be poisoned."

"I'll get rid of it for you." He winked before taking the offending half-eaten takeout container from my hands.

"Thanks Chris." I smiled in gratitude.

"You're welcome Ms. Honey. Now go rest up so we can shoot this episode and go home. I have plans tonight," he mumbled as he shoved the remainder of the chicken salad wrap in his mouth and walked away.

I walked into my trailer, grabbed a bottle of water from the mini fridge, and collapsed on the couch. Pulling out my phone I wondered briefly if it was a good idea, but I decided to do it anyway.

Jake didn't answer.

"Hey this is Jake. I'm busy, so leave a message. I might call you back."

"Hey babe, I was just calling to check in and see what's going on. I'm getting ready to film, so I will see you after the gallery opening tonight. Love you."

The next phone call I made was easier. She picked up on the third ring. "You got any ideas?"

I leaned my head back against the couch and briefly pondered her question. "Nope" was all I had for her. "Just more questions." Cassie was the queen of tabloids. She read them like most read the bible—or a Nora Roberts book.

If anyone could give me the background info I needed, it was Cassie.

"Maria Santos," I said and heard her suck in a sharp breath. "So, it's true then? They dated? And you didn't think to tell me this?"

"What did that twatwaffle say to you?"

I giggled at the word choice but quickly sobered. "She made a suggestive comment and gave me some mystery drink for my supposed hangover."

"*Do not* eat anything that crazy bitch gives you," she all but yelled.

"I'm not a dummy," I giggled. "Chris got rid of it for me."

"Oh, thank God," she sighed. "The word is that she auditioned for your role and trashed the screening room when they gave the part to 'some unknown' instead of her," she informed me. "And, as for not telling you, I'd kinda hoped it was exaggerated. Guess not."

"Oh wow, so now she must be really mad." I ran my hand through my hair, not caring that I'd have to sit back down in makeup again before the next shooting.

"Yup, you walked in and took everything she ever wanted."

"Crud."

"The word you're looking for princess is shit. Say it. Just once. I promise I won't tell anyone," she coaxed.

"That's gonna be a no, nice try though."

"It was worth a shot. So, are you going to get rid of dick head yet?" she asked hopefully.

"They are over though, right?" I asked uncomfortably, thinking back to waking up alone and the no answer to my phone call.

"I haven't seen anything in the rags about Jake lately unless he is with you, darlin'," she grumbled. "That doesn't mean there isn't something going on though. Now that the engagement has been leaked, though, the paps are gonna be following him everywhere. You never know what they might find."

"Which means they will be following me too. How am I supposed to get a quiet divorce with reporters all over me all the time?"

"Shit, I didn't think of that, but I'm sure it will all work out, babe. Don't trip potato chip." She laughed into my ear.

"You're such a dork." I couldn't help but giggle with her. Since my mother's death, there wasn't a soul on the planet that knew me and understood me like Cassie did.

"You love me though."

"Of course," I answered automatically.

"Okay babe, I gotta go make sure people are doin' their jobs. See ya tonight, boo. Mwah."

"Bye hun, mwah back."

COLE

The day was a long one. With my brother's wedding looming above my head, something kept niggling at the back of my mind. I couldn't figure it out and that was what was bothering me the most.

I had phone conference with my father that morning but I couldn't focus. "How is the club renovation going?" he asked by way of greeting.

"Excellent. They are a week ahead of schedule." I smiled half-heartedly.

"Great news. I got a call from your brother this morning." I silently groaned. "He said something strange about investors. I think I would remember if I scheduled investors to come out there."

"Pops," I sighed. "Please? I just don't want to go and meet the latest bimbo after his money."

"Son, Honey is different. She's a good girl. I have never heard her say a bad word about anyone, and she is a very talented actress making plenty of money on her own. They are saying she is going to be huge."

"They have been together, what three months? Something just doesn't feel right."

"Cole, need I remind you of the girl you married and have been looking for the past five years? When you know, you just know." I could hear the smile in his voice. He loved reminding me of that.

Our father taught us everything we knew about impulsive behavior, being the stereotypical philanderer. He and my mom had a messy divorce, then he married and divorced Jake's mom when we were kids and he must have remarried five times since then. I wasn't sure, I had lost track over the years. Thankfully, I only wound up with one sibling from all those unions, and at the best of times my younger brother was enough to make up for at least five.

"No, pops. I have been reminded every night this week." I looked over across my desk to the "calming" fish tank, which wasn't very calming at the moment. "Just don't out me to Jake. I will get out there eventually."

"You better. I think you will like this girl. She is nothing like the girls he's dated in the past."

"You mean she's not a vapid money grabbing whore?"

"Exactly," my father said, not even shocked by my tone or phrase. "I think she will be good for him."

I watched the Nemo-like fish dart from one end of the tropical tank to the other. They didn't have to wear a suit or go visit their playboy brother and his endless parade of blonde bimbo bombshells. "I'll think about making a trip down there. Anything else?"

"Don't work too hard. I'll talk to you later."

"Bye, Pops." I hung up the phone, scrubbing my hands over my face.

Something was up with my brothers' fiancé. When it came to

Jake, wholesome and sweet were not qualities he looked for in a bed partner. He liked crazy. He got off on it. Perfect example, that Latina chick Maria was more his type then this girl my dad described. I knew something was up, but I had my own problems to deal with. Still, if this girl was actually as innocent as my father claimed, I felt bad for the poor thing; she'd wind up an unsuspecting victim in my crazy brother's scheme. But, for all I knew, Pops was wrong and she was crazy just like the rest of them.

My assistant, Ruthie, was on the line, pulling me from my thoughts. She was an older woman and the best assistant I could ever ask for—more of a mother figure really, than an assistant.

"Mr. Hillard," she said through the intercom, disdain dripping from her normally cheerful voice. "Mark is on the phone. He says it's urgent."

"Thanks, Ruthie." I chuckled quietly. For some reason, my sweet-as-pie assistant had a real hard-on against my PI. It was unusual for him to call twice in one week. Picking up the phone, I started getting excited. Maybe he found something.

"This is Cole," I said attempting to keep my calm.

"Cole, you have really stepped in it, man."

"What do you mean?"

"The girl? Her mother was Emma Taylor."

"*The* Emma Taylor? Like the leading lady of Hollywood? Shit, how did you find that out? I thought you scoured LA for any information on her," I asked more than a bit perturbed that it's taken him over five years.

"I broadened my search. She was born in New York City. She has never had anything in her name in LA, and attended boarding school in Connecticut, and then went to one of the finest acting academies in the world. There's nothing about Rissa Taylor since her mother passed four years ago, but she could still live in her mother's house in Beverly Hills. Do you want me to check it out?"

Wow, I never would have guessed she was related to Hollywood royalty. I was starting to second guess my ideas about this girl. "Yeah, keep an eye on the house and see if she's there," I said impulsively.

"Sure thing, boss."

I wondered, not for the first time, what the hell I was doing. Obviously she didn't remember what happened, or she wouldn't have bolted. Looking down at my cluttered desk, I needed to get back to work, but more importantly, I need to find my wife.

Everything else would sort itself out later.

CHAPTER 5

RISSA

I was going to kill Cassie when I found her in the chaos that was her gallery opening. Someone tipped off the press that I would be making an appearance. Cassie set up a red carpet and I had no idea why.

Reporters were screaming at me from both sides asking questions and trying to get me to pose for them. "Honey, where's Jake? What do you think of the rumors that he is still seeing Maria Santos? Do you have a comment?"

The bottom dropped out of my stomach, and I was so thankful security grabbed me and brought me inside before I could say something dumb. One of the things my mother taught me was to be the ice queen, and in situations like this with the press, it was the perfect persona, even though on the inside I was a complete wreck.

"Honey," Cassie said as I walked in the door. "I'm so sorry. I have no idea how they found out you were going to be here."

I looked at her skeptically, but didn't comment. She had no reason to lie to me. We never lied to each other, hence her always telling me about the guys I dated. "It's okay, they just caught me off guard. They asked something about Jake and Maria that had me pausing."

"What did that fucktard do?"

"Rumor has it he's still with Maria. I'm sure it's a misunderstanding. They are wrong. Jake loves me. He wouldn't cheat on me."

"Right, you keep telling yourself that, babe." A saccharin-sweet voice said from behind me.

I cringed. Cassie's eyes were huge, and she had a surprised look on her face.

"Hi Maria, how are you tonight?" I asked politely and put on a fake smile as she pulled me in for cheek kisses.

"Honey, Cassandra." Maria smiled in greeting while Cassie growled and said, "Who let the trash in?"

Maria laughed loudly. "Really Cassandra? You think you're cute don't you? Wait until I tweet about the rude owner of the Manhattan Gallery on Sunset to my ten thousand followers."

"It's all right Cassie, I got you babe." I patted her on the arm. "My hundred thousand followers will love to hear about all the amazing artwork and friendly staff."

"Holy crap! Were you just mean to someone?" Cassie whipped around to me in shock.

Was I? That wasn't actually my intention, I was just trying to defend my friend, but now that Cassie's said that, I can see how that could be interpreted. Looking over at Maria, I apologized, "Oh Maria, I didn't mean to. I'm sorry—that was really insensitive of me."

"Are you for real?" The look on her face was in direct contrast to the artistic beauty of her Dries Van Noten gown. "I'm basically telling you that I am fucking your fiancé and you are apologizing?" She shook her head. "This is no longer fun."

Grabbing a glass of champagne off the waiter's tray, she practically devoured the thing in one gulp before stalking off, probably looking for new prey. Honestly, I had no idea why she was acting like that—I really was sorry. Trumping her in the part for the show, and basically taking her ex-lover, I never should have mentioned the number of followers I had. It was insensitive of me, even if she was lying about she and Jake getting back together.

"Don't do that," Cassie said as she pulled me over to the bar. "You did the right thing. She was being a heinous bitch and is probably the one who spread the rumors to the rags."

The bartender came over to us, and I opted for the wine instead of the champagne. "I think I need to get away for a few days."

"Don't run." She nudged me in the shoulder, practically causing me to spill the glass the bartender just handed me. "Remember what happened last time?"

I shot her a glare and took a hefty gulp. "Don't... we don't talk about that, remember?"

"My lips are sealed. Come on let's mingle." She looped her arm in mine and dragged me around the room.

There were a ton of people, mainly artists and a few business men with their trophy wives. I had to dodge a couple creeps with wedding bands that were trying to flirt with me, but other than that it was a lot of fun and I am certain Cassie made a boatload of money off her paintings.

As the night wore down I was getting tired, so I went in search of Cassie. I noticed people looking at me funny and wondered what the deal was. It wasn't long before a message came through on my phone and I found out exactly what was going on.

The video took forever to load and it was grainy but bright enough that I could make out my bedroom, bed, and sheets. Maria, with her big fake boobs, was there spread eagle for the whole world to see. Laying on top of my comforter, completely naked, and playing with herself. But Maria's display is not what had me staring at my phone, it was Jake walking into the room, fully clothed and watching her.

"No!" I heard someone yell as if from far away. It must have been Cassie because the next thing I knew my phone was ripped from my hand and she was there with two big burly security guys. "Come on, babe." She grabbed my arm and began pulling me. "We will take you out through the back."

"What on earth just happened?" I asked as a million notifications came through on my phone.

"That, my dear, was me not telling you I told you so."

I stood there for a moment, my heels embedded in the carpeted floor. What I saw was real, and Cassie was again correct. "I gotta go," I murmured in a daze.

"I'm coming with you."

"What?" I looked down at Cassie, "No, you can't do that. What about your show?"

"That's what assistants are for. You're my bestie and you just found out that your fiancé is a lying cheating cuntcake. So, we are going to go away and have some fun and forget that douche nugget even exists." I was too absorbed with my new reality and the thoughts of what the next few weeks were going to be like between the press and trying to film with my new ex's current lover, that I didn't even process Cassie's most colorful language about Jake.

"Where are we going?" I asked but she was busy going through my phone.

"Joanie? It's Cassie. Yeah. We are leaving town for a couple days. Call the show and tell them she needs some time off." She paused. "Yep. We are getting out of here. I will make sure she's all right. No I'm not telling you where we are going. Why not? Seriously... because you're her publicist." Pause. "Um, no, I don't trust you not to leak our location to the press. Gotta go. Just make sure you talk to the studio. Bye."

"What are you doing?" Clearly, I was still in shock.

"Clearing your schedule. We are going to Vegas."

I blanched. "No, no, no. That's an insanely bad idea."

"Look at it this way," she whispered in my ear, dragging me out the back door, "you can't get married this time. Been there. Done that. Remember?"

"That is so not funny."

"Yet, it totally is!" She laughed, opening the driver's side door of her car. I just shook my head, then promptly stuck my tongue out at her.

Well, it was better than cursing.

COLE

It was late. Probably around eleven, and I was at the bar drinking away my misery when my phone rang.

"Seriously Jake? Normal business hours," I said into the phone exasperated.

"Dude, she's gone. That crazy slut Maria ruined everything and she's gone."

"Whoa, slow down. What happened?"

"That crazy bitch Maria posted a sex tape on Twitter!" He sounded frantic.

"How bad could it be? It was from before you got together, right?" I asked, but by the silence on the other end I was pretty sure I knew the answer.

"It was in Honey's bed."

That was about the worst thing he could have said. "You. Stupid. Moron. You cheated on her with that skank in her *own bed*? Well kiss that marriage, and the rock you shelled out a million bucks for. Goodbye." My brother was an embarrassment. If what Dad said was true, and this Honey girl was as good as gold, then I was secretly happy she found this out *before* she married Jake.

"The tape was totally misconstrued," he went on defending himself. "It didn't even show me touching her. It was a bunch of bullshit. I found that crazy bitch in Honey's bed and kicked her out."

"It doesn't change the fact that you still cheated on her."

"Cole, you have to help me get her back. I need her."

"Idiot. You should have thought about that before you cheated on her with that disgusting woman."

"Watch it," he barked.

"Wow, yeah if you're sitting here defending the whore, who ruined your marriage before it ever started, there's no way I can help you."

"Wait. The truth?"

"No, lie to me, dick."

"The relationship with Honey is a sham," he confessed. "My publicist was getting pissed because she kept having to clean up my messes, and the label was about to drop me. I decided if I started dating Hollywood's newest good girl it would help clean up my image."

Oh my God, did it really work this way in his world? Who thinks of doing that? Was she in on the scam too?

"Did she know about this? You and Dad keep saying she's such a good girl. I can't see a good girl agreeing to something like that."

Silence.

"No, she doesn't know. I wanted it to look authentic."

"You are a complete and utter tool. Do you know that, Jake?"

He continued, obviously not about to answer my question.

"Anyway, my publicist is the one who said I needed to take it a step further or no one would believe I had really changed. So, I proposed. But honestly, I don't even really like her that much.

She's too vanilla. She's too happy and too… nice." His shudder was obvious even through the phone.

"Are you seriously telling me that you used this girl to get ahead in your career, and you want me to help you get her back? You're a sadistic prick. I'm not helping you drag this poor girl through the mud."

"Come on, Cole? You're my brother. She is just some girl you have never met before, please?"

"Good bye, Jake." I hung up the phone in disgust. I couldn't believe my little brother was such an asshole. How could he expect me to help him ruin some girl's reputation like that? With the sex tape, her reputation was already destroyed, not to mention how the public will react to Jake's cheating. I found myself feeling bad for a girl that I had never met before. Knowing now what the publicist did to help his image, who knew what she would do to manipulate this into making Honey look bad and Jake somehow the hero.

Heading up to my suite, I felt my phone vibrate. "This is Cole."

"The girl is on the move."

"Mark? What do you mean she's on the move? You found her?"

"I found someone at that house, but I'm not sure if who I found is the girl you married. The person I'm looking at is a freaking superstar television actress."

"What? Are you sure?"

"Yup I'm positive. I sent you a picture. Tell me if that's the *wife* you are looking for."

It felt like an eternity before my phone pinged with a text message. All the air whooshed out of my lungs as I looked into the violet eyes of my missing wife.

"That's her. Who did you say she is?"

"What?" He nearly shouted at me through the phone. "Don't you recognize her?"

"I don't watch TV, Mark. Spit it out. Who is she?"

"That, my friend, is Hollywood's newest star… Honey Davies. Rumor has it she doesn't even curse. That's how much of a good girl she is." He chuckled as if it was just a Hollywood PR stunt.

"She doesn't," I replied robotically. "Her mother taught her it wasn't ladylike."

"Shit, so it is her.

The name kept running circle through my mind. *Honey* holy fuck! My wife is my little brother's fake fiancé.

"Shit," I cursed loudly, stomping down the hallway. The guests I passed were looking at me oddly, but I ignored them. I didn't care what they thought. Needing the privacy of my rooms, I continued on, practically running. This was not happening. How in the hell could my wife be the fiancé of my brother?

Fuucckkk.

"You're finally catching on, eh?" Mark asked.

"Yeah, follow her. I want to know where she's going."

"You got it, boss."

After I slammed the door to my suite, I burst into an uncontrollable fit of laughter. My brother and I were in a giant mess. He was trying to marry my wife, who he didn't even like, and I was trying to find my wife, who bailed on me. The same woman I never got out of my system over the last five years.

After getting myself under control and thinking back to the messed-up conversation with Jake, I flinched. Could it really be the same girl? The girl I remember was anything but *vanilla.*

RISSA

The drive to my house was a blur. I was seriously thinking about selling it after that awful video. I was completely numb, no tears, no screaming, and cursing didn't even cross my mind. Cassie was saying something, but I couldn't hear anything over the whooshing in my ears.

"What?" I asked stupidly.

"We are gonna have so much fun in Vegas. You will be like, Jake who?"

"Ugh, please don't even say his name."

"Sorry."

"Let's just get to the house. I need to start a bonfire with anything they may have had sex on."

"Babe? That could be the whole house, and as hot as the Beverly Hills Fire department is, I doubt they would be lenient towards you for burning your own house down."

"Shoot, you're right," I said in all seriousness. "Well, I need to grab some clothes. I will call an exterminator and order the world's largest can of Lysol in the morning, but the bed is definitely being burned."

"Ohh, do you have any marshmallows?' Cassie asked laughing hysterically.

"Like I would eat anything roasted over the mattress that those two slept on."

"I think that must be the most unforgiving thing you have ever said. I approve." Cassie winked.

"Just drive. I want to get this over with. I need a hot bath and a bottle of wine." The alcohol I consumed at the gala wasn't near enough to help me after finding out about Jake's betrayal.

"Now that is the best idea I have heard yet."

When we got to the house, the sensored porch light was on, so I knew someone had been there recently. It wasn't until we got closer that I saw the slim figure with a hand on her hip standing on the front porch.

I cringed. Cassie roared. "Are you fucking kidding me?"

"Cassie calm down. I'm sure there is a reasonable explanation."

"Bullshit. The only reason she is here is because she wants her ass whooped."

I tried to grab her arm before she got out of the car, but I missed. Cassie was marching towards the woman before I could utter another word.

"Crud," I said into the quiet and hopped out of the car and chased after her. "Cassie? Babe? You don't want to hurt her. You're not a violent person."

"Like hell I don't," she shrieked over her shoulder. "This bitch sits here and is all passive aggressive with you, then she leaks to the rags that she is still with *your* fiancé. She has the nerve to woof her shit at my gallery opening, and then when she gets shown up, what does she do? As if all that wasn't bad enough, she leaks a sex tape with your fiancé in *your* bed on Twitter. Believe me, she should have gotten her ass beat at the gallery. She has the nerve to come and gloat on your doorstep? Hell no." She turned to me just before she reached the porch steps and begged, "Let me punch her, just once?"

"No, you're not going to punch her. We are not violent people, Cass."

My friend looked between me and Maria and pouted out, "Fine."

We walked together the rest of the way up the steps.

"I left my panties on your floor. Can I get them please?"

"You stupid skank." Cassie started to lunge, but I grabbed her arm and shook my head.

"I've a better idea." I opened my phone and dialed. "Hi, this is Honey Davies. I have an intruder on my property," I said smiling sweetly, enjoying Maria's face blanch.

"Yes Ms. Davies, we will be there right away," the security officer said into the phone.

"Oh, sir, can you hold on a second? I think she might be leaving." I looked at her pointedly. "Never mind," I said back into the phone. "She's decided to leave on her own."

"Are you sure you won't be needing us, ma'am?"

"Yes I am sure, but could you patrol my house a bit more? I am going out of town, and I would hate for anyone to break in. Oh, and can you call someone to change the locks for me please? Jake Moore is no longer permitted on the property."

"Right away Ms. Davies."

Hanging up the phone, I looked over to Maria, who was still standing there. "I thought you were leaving? Should I call them back and tell them I need the police after all? Can you imagine what the rags will say in the morning when the police report gets leaked?"

"Fuck you, skank," she spat out as she walked down the steps. "But don't worry," she taunted, "I'll get my panties back from *Jake*, after he comes by later."

"Oh darlin', that's so cute that you think they won't be a charred pile of ashes by then," Cassie said, staring at her nails as if she was debating a new color.

I finger waved at her as I unlocked the door and went into my house, which needed a team of twenty in there like immediately—everything needed to be scrubbed down. I had no idea where else they had done it, but I needed rubber gloves, or better yet, a hazmat suit. It was a good thing that I was kind of a neat freak. I knew where all of the cleaning supplies were despite the fact that I had a cleaning service.

"I just need to get rid of my bed and anything else in my room they may have done it on. And, I need to box up the few things Jake left and leave them with security."

"Wait? You're giving him his stuff back?"

"Yeah? Why wouldn't I," I asked confused.

"Because you should burn it. We can take video and post it on YouTube," she said with an evil glint in her eye.

"Remind me to never get on your bad side." I laughed. "I'm not burning his stuff and posting it anywhere. That's just mean."

"Kill joy," she muttered, but with a smile.

I found a pair of cleaning gloves and an industrial sized trash bag in the laundry room and went to work stripping the bed of everything. "I really want to get rid of the mattress too, but I don't want to touch it."

"We can ask the cleaning service to take it out, and we will order you a new one before we get back," she said knotting up the bag with all the sheets and pillows. I had another bag beside me with my gorgeous down comforter, but no matter how much I loved that thing, it was definitely heading for the backyard bonfire.

"I'll call Cliff and ask him to coordinate timing and let the delivery people in."

Cliff was our interior designer friend, who also just so happened to be gay and not just gay, but an absolute diva, and we loved him to death. "Maybe I should ask him to just redecorate the whole room. I don't know if I will be able to step foot in here again after seeing that video, let alone sleep in here." I shuddered.

"Good idea. We can call him in the morning. I know he's not home right now. He supposedly had some important plans already for the night, which is why he was a no show at the opening."

After cleaning up everything that could possibly house anything offensive, complements of Jake and Maria, I looked around on the floor and sure enough there they were. A pair of black lace panties. I honestly thought I was going to be sick as I picked them up with a pair of tongs that I grabbed from the kitchen on my way to the bedroom.

"That fucking skank," Cassie swore when she saw the offending object.

"Yeah," I replied as I dumped them in the bag with the tongs and all. Anything touching anything would be burned with the rest of it.

Cassie walked out of the room with the two bags of trash, while I grabbed a box and dumped all of Jake's stuff in it. His cologne bottle may have broken on the way in the box. Oh well. It smelled like him and I heaved.

"What are you doing?" Jake asked from behind me.

Turning around slowly to gain my composure—I was an actress after all—I said, "What are you doing here, Jake? I figured Maria would have told you that I don't want you here." There, that was adult of me. No swearing, no yelling, just stating the facts.

"You saw the tape?" He had dread in his voice.

Looking him directly in the eye, and hoping it would be for the very last time, I stated, "Everyone in the world saw the tape, Jake. You made me a laughingstock. I want you to leave." Turning around, I couldn't look at him a moment more. I might throw up for real if I had to.

"It's not what it looks like, Honey! I don't know how she got in here, but when I found her I kicked her out."

"Save it Jake. Please just leave me alone." A tear threatened to fall, and I couldn't let that happen.

Another one of my mom's rules… never let anyone see you cry. I needed to be a good girl, but an ice queen at the same time. Emotions, especially in this industry as my mom knew full well, could be used against you.

"Please, baby," he begged, and I gasped quietly.

"No, not going to happen, Jake. Just take your things and leave. And, don't come back."

"Wow, no forgiveness for someone you supposedly love? For someone you were going to *marry*? I thought you were better than that."

I started to see red, so I whipped around and glared daggers at him. A traitorous tear fell down my cheek and I swiped it away.

"You don't get to demand forgiveness when you had that woman—any woman, Jake—in my bed. How would she even know where I live, if it weren't for you telling her? Huh, Jake? How could she have even gotten in here, if it weren't for the key you have?"

Cassie walked in then not really paying attention to the fact that Jake was here. "What's taking so long?"

She looked up and all the blood drained from her face before she started screaming, "You fucking bastard! How dare you show your stupid fucking face here after what you did? Get the fuck out, *now.*"

"It's nice to see you too, Cassie."

"Honey," she ordered, all while keeping her glare on Jake, "call security and demand why in the actual fuck they let this ass clown in here."

"Calm down, Cass. He was just leaving." I shoved the box into his chest and he grabbed it before it fell to the ground. Glancing down at my hand, I pulled the ring off my finger and threw it at him, hitting him square in the forehead, and I watched it roll away. He didn't even look for it.

"Whatever, Honey. I never really liked you anyway," he

dropped that bomb before turning around and storming out of the room. When the front door slammed shut, I slumped to the floor, tears falling freely down my cheeks, and Cassie kneeled down and wrapped her arms around me.

"Don't cry over that fucking asshole, babe. Let's go start a fire. That will make you feel better."

I shot her a watery smile and wiped my eyes. Getting up from the floor, I made a decision, I wasn't ever dating again.

"What's wrong with me? That's two of them, Cass. I don't want to lead the life my mother did."

"There isn't a thing wrong with you. It's them. Men are dicks, and you are in no way like your mom—may the true Ice Queen rest in peace."

I laughed and hugged her again. We walked out to the backyard, and I noticed all the bedding in a pile in the middle of the fire pit. Cassie must have been busy because the whole pile reeked of lighter fluid. If we weren't careful, we would be getting a visit from the local firemen, but alas, I was now officially off men entirely.

"The honors are yours." She handed me a box of matches with a flourish. Unable to stop myself, I swiped that stick across the side of the box, and sure enough right at the same time a breeze blew it out. Undaunted, I took another match and ripped that one across the side as well, and when that little flame caught, I threw it on the pile before me and watched in awe as my past metaphorically went up in flames.

Cassie was right, I got a sick kind of pleasure watching the fire burn. The glare from the orange flames glowed brightly, and I could feel the heat on my skin as a piece of my life became nothing more than ash. I looked over and smiled, seeing Cassie with her phone out taking video of the fire.

"You are not posting that," I said, knowing exactly where her thoughts were going.

"Of course not," she replied putting her phone away. "But, I did zero in on the panties burning and sent a copy to that skank, Maria."

"You are truly evil."

As we walked back in the house, Cassie's phone rang and she looked at it skeptically before handing it to me. I looked down and noticed Cliff's name on the screen.

"Hello," I croaked. I knew this was going to be a tough one. Cliff was so sweet.

"Riss, babe. How are you feeling?" he asked me gently and I couldn't stop the sniffle. "That good, huh?"

"I've been better."

"If you need anything, anything at all I want you to call me immediately. M'kay?"

"Actually? Do you have any openings in the next week? I'm going to get out of dodge with Cassie for a bit, to lay low, but I need my bedroom redecorated before I get back. I don't think I can handle sleeping in there after... that."

"Absolutely darling. When I am done, you won't even recognize it. Have Cassie text me the number for your cleaning service, and I will make all the arrangements to have the house bleached," he said sincerely, and I blew out a relieved breath. "I always knew that Jake was no good," he added.

"Yeah, and apparently, I'm the only one who saw any good in him, but it seems as if I was duped."

"Don't be too hard on yourself, babe. I know you only want to see the good in everyone. It's one of the things I love most about you. Don't turn into a cynical old hag like Cassie..."

"I heard that, bitch."

"Love you too, pumpkin." He laughed lightly through the speaker phone. "Riss, I will come by the house first thing and get started. Don't forget the cleaner's number. Ta ta for now, darlings."

"Mwah," we said in unison back.

Cassie grabbed her phone back and started punching buttons,

while I raced back up to my room and started packing. It didn't take long to throw some clothes in a suitcase, and in no time we were in her car driving to the gate.

"Shit," Cassie exclaimed. I could see she was clearly irritated, but it took a second before I realized what was going on. "Get down."

I looked at the gate and saw at least ten men with cameras waiting to get pictures of me. With all that was going on, I hadn't even thought about the press that could be camping outside the secured gates.

I bent forward, resting my head on my knees, and hoped like heck that they didn't see me. It was a faint hope, and when the gates opened, Cassie gunned the engine, laughing maniacally as a couple of the photographers had to jump out of the way.

"Stupid bastards. Bowling for paps!" She floored it, and then yelled over to me, "They are getting in their cars. We are gonna have to drive fast."

As if we weren't already.

"Where exactly are we going again? We aren't driving all the way to Vegas?" I asked righting myself in my seat. "That could lead them directly to us."

"No, we are going to LAX. I chartered a plane."

How in the hell had she managed that in three short hours?

"Awesome."

COLE

Violet eyes were staring up at me with a hunger I hadn't seen from her before. Hovering over, I had her tiny wrists in one hand pinned to the bed above her head. My other hand was sliding down her milky white skin.

"You're so wet for me," I groaned out, sucking her nipple into my mouth. The noises that came from that sexy little mouth were music to my ears, and I smiled against her breast.

I slipped a finger into her and she started thrashing, her gorgeous blonde hair fanning out on the pillow. Eyes closed and moaning, I asked against her nipple, "What do you want, princess? Tell me."

"You. I want you inside me, now," she begged on a breathless moan.

"Tell me again, princess, what do you want me to do to you?"

"Have sex with me."

I tsked behind my teeth, then bit down lightly in punishment.

"You can do better than that. Do you want me to fuck you?" I rubbed her clit just enough to get her close.

"Yes!" she screamed into the quiet room.

"Say it." It was a command. I had every intention of corrupting this girl. When she remained quiet, I sucked her nipple harder and grazed it again with my teeth. "Come on princess, if you don't say it, I'm going to stop."

I punctuated those words with another flick to her clit. She keened loudly. "Don't. Stop."

"Say it."

"Fuu... I can't." She was shaking her head back and forth, writhing under my ministrations, but I wasn't letting up.

"You can. You will. It's just two little words, and then I'll stop torturing you, and give you what you need." I flicked her clit again, and I thought her eyes were going to roll back in her head. She glared down at me.

"Fuck me, Cole." I smiled, almost coming myself right then and there when those words left her mouth.

I woke up in a cold sweat and rock hard. My phone was ringing and I cursed the asshole on the other line, waking me from the best sex dream I ever had.

"Someone better be dead," I answered without even looking at the caller ID.

"Just my career," Jake deadpanned into the phone. "I'm the slime ball of Hollywood."

"You brought that on yourself," was my honest reply.

"Thanks brother," he sneered back.

"What do you want me to say?" I sat up in bed, unable to have this conversation with my asshole of a brother, lying on my back. "You probably just ruined that girl's reputation. Because you're an asshole, who can't keep it in his pants. I don't feel a bit sorry for you. It's time to grow the fuck up. You can't treat people like that."

"Ruined her reputation?" His laugh was derisive. "Hell no. Have you seen the rags this morning? They painted her as a martyr. The good girl that got played by the playboy! Everyone feels sorry for her. I haven't been able to leave my house, and there's a swarm of paparazzi outside the gate waiting to pounce."

Refusing to get out of bed, and with every intention of getting my brother off the phone as quickly as possible, I asked, "Jake? Is there a reason for this call at six o'clock in the morning? Outside of you whining at me for something you totally deserved?"

"I need to get out of LA for awhile. Can I come crash with you for a couple days?"

I groaned. The last thing I needed was my little brother drunk at my hotel and getting in trouble. "Why don't you go to Miami and stay with dad? It's a lot less conspicuous and further from LA."

"That's actually a good idea. Thanks, brother."

"Sure anytime. Now, I'm going back to sleep." I hung up the phone.

But no matter what I did, I couldn't get back to sleep, so instead, I got up and took a shower, while memories of that sweet little body in my dream had me pulling on my cock until I came with a shout. It wasn't as good as it would have been if I had her there with me, but it would have to do for the moment, until I reconnected with my lost wife. And, I had *every* intention of doing just that.

Dragging through my morning routine, I got dressed and sat with my laptop on my L-shaped sofa. My brother was melodramatic at the best of times, but a quick google search proved that he was not exaggerating in the slightest. TMZ headlines painted the exact picture that Jake had described. Funny how they actually got this story correct.

There was a picture of my Rissa holding her phone with a look of devastation on her pretty face. The headline read *Nice Girls Finish Last*. Every site I went to there were pictures of her. It was like watching the night playback through the images. One of her and another girl talking to that psycho Maria, who was glaring at her. Some from the art gallery, another of a woman dragging her from the gallery. There was even one of Maria confronting her in front of a large Beverly Hills mansion, and yet another of that same friend driving out of through the gates, with whom I assumed was my wife hunched down in the front seat trying desperately to avoid any more photos.

The rage bubbling up in me forced me to close the laptop. Tossing the computer to the side, I stood and began pacing the room. My idiotic little brother destroyed her life, and those stupid photographers were following her trying to get pictures of her in distress. I almost didn't hear my phone ring through the blood rushing in my ears.

"*What?*" I barked into the phone.

"Good morning to you too."

"Mark, what do you have for me?"

"Sounds like you've had a rough morning."

"Yeah, so I need some good news."

"Sorry boss, I lost her. They chartered a plane and took off. I tried to find out where the plane was headed, but no luck."

"Shit," I growled. "Have you seen the press?"

"Yup, it sounds like she's running from all this madness."

"That's exactly what she's doing. How am I supposed to find her now?"

I heard him huff out a sigh, which matched my own. "I'll see if I can dig anything up. Be patient, we'll find her."

I plopped my ass back down on the couch and looked up at the ceiling. This was turning out to be a shit day.

RISSA

The flight to Vegas was so much faster than driving there. I was glad for the quiet even though my mind wouldn't turn off. The video was on constant playback in my head. Cassie still had my phone, but we had to shut it off because the Twitter notifications alone were driving me crazy. Then there were the Facebook and texts coming in, everything too overwhelming throwing me over the edge.

"Don't they know I'm humiliated? Why can't they just leave me alone?"

"They're vultures, babe. They don't care about your feelings. It's all money and sales. Just ignore them."

"That's easy for you to say. It's not your life they are splashing all over the internet."

"That's it. No phones," Cassie vehemently declared. "We are going to have fun and we aren't going to worry about any of the drama. We are under no circumstances looking at the gossip rags."

"Sounds good to me. I hope the hotel has a spa because I could use a spa day." I groaned and leaned my head back against the headrest.

"Of course it does. It's Vegas. I booked us a full day of appointments tomorrow. The VIP treatment."

"You're the best," I said honestly.

"I also got us on the VIP list for Voodoo." She winked at me to which I covered my face with both hands, knowing this was going to be a tough argument.

"Do you really think going to a club is the best thing for me right now?" I peeked at her through my fingers. She was nodding her head excitedly.

"We will be in the VIP section. No one will be able to see you and take pictures or video."

"Ugh. You're killing me. The last thing I want to do two days after my fiancé gets caught cheating is go clubbing."

"Don't care. It will be good for you. You can show the world that you aren't going to let that cunt-o-saurus and the man whore get to you."

I burst out in laughter at that one. She had some colorful insults to be sure, but that was the best one I'd heard yet.

"What did you call her?" I asked breathless after my fit.

"A cunt-o-saurus. What?" She tried to keep a straight face but it didn't last long before she was cracking up right along with me.

"That's the best one you've come up with yet." My eyes were watering I was laughing so hard.

"You really should look up the Urban Dictionary, swear, those insults are the best."

I looked over at her to see if she was kidding. Nope, straight face, completely serious. "What would I need that for? I have you to throw insults at anyone and everyone who messes with me." I winked back.

"Aww! Compliment received. I will gladly hurl insults at anyone you want."

"Plus," I added, "they are always good for a laugh."

The plane touched down not long after that and Cassie booked a

Town Car, which was waiting for us. The price of that charter was probably ridiculous, but avoiding the public was my number one priority at the moment. No matter what Cassie said, I was sure word would get out sooner rather than later, but for now, my only need was a hot bath, a book, and a bottle of wine, or three.

"Don't forget your hat and sunglasses," Cassie reminded.

"Oh yeah, I'm still not used to this hiding stuff."

"Well, you never had paps all over you before. Get that shit on so we can blow this popsicle stand."

I put on the old beat up baseball cap and the oversized sunglasses. They looked silly seeing as it was after midnight, but my eyes were one of my most recognizable features. You would have thought I was related to Elizabeth Taylor, they were such an odd shade of violet. Between that and my blonde tresses, I was now too recognizable to be mistaken for someone else.

We walked into the mostly empty airport and were rushed through security and out to the waiting car. I didn't think I had seen anyone pointing or whispering, so I was reasonably sure we got through the airport undetected. Surprisingly, the traffic at a little after midnight was horrible. I guess Vegas works on a different time schedule than the rest of the world. Considering the last time I was here I left with massive gaps in my memory, I wasn't one to cast stones.

The lights from the strip assaulted my eyes, and I watched the fountain at the Bellagio for a moment as we passed. It was beautiful, and not having stepped foot back in this state in five years, I found myself getting excited by the prospect of spending a week in Vegas with my best friend.

The hotel security guards brought us through the back entrance to the hotel and took us to the private elevators that led to the suites.

The suite was amazing. Plush overstuffed couches sat in front of a huge flat screen TV. There was a bar and a kitchen. It had three bedrooms and each had its own en suite bathroom with huge whirlpool tubs and unbelievable walk-in stone showers.

After the most incredible bubble bath of my life, I walked back into the living room in my fluffy white bath robe and plopped on the couch, ready for glass of wine number two.

"So much for having my room redecorated, I'm going to have it remodeled. I need a bathroom like that."

"Right? The jets in the bath tub were heavenly," Cassie said leaning back in her spot on the couch. She had her bath robe on too and was toweling off her long black tresses.

I reached for the remote to turn on some mind-numbing reality show, but Cassie snatched the remote before I could get to it.

"Hey," I grumbled.

"Rissa, you really don't want to turn on the TV."

"You looked at your phone." Understanding dawned. "How bad is it?"

"You're everywhere." She sighed, pouring herself a glass, then got up to go raid the bar for snacks. "They even got pictures of us talking with that bitch at the gallery."

"Oh my God." I took a few sips then carefully placed the glass on the coffee table. Leaning back on the back of the sofa, I groaned and covered my hands with my face, unable to take anymore news.

"It looks like the headlines are all slamming him, but I figured you don't want to be sidelined with it."

I peered at her through my fingers and saw her evil smile. "They are slamming him?"

"Cunt-o-saurus too! They are pretty much the most hated people in Hollywood right now."

She was piling up the snacks on the coffee table like this was some celebration. "I don't even know what to say to that." I lifted myself off the couch and looked at her. "I'm sorry Cass, but is it okay if I go to bed? It's been a long day."

"Night pumpkin." Literally, I had the best, most understanding friend in the world. "Try to sleep; we have a full day at the spa tomorrow."

Before heading down the hall to my end of the suite, I bend down and gave her a hug. "Night."

***

The next morning started out great. We had a full set of treatments planned for the day—the deep tissue massage was like heaven on earth. I was waiting to get a facial when I overheard a conversation between two girls walking by the waiting area.

"Did you see the pictures? She was at an art gallery when she got the video," one girl said.

"Poor thing. It's nice that she had a good friend to get her out of there. Did you see that look on her face? She was devastated," the other girl replied.

"What a pig. Making a sex tape with that skanky Maria days after he proposed to poor Honey."

Cassie looked at me and something on my face must have showed my feelings about the situation because she got up.

"Hey, didn't your parents ever teach you to watch what you say? You never know who will be around to hear it," she said to the girls and looked at me pointedly. Their eyes lit up in recognition just before she slammed the door closed.

"At least you have a good friend." She chuckled.

"Wow, I should have realized this was going to follow me everywhere. Maybe going out tonight isn't such a good idea."

"Nope, we are going because you need to show them all that you are better than them and their games," Cassie replied adamantly.

The rest of the day was relatively calm and relaxing, but the dread never left me. I didn't want to go out and pretend this whole situation wasn't destroying everything… wasn't destroying me. The thing that was weirdest about how I was feeling was that I didn't care in the slightest about the end of the relationship I had with Jake. The only thing that really bothered me was that it happened for the world to see, and now they all knew I lacked whatever it took for someone to love me.

People were pitying me. Pity sucked. It was the last thing I wanted.

COLE

I walked through the hotel lobby as if on autopilot. The staff must have known something was up with me because they were avoiding me like the plague. Either that, or they heard that I had snapped at a couple of bell hops who were being a little rough with some guests' bags, and decided that I was in a mood, which they were right about.

Walking past the bar, I heard one of the cocktail waitresses talking excitedly to the bartender. "I got a look at the VIP list for Voodoo tonight, and you are never going to guess who is on it."

"Who," he asked distracted.

I stopped and tried to listen to her excited whispers. "Honey Davies," she nearly squealed.

"You really think she is going to be at a club in Vegas right after that jerk screwed her over?" he asked skeptically, while hustling to fill out the drink orders.

My heart nearly stopped when I thought about it. It made perfect sense. Five years ago she'd taken off to Vegas after a failed relationship. It was entirely possible that she would do that again.

I walked over and leaned down close to my employee's ear. "Natalie." She jumped and turned around immediately, her eyes holding a hint of terror as she saw my thunderous expression. "Y-yes," she stuttered.

"VIPs expect discretion at our hotel. You can't go spouting off about them at the bar in front of other guests, especially those who are as famous as she is. This is your only warning. Do I make myself clear?" I asked with barely controlled rage. She nodded and shrunk down more than humanly possible, eyes wide and terrified.

"Yes, sir. Sorry, sir." She scurried off with a tray the bartender handed her.

"If I hear that rumor has spread, both you and Natalie will be looking for different employment," I told the bartender. The only response was a curt nod.

Satisfied, I made my way downstairs to Voodoo. With the size of the hotel, and wanting guests to stay here to spend their money, a few years back, I'd opened up a high-end bar to cater to both traditional and exclusive guests. One of the perks for those guests needing privacy was a VIP area separated out with blackout windows, so they guests could enjoy an evening out, yet remain concealed.

However, it appeared I now had a bar manager to yell at and was unsure if there'd be a need to hire a new one.

"Larry," I barked when I made it to the club, which didn't open until 10 p.m.

"Yes Mr. Hillard." The club manager came out from behind the bar. When I hired him, he came in with excellent references and more importantly, had the image I was looking for. However, if he crossed this line, he was gone.

"Who has access to the VIP lists?" He flinched.

"Just me until the club opens and then head of security has it, why?"

"I just heard Natalie from the main bar gushing that she got a look at it and talking about a certain star, who is going through the ringer at the moment, being on the list." I glared at him and tapped my foot. "Give me a reason that I shouldn't fire you for breaking confidentiality."

"Uh… you need me. I make sure this club runs smoothly." The idiot was actually starting to get angry. With me!

"This is Las Vegas. Club managers are a dime a dozen here and most of them know enough not to divulge the VIP list just to get laid by a pretty little waitress," I said pointedly.

"You'll be sorry if you let me go. There isn't anyone that can run a high-end club like I can."

"Whatever, get out of my hotel. You're fired."

He glared at me and stood his ground. "You'll regret this."

Ignoring his threat, I looked around and saw club security standing not too far away.

"Eric? Can you come escort Larry off the premises please?"

"Sure thing, boss." He smiled wide. Eric was a behemoth at six feet six. We had been in the marines together, and when he got out I gave him a job as head of security. He looked more than happy to escort the smarmy Larry out of the hotel.

"When you're done I will be in the office. Come see me."

"You got it."

He pushed a disgruntled Larry out of the club and I sighed in relief. Looking around, I didn't see the assistant manager anywhere.

"Where's Tim?" I asked the girl behind the bar.
"Larry fired him last week. He said he could run the whole place by himself."

I growled. There was no way I could get a new manager in there in three hours. I stomped into the office and called Ruthie.

"Ruthie, could you get the old assistant manager for Voodoo on the phone please? Ask him to come in as soon as possible for a meeting?"

"Yes sir," she replied and hung up the phone.

I leaned back in the chair and waited for Eric to return from taking out the garbage. It wasn't long before he lumbered into the office and plopped in the chair across from me.

"What can I do for you, Boss?"

Stop with the boss crap; there's no one else in here," I ordered. "Have you seen the VIP list for tonight?"

"I just got my hands on it before you laid into Larry, why?"

"Did you see who was on it?"

"I sure did. She was engaged to that worthless brother of yours for like five minutes, right?"

"Yeah, I need you to keep an eye on her tonight. No one gets within fifty feet of her with a camera, got it?"

"Sure thing. What are you going to do about a club manager?"

"I have Ruthie calling Tim in to see if he wants the position."

"Tim was swooped up by the Venetian. He won't come back," he informed me.

"Shit. That was fast. What am I going to do now?"

"You're gonna have to do it yourself until we get someone in here. My friend Nikki can do it, but she's out of town until next week."

"She any good? I'm not going to wait a week to hire someone unless they are worth the wait."

"She used to run that trendy club that all the stars go to in LA. She's the best. She left because she was tired of Hollywood. Said she needed a change and came here."

"Good enough for me. Get her on the phone and persuade her to come back early from wherever she is. I will send the jet to pick her up. I just need someone in here ASAP."

"I'll ask her, but I doubt she will cut her trip short."

"Do what you can for me? I need a new manager in here like yesterday," I said standing up. "I can't run the club and the entire hotel by myself."

"You got it. I will get her here as soon as possible."

"And don't forget about Honey. No one gets near her."

"No problem."

After he left, I plopped back down into my seat and scrubbed my face with both hands. This day just kept getting worse. Now, I was going to have to hang out in the club all night.

The only consolation was that Rissa would be there; she was somewhere in Vegas at that very moment. I got a thrill just thinking about the fact that I would be seeing her that night. After all these years of looking, I was finally going to see my wife again.

The need to protect her was strong, and I wondered if I should have extra security in the VIP area. I shook my head knowing that Eric was more than capable of keeping the vultures off of her.

I just hoped I stopped that rumor before it spread anywhere else. The last thing she needed was the press finding her and posting more garbage about her break-up. I sighed and got back to work. It was going to be a long day.

RISSA

It was about ten o'clock, and we were driving down the strip dressed to the nines. Despite the flurry of nervous energy running through me, the spa had relaxed me and I was ready to relax and have a good time. Cassie assured me the VIP area at Voodoo was private if not a bit exclusive, so my nerves weren't running too high.

The minute we pulled up to the valet stand and we were greeted by a big burly security guard instead of the valet, I knew something was wrong. The massive giant opened my door and helped me out of the car.

"Ms. Davies, my name is Eric and I will be your personal security for the evening," he said with a kind smile.

"Personal Security?" I balked and looked over at Cassie, who only shrugged.

"Yes ma'am. Hotel management offered my services to you this evening so that we could make sure your night was enjoyable and free of unwanted interruptions."

"Thank you, Eric. I will have to send the manager a note to say thank you for going above and beyond for me." I patted his hand. For a behemoth, he was quite the softy.

"That won't be necessary. He will be in the club tonight. I will have him come by so you can thank him personally. Now if you're ready to go in, I would be happy to escort you." That smile of his was disarming.

He held out both arms for us to take. Cassie was more than happy to take his arm and cozy up to his side. I snickered to myself—she was such a flirt. I accepted his offered arm and we walked into the hotel where I was immediately bombarded with people.

There were smart phones in my face, fans screaming asking for my autograph, or telling me how much they hated Jake and they would never listen to his music again.

I looked up questioningly at Eric, and he tucked me into his side and pushed through the fans covering my head with one arm as he dragged Cassie along behind us. It was hard to walk in the six-inch stilettos, and I managed to barely keep up with his long strides. Finally, we made it into the club and up the stairs to the VIP section. I blew out a breath and fixed my hair.

"Shit," was the first thing Eric said after safely getting us into the lounge. "The boss is going to be pissed. I'm so sorry Ms. Davies—everything was clear when I walked out to meet you. I don't know exactly what happened between the time I left and when we walked back in." He shook his head, and I could see his frustration mounting. "I will have a bottle of champagne brought out right away, complements of the house. Please accept my apologies again; I hope you still have a good time tonight."

"It's fine." I leaned back to look up at him. Even with my heels the man was still towering over me. "I half expected to be seen here tonight at some point." I tried for a reassuring smile.

56

"If you need anything, I won't be too far away."

"Good to know," Cassie said with a flirtatious wink, and I swear the big guy blushed ten shades of red.

I looked at Cassie who was fanning herself.

"Holy hotness, batman," she said. "The things I would do to that man."

"Did you see him blush?" I giggled.

"Who cares? Did you see all those muscles?" She was practically licking her lips. "I bet you he looks amazing naked. And that mouth? Ohmygod. I think I just came."

I nudged her shoulder. "You're gross."

"I just want wrap my legs around his head and mmm…"

Standing at the high-top table, I picked up the napkin and threw it at her head. "How long has it been?"

"In general? Or with someone *that* gorgeous? Because if it's the latter? Never, I have been waiting my whole life for that delicious piece of man meat."

I burst into a fit of giggles and Cassie laughed with me as Eric came back and set a chilled bucket on the table with two champagne flutes.

"Glad to see you ladies enjoying yourselves." He winked at Cassie and she looked like she was going to spontaneously combust.

"You look hot, Cassie." She deserved to be teased in front of Eric. "Maybe you should take some ice from the bucket to cool down."

"Are you hot, darlin'? I can get you something to cool you down or you can go out to the patio and get some air," Eric asked sweetly, and I couldn't tell if he was being serious or not.
She kicked me under the table. "Ow."

Eric looked confused as he opened the bottle, looking between us curiously. He shook his head, clearly not picking up on Cassie's obviousness, and poured us each a glass.

"Thank you, Eric." I smiled at him as he handed me the glass.

"You're welcome, Ms. Davies." He flashed me a grin before handing Cassie hers.

"Toast, to new friends." We clinked our glasses together, and Eric gave us one last skeptical look before leaving us.

"You bitch, what was that?" Cassie hissed at me.

"I was trying to help your game."

"My game is just fine without your help thank you."

A night out with my bestie was exactly what I needed, and in a place where the press had no idea where I was. I knew that wouldn't last long because of all the people at the hotel when we got there, but regardless, I decided to enjoy the night while I could because no telling what tomorrow would bring.

"Let's dance," I said excitedly and finished off my glass of champagne.

"I think that's the best idea you have had all night." Cassie grinned at me.

When we got up from the table, I noticed Eric watching us as we made our way to the VIP dance floor. I finger-waved at him and he saluted me which set me off giggling again. He really was cute. Just, not my type. But, since I was going to be a single-forever-cat-lady, I guess I no longer had a type, though technically, I still had a husband.

I was surprised to see the dance floor was packed with bodies. It was a Wednesday night but I guess that didn't matter in Vegas too much. I tried to keep Cassie to the outer edge of the dance floor, but we were quickly sucked into the group of writhing bodies. It was only a minute before the music overtook me and I no longer cared about anything but swaying my hips and letting the music flow through me. It was exhilarating. That was until some sleaze wrapped his arms around my hips and started grinding against my butt. I tried to extricate myself as nicely as possible, but he wasn't taking the hint.

Where was Cassie? She would have some colorful words for him. After twisting around back and forth looking for her, all while elbowing the guy to back off, no matter what I did the guy wouldn't get his hands off me.

A mild level of panic was setting in. Cassie was missing, and this jerk was not taking no for an answer. As I was about to nail him with my heels, I felt him being ripped off me. I stumbled back a little and somehow managed not fall as I turned around to piercing blue eyes. I knew those eyes, but from where? They looked eerily familiar. Behind him, and only about two inches taller than blue eyes, was Eric hauling the annoying dancing guy away.

"Thank you, he just couldn't take a hint." I blushed and looked down, yet I still felt his stare boring into me. Gathering the courage to at least face the man who helped me, I looked up into those eyes. "Do I know you?"

COLE

I watched her. Yeah, I know it was creepy, but I didn't really care. My long-lost wife was in my club in my hotel. So close, yet so far away. The green sequin mini dress she was wearing hugged her slight curves, and I was rock hard as my mind played out how exactly how I wanted to remove it from her body.

I watched as she and her friend laughed together and chuckled when I saw the other girl checking Eric out. Rissa was beautiful and vibrant when she laughed. I was insanely jealous of her friend in that moment. I wanted to be the one to make her laugh like that.

"What's your deal?" Eric bumped me in the back, and I jumped. "For such a big guy, you're a stealthy bastard."

"You were in basic too and can be just as stealthy. Don't change the subject. You're staring at Honey like you want to eat her. What's your deal?"

It was hard keeping secrets and even harder keeping them with a guy you served with. I trusted no one in the hotel like I did him, but I was still reluctant.

"Nothing, just making sure no one bothers her."

"Bullshit. That's what you have me for. What's the real reason?"

I sighed before confessing, "Remember the girl I married? The one that disappeared?"

"Yeah... the one you have been pining for the last five years?" He was looking down at me like I'd lost my mind.

"That's her."

"Who? Honey?" I nodded.

"You got yourself into a huge mess there, man." He whistled long and low.

"Tell me about it."

"What are you going to do?"

"I guess just keep an eye on her while she's here."

"You're not gonna try to talk to her?" he asked, baffled.

"No, she just got out of a relationship. I'm sure you heard... with my asshole brother. Let's just say complicated probably doesn't cover it."

Eric wasn't one to give advice or talk out of turn, so when he took a few minutes, I figured he was going to just let it be.

Looked like I was in for another surprise tonight.

"Cole." He was glaring at me intently. "There's no time like the present. If you don't talk to her now, you may not get another chance. Are you willing to risk another five years?"

"Wait. Eric, where did she go?" I asked suddenly terrified. Her friend was at their table looking around presumably for Rissa. I walked over to her.

"Where's R... Honey?" Her friend gave me an odd look. It wasn't until she noticed Eric standing next to me that she relaxed a bit.

"I don't know. I lost her on the dance floor."

"Stay here, we'll find her," Eric said reassuringly and squeezed her arm.

She smiled up at him gratefully. "Thank you."

61

I didn't wait for Eric. I took off to the dance floor with him following behind me and noticed her almost immediately. She was struggling to extricate a man from her ass, and I saw red. The douchebag wasn't taking no for an answer and continued to grind into her as she attempted to elbow him away. At one point I saw her looking around wildly for help, and I tapped Eric on the shoulder pointing to where she was standing.

Just as I thought he would, he moved like a raging bull towards the man, but I got there first. "Get your damn hands off of her," I yelled, grabbing him by the shirt and pulling him roughly back.

Now free, she stumbled forward, and I reached out a hand to steady her. The minute our skin made contact, I froze. She looked up at me, and I couldn't do anything but look into her gorgeous eyes.

"Thank you, he just couldn't take a hint." She blushed and it was the sexiest thing in the world. I wanted to see that blush over her entire body. "Do I know you?"

"My names Cole, Ri… Honey." *Shit.* I nearly slipped and called her Rissa again. She looked at me curiously, but eventually smiled. "If you would like, I will escort you back to your table."

"I would like that Cole." She grabbed onto my forearm and let me lead her off the dance floor. "Do you work here?"

"Something like that." I laughed when she wrinkled her cute little button nose.

"What do you mean by that?"

"My father owns this hotel. I run the whole place," I replied, a little embarrassed.

"Oh."

I guided her over to the bar and pulled out a stool for her to sit. "So, what are you doing pulling random creeps off me in the middle of the night?"

Sitting down next to her, I nodded for the bartender to bring us a couple of drinks. "I had to fire the club manager today, so it's up to me tonight." I replied cryptically, not wanting her to know the manager was basically fired because of his bad decisions regarding her.

"That's too bad, but I guess it worked out for me." She teased then gave me a little wink. *Huh, was she flirting with me?*

The bartender placed a glass of champagne in front of her and a whiskey neat in front of me. "It certainly did. This drink is on me." I held up my glass for a toast. "And let me apologize for security not doing their job." I flashed my most charming smile, one I was hoping to have her in a puddle of goo on the floor.

"Oh no." She grabbed my arm and looked at me with pleading puppy dog eyes. "Eric's not going to get in trouble is he? It's really not his fault."

"Don't worry about Eric. He's not in any trouble. He was actually talking to me when that happened, so it's just as much my fault as it is his," I assured her and happily noticed she didn't remove her hand from my arm.

There was the same electricity between us that I remembered from before. Deciding to keep her talking, I asked, "Is this your first time here?"

"At this club? Yes. In Vegas... no." Her hesitant answer had me curious if she remembered anything.

"Oh? You come here often?"

"No, the last time I was here was about five years ago," she said and then stopped.

She looked at my quizzically. "Do I know you from here?"

RISSA

I was so confused. I swore he nearly called me Rissa, but that wasn't possible. Only my closest friends called me that—even Jake didn't know my real name. I'd had my name legally changed four years before at the insistence of my publicist, since I refused to use any connection to my late mother's fame. If I was going to follow in her acting footsteps, any success needed to be from my talent, not my heritage. Funny though, as the whole reason I came out to Vegas in the first place was to run from Wes, who wanted nothing but to use my mother's fame. Now here I was again, running to Vegas, and I had the sinking feeling my past was about to catch up with me.

Grabbing his arm, I felt a current of electricity run through me; there was something about this man. "Do I know you from here?"

He looked away uncomfortably and a bit disappointed, but why? We'd just met. He didn't seem like the type to care about my fame.

"Honey," Cassie squealed and tackled me from behind, nearly knocking my chest down into the bar. "I'm so glad they found you."

She seemed a little tipsy, but there was no way she could possibly be that drunk yet. "I'm fine. Cole and Eric took care of the guy."

"Cole?" she asked and turned to look at him with what appeared to be a flicker of recognition in her eyes, but she furrowed her brow and seemed to think better of whatever errant thought had crossed her mind. "Well Cole, you must join us for a drink." She didn't allow him to decline as she pulled us all to the table. He was sputtering something about work, but in true Cassie fashion, she shushed him and continued marching through the crowd, pushing anyone who dared step between her and her desired goal.

Letting her drag me, I winked at him. "Trust me, it's easier if you just go with it."

"She is incredibly strong for such a little thing."

"I heard that, Rissa!" She practically sang it out.

"Rissa?" Cole looked down and said quietly.

"It's my real name, but Cassie isn't supposed to shout it all over the club."

Practically tripping to get to the table, she shrugged before yelling, "Sorry, it slipped."

"I think it suits you much better than Honey," he said silkily, shooting me a charming smile and I melted. I needed to watch out for this one. He was going to ruin all my plans for becoming a spinster.

"Okay, you two, enough with the googoo eyes." Cassie was practically cackling and broke whatever spell his eyes had me under.

After dragging us through the crowd and to our table where the bottle of champagne and our old glasses still stood, Cassie grabbed her drink and I smacked her hand, stopping her. "You left your drink there while we danced? Are you crazy? Don't drink that."

"Shit," Cole cursed from beside me, and I looked up at him startled. "I watched her pour that from the bottle before we went looking for you."

"Cassie, how many glasses of champagne have you had, hun?"

"That's my second, why?"

Something was up. Cassie, while not a rager, could definitely handle more than two glasses of champagne, especially since we'd been dancing the better part of two hours. "You're acting crazier than normal, babe."

Looking over to Cole, I whispered, "Do you think someone put something in it?"

"Pfft, why would anyone drug me?" Clearly her hearing wasn't affected, but she slurred it out and started to stumble back. Eric walked up right in time to catch her before she fell on the floor.

"What's going on?" Eric looked between us, cradling Cassie in his arms, who looked like she was moments from passing out. "I've been watching. She hasn't had enough to be this drunk."

"Grab that bottle and call the police. I'm going to take the girls upstairs and call a doctor to come check on her," Cole said authoritatively. "I want surveillance video sent to my personal computer."

"Yes, sir," Eric said and handed over my now unconscious friend to Cole and took off.

Cole adjusted her in his arms and nodded for me to follow him. While attempting to keep me out of sight, he explained there was no other way than through the main club, which was packed. Trying to duck my head and be as inconspicuous as I could, clearly didn't work all that well when a very drunk guy grabbed my butt, hard. I yelped and Cole turned on his heel—ready to do, I have no idea what, since he was carrying Cassie in his arms—and glared at him, and I had to literally pull him away from the guy. He was like a stone statue, then finally conceded and we made it to the front of the club.

"Shoot," I said as I spied all the people in the casino who now had their phones out just waiting to get a picture. "Is there another way out of here, instead of going through the casino?"

"Yeah, that's where we're headed. Follow me."

It was nearly impossible to keep up with him. The club was packed and I was wearing some extremely high heels. We walked into a room just behind the bar area, receiving curious looks from the bartenders and waitresses as we passed, but I was too worried about my friend to care. I had a feeling I wouldn't be turning on a TV or my phone for awhile, though. I could see the headlines *Honey's Night Out Ends in Disaster.* Or, *Hollywood's Good Girl Not so Good in Vegas.* Can I say #cringe? This could get all the heat off Jake and Maria and switch it to me. #PRdisaster.

There was a service elevator in the back room, and the three of us got inside a surprising large space. Reaching over to swipe the hair away from Cassie's eyes, it was obvious something was very wrong. My friend was dead-to-the-world passed out and Cassie was a light sleeper. She had a no sleepover rule because of it, claiming if the guy tossed and turned he would keep her up all night denying her much needed beauty sleep. I laughed to myself. *She would definitely get her beauty sleep tonight.*

"Maybe we should take her to the hospital?"

"That's the last thing you want to do."

"What do you mean, Cole? You have no idea what she was given. She could die." I may have shrieked that last part out, I wasn't sure, but by the whip back of his head, I guess my reaction shocked him.

"Hey, hey, hey. Calm down," he said soothingly, trying to lift my friend up in his arms more. "As soon as we reach the room, I'm calling a doctor that makes house calls. They have at home date rape drug kits now, so I'm sure he will be able to figure out what's happening with her, and if she was administered anything. Don't worry, I'm not going to let anything happen to your friend."

Nodding stiffly, I looked into his eyes and softened. We were lucky, Cassie and I, that he and Eric were there.

"Thank you." I sighed and rubbed my hand along his rock-hard biceps. He shuddered at my touch, so I quickly removed my hand, not wanting to offend, but yet, there was something going on with this impossibly gorgeous hotel owner.

When the elevator doors opened a sense of déjà vu struck me, hard and I stumbled. "You live here?"

His face looked impassive, but his eyes looked, hopeful? "Yes, is something wrong?"

The hallway the elevator opened up into looked exactly the same as the one I fled all those years ago. I cringed. The morning I left, I just ran and all the hotels on the strip looked different from day to night. Was it possible that this was the same hotel and the same man I had fled?

What are the odds of that?

COLE

I was staring into her eyes, willing her to remember me. "Y-yes," she stammered. She was cute when she wasn't sure of herself.

"Are you sure?" Inching closer to her, I smirked. "You look like you've seen a ghost."

My wife steeled herself, squaring her shoulders; she was going to be a tough nut to crack. I would though—if it was the last thing I did.

"I'm fine. I just don't know which way I'm going." She glared at me, daring me to tease her anymore.

"That way." I nodded—in the only direction we could go.

Stomping down the hall to my penthouse apartment, I fully enjoyed the show, with her perfect ass swaying as she marched to the door, and dear God, those legs in those heels...

She abruptly turned on her heel, and asked indignant, "Are you staring at my butt?"

"No. That would be rude." She rolled her eyes, knowing better. But seriously, I didn't care, and she was in fact my *wife*. I had rights, didn't I? But instead of bringing up that topic, I said, "I need you to grab my wallet out of my back pocket."

"What? No."

I rolled my eyes in return then looked down at the unconscious form in my arms. "Focus Rissa. I can't reach it, or I will drop Cassie."

She looked at me curiously, before walking behind me. Long minutes passed, and I hoped she was staring at my ass with as much appreciation as I did hers. "Now who's staring at whom?" I winked over my shoulder at her.

She turned a beautiful shade of scarlet and I laughed out right, hoping she'd cop a feel when she reached in. No such luck, just grabbed the wallet roughly and yanked it out.

"Which one is the keycard?"

"The grey one tucked into the money slip." Unable to meet my eyes, I chuckled inwardly. She definitely was a good girl and it was going to be my pleasure seeing how bad she could be.

A quiet gasp came from her as she looked around my suite. She looked ready to bolt.

"Everything all right, princess?" I asked quietly. "I really need to put your friend down and call the doctor."

She nodded woodenly and took a step into the apartment. "What? How is this possible?"

"How is what possible?" Giving her an innocent smile, I made my way down the hall to the second bedroom.

Huffing while she marched the rest of the way into the room, I knew her head was ready to explode with questions. God, she was adorable when angry, but I really did need to put Cassie down before I dropped her.

"Give me a minute to get her settled and we will talk, okay?" She nodded once, and then plopped down on the couch.

Laying a still unconscious Cassie down on the bed, I shook out my arms trying to get the blood flowing before grabbing my phone from my front pocket. "Dr. Parks? I have a problem. A high-profile guest in my club was drugged tonight. At least that is what I think happened. Is there any way you can come check her out?"

"Sure Cole, I will be right there," the grizzled old voice replied. Thank you, I will have someone on standby to escort you to my apartment."

"All right, see you soon."

When I walked back into the room, Rissa had her head tilted back and she was muttering to herself. Instead of listening to what she was saying, I was focused in on the smooth column of her neck and how badly I wanted to lick my way from its base to her ear and whisper all the dirty things I wanted to do to her. A throat cleared and pulled me from my salacious thoughts.

"What are you thinking?" she asked shyly.

"You really don't want to know." I shook my head to clear it and grabbed the club chair and dragged it closer to her. Far enough that I couldn't touch, but close enough to keep her near. "The doctor is on his way."

"How long have you lived here?"

"About six years. I moved in when my dad promoted me to hotel manager."

"Do all the suites look like this one?"

Here was the moment of truth.

"No. They are all different." No reaction, she just sighed and looked away.

RISSA

I knew it was him. The second we stepped into that hallway and off the elevator, I knew I'd made a mistake. My earlier intuition of Cole was correct.

When I opened the door, the memory was so powerful that I felt like I was cemented in place and no amount of struggle could release me from my spot. His quiet laugh had me moving again which made me stomp into the room and glare. The dreaded feeling that Cole remembered much more than I did, knew much more about my life than I did. I hated it, especially when I felt like he was in on a secret I should have been part of.

He seemed like a sweet, caring guy that I didn't want to hurt, and if truth be told, we pretty much did the same thing to each other, asked passive aggressive questions that we probably already knew the answers to, but it was time for the truth.

"What's going on here? You're him, aren't you?"

"Him who?"

Standing up from the couch, I nearly shouted, "Don't play dumb with me. You're the guy. The guy that I got drunk with and married five years ago, aren't you?"

He sighed and looked to the ceiling before answering, sitting there still for so long I wasn't sure if he was going to answer. "Yes."

"And you knew?" I accused. "You remembered?"

How on earth did he remember? Why would he marry a complete stranger if he was sober enough to remember?

He put his hands on his knees as if he were an old man and hefted himself up from the chair and walked the five paces until he was towering over me, the scent of him nearly making me dizzy. "I never forgot a single moment with you." His soft blue eyes were pleading with me, yet I was still confused.

"I don't understand."

Abruptly, he turned and walked to the bar. "How about a glass of wine? It will calm your nerves and then we can talk about this."

Was he kidding? Did he think alcohol, the original cause of this debacle, was going to calm me? *Ah, fudgecicles.* "Sure."

As he poured the wine in the glasses, I watched him. How is it that he never saw me on TV? I wasn't conceited, and I hated seeing my face plastered everywhere, but the PR people were tossing me out there like bait, trying to scoop up every last dime, using my face until the next new it-girl arrived. So how was it possible he could have missed me or not known about me, yet he said he never forgot a moment?

"Thank you."

"You're welcome," he said after handing me the glass, and then led me to the couch. This time he sat next to me, so close our knees touched. His touch was electric. We sat in silence for long minutes sipping from our glasses. There were so many questions running through my head, I had no idea what to ask first.

"Why didn't you ever find me?"

"Please." He let out a frustrated sigh and ran his hand through his hair. "I only found out who you were last night. I have been searching for you for five long years—since the moment you fled, Rissa."

"How is that even possible?" I asked in disbelief.

He shrugged. "I don't watch TV, I stay away from the gossip rags as much as I possibly can, and I've done nothing but work and look for you." It looked as if he was going to say more but he stopped himself. I wondered what he wasn't telling me, but decided to let it go because I didn't really know him and had no right to his secrets.

"If you weren't as drunk as I was, then why did you marry me?"

"I *was* drunk; I just wasn't as drunk as you." He put his glass on the coffee table in front of us, knee up on the sofa, now half turned to face me. "It was extremely impulsive of me, but I just had the best, and craziest, night of my life with an amazing beautiful woman... and I didn't want you to leave."

"Craziest?" I asked with a laugh.

"That's the part you picked up on?"

"I'm still processing the other stuff." I bumped him with my shoulder playfully.

When he reached up and tucked a strand of my blond hair behind my ear tenderly, I jumped at the shock of electricity that coursed through me and I spilled my wine over the both of us.

"Shoot, that's cold" was my first thought before realizing the red wine was seeping into the fabric of my dress.

He launched himself off the sofa, grabbed a few towels and handed them to me. "I'm sorry, I didn't mean to startle you."

"Why are you sorry? I'm the clumsy one."

"Shit, it looks like it's going to stain. I have a shirt and some shorts you can wear, and I'll send your dress out to get cleaned."

"Thank you, if you're sure?"

"Of course, come with me." He held out his hand and I stared down for what seemed like a full minute before I grasped his hand in mine. Stopping in the doorway to his bedroom—an all too familiar sight—I watched him move gracefully toward the closet. The sight of his butt was again in my line of vision, as he walked to a closet, grabbing a white T-shirt from the rack and then rifling through a drawer for some drawstring shorts. He looked satisfied with his choice as he walked back over and handed me the bundle.

Before making his way out of the room to give me privacy, he said. "You can take as long as you want. I'll call down to the front desk and have them send someone up for the dress."

"Thank you, Cole."

I sat down on his bed and sighed.

What have I gotten myself into?

COLE

After dialing the front desk and having them send up a concierge to collect her stained dress, all the while pacing with how this night became so damn complicated, I finally decided to sit down and try to relax. What the hell I was going to do now? Why did I stop myself before I told her who my brother was? But I knew why… knew what she would think about me being related to that ass, and the inevitable disappointment would be in those violet eyes.

A knock sounded on the door. I looked down the hall to see if Rissa was ready with her dress for the concierge, but as I opened it, a weathered old man with leathery skin and a kind small stood there staring at me behind wire framed glasses. He looked tired and I instantly felt guilty about calling him.

"Good evening, Dr. Parks. I'm sorry again about calling you so late."

He patted me on the hand, walking past me into the suite. "Not a problem, my boy. Where is the patient? I'll need to take some blood and send it to the lab."

Cassie was still laid out on the bed, still as a stone, and a horrible thought crossed my mind before she moaned loudly.

"We may have to send her to the hospital to pump her stomach," the doctor broke through my thoughts.

"You think?" I asked with dread. Riss couldn't go to the hospital and it wasn't likely that she would leave her friend.

"It's the fastest way to get the toxins out of her system. How much alcohol did you say she had?"

"Only two glasses of champagne."

"Let me take some blood first. I'm sure the police will want the results."

He went to work taking a couple vials of blood and sealing them for transport while I paced.

"Is she going to be okay?" A soft voice asked from behind me and I tensed.

Turning around I was struck dumb by the sight of her standing there in my clothes. The dress had looked spectacular on her, but a very male primal possessive feeling came over me as those milky white, toned legs and barefeet with green polish walked toward me. My eyes traveled the length of her, and I saw the place where the hem of my shirt met her thighs. "Was there a problem with the shorts?" My voice sounded strangled to my own ears.

Clearing my throat, I looked up and saw a blush cross her pretty cheeks. *This girl is going to kill me.*

"They didn't fit," she replied, shy, not quite looking me in the eyes.

"There's going to be police and my security guys up here soon. I would prefer it if you had more clothes on." My tone was gruff, but she was seriously killing me and there was no way in the fucking world, I was about to let a bunch of men look at her like that. My eyes only.

However, the look of hurt in her eyes by the obvious anger in my voice was enough for me to soften. "No, no, no, you misunderstand. We wouldn't want rumors to spread would we?"

Realization dawned on her pretty features before she ran from the room. Hopefully it was because she realized the image the tabloids would get of her, rather than her being upset with me.

"Okay, I'm done." Once again the good doctor cut through my inner turmoil.

RISSA

I watched him peruse my body with something like hunger in his eyes, and it made my knees weak just thinking about it. When he asked about the shorts and said I should put something on, I thought I might cry from humiliation. It wasn't until he explained why that the ice bucket called reality was poured on my head. I'm not a normal girl anymore and the tabloids would love nothing more than to hear my fall from grace—my inevitable failure to remain the good girl, the ice queen.

I ran back to his bedroom and found his shorts that I'd discarded laying on the floor. Grabbing them, I slipped them on my legs and synched the strings as tight as they could go. They were still too big, so I rolled the waist over a few times, giving me that nice muffin top look. If I swore, now would be about the time, and wouldn't Cassie just find that hilarious.

I had no idea why I was reacting to him like this. My life was going to be that of a spinster, the old lady with a thousand cats.

Well, except, I hated cats. After that embarrassment with Jake, the weasel, my life plan would be boring, but at least it would be safe and comfortable. And now, the husband I don't remember comes in and ruins my perfect plan.

Through the open door I heard something muffled sounding coming from the guest bedroom, it sounded as if someone was puking her guts up.

Racing down the hall, the noises got louder as I went further into the room. *Cassie's definitely puking.*

When I walked into the bathroom, I saw a very green looking Cole hunched over the toilet, rubbing Cassie's back as she continuously wretched. Moving him out of the way, I held back her long dark hair away from her face, and motioned for Cole to get a damp washcloth.

"Is she going to be all right?"

"Yes miss, as soon as the toxins are out of her system she will be better," the doctor said kindly. His expression was curious. "You must be the high-profile guest that Cole mentioned?"

"Yes sir, my name is Honey Davies."

"I know who you are, dear, my wife watches your show every week."

"If you think she'd like it, I can sign something for her?"

"She would love that, thank you." I couldn't believe I was actually having this ridiculous conversation while my friend was heaving her guts up, but clearly my new reality was altered.

The retching finally stopped and Cassie placed her head on the side of the bowl, grunting out. "What in the actual fuck happened to me?"

"You were drugged, hun," I replied and smoothed the hair back from her face, and handed her the washcloth. "Feeling any better?"
"Like hell."

"Well, you done puking your guts up?" I giggled because the doctor was right, she was going to be fine.

"Shut up," she hissed. "Yes, I want to sleep for a hundred

years."

"Let's get you up then," Cole said with obvious relief in his tone and reached down scooping her in his arms and carrying her back to the bedroom.

I watched him leave with pure female satisfaction. The man really did have a great butt. #lovetotakeabite. I was so distracted that I forgot Dr. Parks was still standing there until he cleared his throat. Dear God, what was happening to me. Clearly, Cole was making me a hussy.

My face was probably scarlet from being caught staring at my—Oh My God—*husband's* backside. "Sorry."

"No problem, dear," he replied with a twinkle in his eye and a smile on his face that just made me blush more. "Here is my card. If you have any problems while you're here. Call me."

I nodded my thanks and took the card. He walked from the room and I sat there in silence for a minute attempting to get my bearings until the smell finally registered and I almost gagged.

Walking quickly to the foyer, I noticed my purse on a little table by the door and I froze. Something as innocent as my purse should not be so meaningful, but it looked and felt like it belonged there. I shook my head to clear it. Grabbing a pen, I walked to where Dr. Parks was standing and grabbed a blank sheet of paper from Cole's kitchen island. "Can I use this?"

"Sure."

"What's your wife's name?"

"Oh dear, how sweet of you. Her name is Beverly, and she will be so pleased." Dr. Parks smiled.

"No problem. It's the least I can do since you took such good care of my friend."

"How lovely. Thank you. She will love this." He waved the piece of paper that bore my little note to his wife as he left the room.

"My pleasure."

I walked into the bedroom and noticed Cassie on the bed,

already back to sleep. Slipping back out of her room, I followed the steady cadence of Cole's voice.

"Thank you," he said as he closed the door. He turned and was startled by my sudden appearance. "That was the concierge, who will take your dress to the dry cleaner here in the hotel."

"Thank you."

"No worries, it was my fault that it happened in the first place." Reaching up and rubbing the back of his neck, his muscular forearm was clenching back and forth.

Thoughts of our nickname for him came unbidden and I began to giggle.

"What's so funny?"

"Nothing."

"Something's funny," he said stalking towards me. I took a step back without thinking and my laugh cut off abruptly at the fire in his eyes.

"Okay, okay." I put my hands out to stop him, then covered my face with them as I muttered, "When I woke up here all those years ago, you had your arm wrapped around me. It was the only part of you that I saw." Peeking through my fingers I noticed him stalking closer. "Cassie and I call you 'the forearm.'"

He continued his approach. "You called me the forearm? Like what, some superhero name?" He chuckled and was now standing bare inches from me. "Now that you have seen the rest of me, I'm sure you can think of some sexier things to call me."

That sexy smirk of his was going to be my undoing. I couldn't believe he was there—two inches from my face. The worst part of all was how badly I wanted him closer.

"I don't know… it's a great forearm," I said lifting his hand and tracing up the corded muscle in his arm. A nervous laugh fell from his lips—lips that were now less than an inch from mine and I wanted him to close the distance. His eyes clouded over and I was sure the blue was darker with his lust. When the most inopportune knock came from the door, Cole cursed and I certainly wanted to.

Whatever spell we had on each other was broken.

"Where is she?" A very irritated Eric stormed through. "Has the doctor been here yet?"

"She's sleeping in the guest bedroom," Cole replied shutting the door. He had an irritated scowl on his face, with a barely controlled hunger simmering below the surface. "We almost had to take her to the hospital to pump her stomach, but thank God she started retching. Dr. Parks did take some blood and he'll let us know what drug she was given when he gets the results back."

"The police are downstairs. They want to talk to you both. Should I have them brought up?" He looked at me curiously. "What happened to your clothes?"

"Wine, the dress just went to the cleaners."

He nodded and then moved towards the door. "I will bring the cops up then."

As soon as he was gone, Cole walked over to me slowly, all predatory grace, and I found myself for what must have been the third time in a few hours, watching his fluid movements. What a mistake.

Grabbing me in fierce embrace and tilting my chin up so that I would meet his eyes, he whispered only a breath from my lips, "Stop me."

I shook my head. That was the only encouragement he needed before he crushed his lips to mine. It was possessive and it was dangerous, but I couldn't stop from melting into it. He cupped my face in both hands and deepened the kiss. I was drowning. I had never been kissed with such fierce possession before, never felt anything like it.

At some point I moaned into his mouth and he broke the kiss breathing hard. "We have to stop."

His eyes still held that hunger and fire but then he dropped his hands from my hips, and I stepped back reluctantly.

"Rissa? Where the hell are we?" Cassie said from behind me, I turned to her startled.

"Hey, I thought you'd be sleeping for the next two days." I turned plastering a fake smile on my face, but it was one she knew too well. It was a plastic Hollywood smile, the one I reserved for the press and when my world was crumbling around me.

"I feel like shit. What happened?"

"What's the last thing you remember?"

"Dancing," she replied as I walked closer. "Who is that?" She whispered the last question and I blushed.

"That's 'the forearm.'"

"Are you serious?" Her eyes bugged out and I heard Cole chuckle from behind me.

"You really did call me the forearm."

"This is Cole, Cassie. This is his place, his hotel. You were drugged at the club, and Cole promised to help us find out what happened."

"Oh." She looked at me in confusion. "Cole? Do you have any water? I feel like I swallowed glass."

"Sure thing, I'll be right back." He smiled at me as he left the room.

"We need to go," she said to me as soon as Cole was out of ear shot. "And what the hell are you wearing?"

"I spilled wine on my dress. He sent it down to have it dry cleaned."

"Whatever, we need to go, now."

"No, the police are on their way up to take statements about what happened. Plus, I cannot go walking around Vegas dressed like this. The tabloids will go insane."

"Shit. You're right. Obviously being drugged has taken a mental toll on me, but are you sure he is who he says?"

"Eric has been taking orders from him all night. If he didn't run the place, I'm sure we wouldn't be in this fancy apartment and Eric wouldn't have let him boss him around." I didn't want to tell her that I remembered this place. Knowing Cassie as I did, she would just tell me that one hotel suite looked just like any other and I was probably just confused.

"Good point. Where is Eric?"

"He's bringing the police up here," a gruff voice said way too close to my ear. Cole smiled and handed the bottle over to Cassie. "Did I scare you, princess?"

I made a disgruntled sound in the back of my throat. "Don't call me that."

"Why not? Aren't you Hollywood royalty?" he teased.

Cassie gasped and shook her head at him. I hated that term, which was also one of the main reasons that I changed my name, not wanting to be cast in roles just because of my mom.

"I was just teasing you. I'm sorry. I like that nickname though." He nudged his shoulder with mine.

"You're not gonna stop calling me that, are you?" I asked in resignation.

"Nope," he replied with a pop.

Cassie started laughing, looking between the two of us. "I think you might have met your match, Rissy."

"Why do I keep you around?" Clearly my friend was feeling much better. I guess puking up everything in your system, really was a cure-all.

"Comic relief?" She grinned. "Oh wait. I know why. So I can curse out your enemies for you."

"True."

Cole was looking back and forth between us with a bemused expression. "You two are cute together. You," he said pointing to me, "have this whole angel thing happening," then he pointed to Cassie, "and you, definitely got the devil thing going on."

I caught Cassie just before she launched herself at him. "Be nice," I admonished him.

"Sorry." He did look chagrined after seeing Cassie's reaction. "It really was meant as a compliment. I can tell how much you two care about each other. It's nice."

"See Cass, he didn't mean anything by it." I smiled but she

didn't seem convinced.

COLE

I was a little terrified of Cassie, who seemed like a loose cannon, and dealing with loose cannons was something to avoid in my line of work. Cassie, though, clearly loved Rissa and their sisterly affection was obvious. Winning over Rissa meant winning over Cassie.

Then the pounding started at the door, I turned and opened it. Eric was standing there with two uniformed police officers. Reaching out, I shook both of their hands and ushered them inside.

"Officers, this is Cassie. She is the young woman who was drugged this evening," I said as I led them inside to where the girls were sitting on my couch.

Both officers stopped dead in their tracks when they saw Rissa. I nearly growled out loud.

"Gentlemen, I trust there won't be a problem with Ms. Davies anonymity." I looked at them both pointedly.

"Absolutely. We are professionals, Mr. Hillard. I assure you nothing will be said about Ms. Davies' presence here."

I nodded curtly and walked back over to Eric, who was

watching Cassie carefully.

"How's she doin'?" he said to me quietly while the officers made their introductions.

"She seems fine. She was more worried about R… Honey." The interest in his eyes made me a bit nervous. "What did the cameras pick up?"

"Not a damn thing," he replied frustrated. "There was no clear picture from any angle. It was dark and that added to the lack of visibility."

"You gave the bottle to the police?"

"Yes, but there isn't anything they can do unless we have a witness to the crime or surveillance. There were a lot of VIPs in the club tonight; it could have been anyone."

He was still watching Cassie, completely distracted, then tensed when she laughed at something one of the officers said. "You got a thing for the tiny ball of fire?" I chuckled.

He looked over at me like he forgot I was standing next to him. "What?"

"Admit it. You have a thing for Cassie."

"I'm just making sure she's all right," he said evasively. "That is what you told me to do tonight, right? Make sure the girls weren't bothered."

"Yeah, and I'd say we both failed epically at that my friend."

I clapped him on the back and he flinched. I wasn't sure whether it was my words or the back slap, but I had a feeling it was the former. I knew Eric took his job seriously, and me telling him we failed was probably not the best thing to do. Former marines, were still marines for life and failure wasn't a word we liked having in our vocabulary. On the battlefield, it meant someone might not make it home, and tonight could have been a disaster had Rissa not noticed something wasn't right.

Eric cleared his throat. "What?" I barked with an edge in my voice.

"You do realize this could all blow up in your face right?"

"I'm well aware of that."

"Yet, you keep staring at her."

"Fuck man," I whispered back. "I can't stay away from her. And technically, I saw her first."

That got a loud laugh out of him. Everyone turned to us and heat crept up my neck. If I didn't know better I would have thought I was blushing.

"Did you call dibs?"

"I married her, you ass."

"Good point." He sobered a bit, but I could still see the mischief dancing in his eyes.

"What is it?" I sighed.

"You're in the middle of some real-life Jerry Springer shit."

"That I am." I chuckled. "You gonna ask Cassie out?"

I swear I had never seen the big man embarrassed before, so when his cheeks flamed pink and he shook his head, I hunched my shoulders to keep my laugher hidden. Cassie glared at me as if she knew we were discussing her. There was some major work to be done there, getting her to approve of me.

"Nah man, she's way outta my league."

"That's bullshit," I replied adamantly.

"Look at her. She's beautiful. I don't stand a chance."

He looked at her longingly, and I wanted to slap him upside the head. "You're a marine damn it. Start acting like it."

Would he take the bait? It took mere seconds before I saw the determination slide over his features.

"Hoorah," he replied.

"Hoorah," I answered him back.

RISSA

I kept finding myself looking over at the two men whispering quietly to each other, not even paying attention to the officers, and I swore—well, not really—if Cassie elbowed me in the ribs one more time, one of them was going to break.

There was something magnetic about Cole Hillard. He was graceful in his movements but calculated at the same time. He was an enigma, and I couldn't keep my eyes off of him.

"Ms. Davies?" the officer who had introduced himself as Officer Clark asked.

"I'm sorry, what?"

"What made you think Ms. Micheals had been drugged?"

"Oh, well, we had only had one glass of champagne before we decided to go dancing. After Cole rescued me from the dance floor, I noticed Cassie was acting drunk, like really drunk, and I knew there was no way after only a glass or two she could have been that gone. When she went to pick up her half-full glass that was left on the table, I knew something was wrong. We both know never to drink anything left out, for just this reason." I proceeded to replay the remainder of the events of the evening to them.

"All right ladies. I think we have everything we need," Officer Carter said standing. "Do you need a ride to your hotel?"

"No," Cole chimed in before we could answer. "They will be staying here for the night."

"But…" Cassie started before she was cut off.

"You need to be monitored after tonight. You were drugged," Eric said pointedly.

Never in my life had I ever seen Cassie back down so quickly. I had no idea if it was because it was Eric insisting, or something else. My friend, who has the dirtiest mouth and a penchant for making up insults on the fly, did nothing but sit back in her seat and cross her arms over her chest glaring daggers in Eric's direction.

"There is plenty of room here," Cole said in an attempt to placate her. She simply huffed and looked away.

"Thank you Cole." I smiled and watched as he reached up and grabbed the back of his neck in what I was realizing was his nervous gesture. His sun-kissed skin was tinged pink and I wondered what on earth could cause such a confident man to blush like a teenager. It was endearing and incredibly hot all at the same time. I had no idea what was going on, but he was pulling my emotions in every possible direction.

"Well then, if that's everything we will be on our way."

"Yes thank you, Officer. I think that's everything." Offering my hand to each officer, I couldn't help but cringe at the look of excitement on the men's faces.

Poor Cass looked as if she was going to pass out again. "Why don't we get you to bed, hun. It's been a rough night."

She nodded and let me lead her back to the spare bedroom. I noticed Eric take a step forward before Cole put a hand on his shoulder and shook his head imperceptibly. I was grateful for that.

I didn't think Cassie would want him to see her like she was. She had the beginnings of a crush on him, and it was clear that feeling was reciprocated. Plans on how we could spend more time with these men began to form in my mind. I liked Cole; he was intriguing, and honestly, I wasn't sure if I wanted to walk away just yet.

"What are you smiling about?" Cassie grumbled as she laid down in the bed.

"Nothing," I lied.

"For such a 'nice' girl, you have a devious smile." She actually did the air quotes and I rolled my eyes.

"I just thought it might be fun to hang out with them while we're here."

"Come on, Riss. You just broke up with the douchebag. You really want to jump right into something else or should I say, *someone* else? But again, he is your *husband*."

"Shut it. And, who said I was jumping into anything? I'm just talking about having a little fun."

"Do tell."

"I'm tired of being the good girl. I want to get a little crazy."

I hadn't realized until that moment that was exactly what I wanted. I wanted to go out and do something crazy. Make out with a stranger in public just for the heck of it. Get drunk at a club and let loose. I had never wanted to do anything like that before—and with how I was raised, acting out was completely unacceptable—so I figured with my very public break up I was allowed a little girl-gone-wild moment. Cassie was looking at me like I had grown a second head, but I didn't care.

"Crazy? You?"

"Yup, I think that's exactly what I need."

"All right then," she said closing her eyes. "We will start tomorrow. I'm too tired to be crazy tonight."

"Get some sleep. We're going shopping tomorrow."

"Why don't I like the sound of that?" she murmured.

"It will be fun, I promise."

As I walked down the hall in search of Cole, I thought about the first crazy thing I could do. It wasn't like me at all and I didn't think I could pull it off, but the mere thought of him had my blood running hot and my lips began to tingle. It had been two hours since the kiss, but my lips felt like he just pressed his soft warm lips to mine.

I had never been kissed like that before. It was hot and primal. I wanted to do it again... do it forever. So lost in my own thoughts I didn't notice anyone there until I walked into a wall of solid muscle. Putting my hands up I grabbed his pecs to steady myself.

"Sorry, I wasn't paying attention."

"I'm not," was his rumbling reply.

I still had my hands on his pecs and must have pulled him closer because he stepped forward, sliding his hands from my arms and placing them at the small of my back. I was so entranced by his blue eyes I barely noticed the movement. He leaned forward and placed a feather light kiss on my lips that left them tingling even more, and then he stepped back. Instantly feeling the loss of his warm body, I groaned in disappointment.

"Good night, Riss. You can sleep in there," he said then walked into the other room. I balked when I realized what had just happened. The room he pointed to was his room. I didn't know what to think about that, but at that moment I was too tired to care.

When I laid down in his big bed and rested my head on his fluffy pillow all I could think about was Cole. The bed smelled distinctly of him and I wanted to breathe it in and smell it for the rest of forever. The thoughts jarred me. Hadn't I just been in love with Jake? Why was it that after only two days I was able to have thoughts about another man? Thinking about my feelings and really trying to analyze them, I realized I never loved Jake—not in the way you should to marry someone. That relationship was based on a lie—even though I never knew it—and the weight I'd been carrying lifted when that thought hit my brain. There was nothing to mourn over, and my feelings for Jake were always somewhat indifferent anyway.

Cole and I could just have a good time; it's not like we lived in the same place. Once my week here was up, I would go back to Hollywood and he would stay in Vegas. Quickly divorce and we'd never see each other again. No big deal.

As I closed my eyes and went to sleep, I tried not to dwell on the reason that made me sad.

COLE

This was a big mistake. It was one thing knowing she was somewhere in the city, but it was a completely different thing altogether knowing she was in my house, in my bed, wearing my clothes.

It was a restless night full of erotic dreams, all staring Rissa. I woke up early in the third bedroom and decided that a cold shower was in order. I couldn't get the images out of my head as the freezing water sprayed my body, which did nothing to dissuade the huge erection I was sporting. I was so hard it hurt. I punched the stone wall of the shower and pain shot up my arm. It was a nice reprieve, helping me to calm myself down. I needed to get my head on straight. There was work to do, and if I didn't get her out of my head then nothing would get done.

Concentrating better after finishing up my shower, I walked back into the adjoining bedroom and cursed. "Shit, I don't have any clothes."

There was nothing I could do but go to the master bedroom and get them. Tugging on the towel wrapped around my hips and making sure it was secure, lascivious thoughts were once again running through my mind as I walked down the hall. Maybe if I wrapped the towel around me harder, it would keep the evidence of my desire down… like literally down.

I winced as I knocked on the door with my busted hand, then waited a few moments and knocked again—this time with my other hand. When Rissa didn't answer, I freaked and went charging through the door to see what happened. That was a big mistake. I plowed right into a soft body and we both went down. I was able to turn us so I would take the brunt of the impact as we went tumbling to the floor. All the air whooshed out of me when Rissa landed on top of me.

The first thing I noticed was that she was wet and had nothing on but a towel and I felt myself hardening even more. Good Christ.

As I looked into her violet eyes they danced with merriment. I couldn't help the loud laugh that escaped me after that.

"You didn't answer the door," I said dumbly.

"I was in the shower." She laughed but it was cut off when she noticed something long and hard between us, and her eyes held a different emotion. A strand of hair fell into her eyes and I reached up to tuck it behind her ear. As my fingertips grazed across her cheek, I felt her shudder at the contact.

That was all the encouragement I needed. I reached up and took her lips in a searing kiss. Her shock only lasted a second and then she was kissing me back. The kiss got hot quick, and before I knew what was happening I had her rolled over on her back and was sucking her bottom lip into my mouth before I kissed a trail down her neck to her collarbone. She moaned when I nipped her lightly and I smiled against her skin.

"You like that, princess?" I asked as I started to remove the towel she had wrapped around her chest.

"Mmmm, yes," she groaned and weaved her fingers through my hair, pulling me down to her chest again. I chuckled lightly and wrapped my lips around one pert nipple and used my fingers on the other.

She sucked in a breath and I stilled thinking she was going to ask me to stop but she didn't.

"Don't. Stop. Cole," she panted.

"I had no intention of stopping."

With her approval, I moved my hand down her belly and lower still until my fingers were caressing her slit. My thumb rubbed small circles around her clit and she screamed my name as she came undone.

"That's one," I smiled at her.

"What?" she gasped.

I wasn't talking anymore because my mouth was tracing a path down her skin. It wasn't long before I was at the juncture of her thighs. She was writhing and moaning and it was the sexiest damn thing I had ever seen in my life. Even my dreams hadn't been this erotic. I was hard as stone, but I wasn't ready to take her yet. My tongue veered off course and licked her inner thigh before I nipped it with my teeth. She groaned again and pulled my hair in an attempt to bring me back to where she needed me. I let her and slowly leisurely licked her up and down.

"Cole, I need you."

"What do you want, Rissa?" I asked with a knowing smile.

"Faster, harder, please," she begged.

\I rewarded her. Sucking her clit in my mouth hard, she screamed my name. I had never heard anything so goddamn sexy in my entire fucking life. She pulled my hair up roughly and I smiled that sexy smile that made girls melt.

"Two," I said and smirked at her.

"I need you inside me."

"What do you need, princess?" I asked and then stuck two fingers inside her. "Is that what you want?"

She shook her head emphatically. "No," she moaned.

I nuzzled her thigh. "Tell me what you want."

97

"I want your… your manhood inside of me," she squeaked out, and I burst into laughter.

"I'm sorry princess, you're gonna have to do better than that." I continued her torment, licking up and down her inner thigh as my fingers stilled. "You can't say it, can you?"

"Say what?" she groaned and ground against my fingers, trying to get me to move.

"Cock. Is that what you want? My big hard cock inside you?"

"Yes please."

She looked down at me and I nearly complied just from her shy smile, but I held firm even though I groaned out, "Say it, princess," as I thrust my fingers in and out of her. I was staring into her eyes and she looked uncertain before she shook her head emphatically.

"Okay then." I smirked and eased up before sucking a nipple into my mouth and bit down gently. She cried out and thrashed her head from side to side as her pussy clenched tightly, gripping my fingers.

"That's three. Say it, princess tell me you want my big cock inside of you. I know you can feel it resting on your thigh. I know you want it as bad as I do. All you have to do is tell me," I coaxed.

"God Cole, you're so frustrating." She pulled my hair in an attempt to pull me up. "Yes Cole, I want your… cock inside me," she whispered.

The smile that spread across my face was smug as I slid up her body. It didn't last long though. As soon as my dick was near, she reached down, squeezed it and positioned it at her entrance, arching her hips. I was lost. This time she smiled smugly and rolled her hips bringing me in that much deeper. I groaned and kissed her fiercely, taking her bottom lip into my mouth once again and grazing it with my teeth before I thrust into her hard and fast. It was as if I were a man possessed. I don't know where it came from, but I couldn't stop myself from pounding into her again and again. She screamed my name one last time and I pulled out as hot wet jets of cum splashed across her belly. It had almost been too late, forgetting myself in my haste to consume her. Her eyes were glazed as I collapsed beside her and realized for the first time that we were on the hardwood floor of my bedroom with the bed literally three feet away, and I busted out laughing.

"What's so funny?" She glared at me and I shook my head as I continued to laugh. I pointed at the bed and she giggled softly in understanding, then dropped her head back down on the ground with a thump and gave me the stink eye. "Shit. I need another shower."

"Sorry about that." I grimaced. "I got carried away." I wasn't about to tell her what it did to me. The possessiveness I felt knowing that I had marked her. It was insanely hot and I needed desperately to stop thinking thoughts like that, or I would be hard as a rock for the rest of the day. I had a feeling that I was going to have a perpetual hard-on whenever she was around.

"Rissa?" I heard Cassie call from the hall.

"One minute," she called back and I jumped up off of her. I reached down to help her to her feet and she smiled in gratitude.

I couldn't take my eyes off of her. When she put her hand in mine and I helped her to her feet, a shock went up my arm and straight to my balls. Even the most innocent touch had my mind turning to mush. Reaching down to grab our towels, and handing her one, she said, "Thanks."

"This is not how I imagined this morning going."

"Really?" She smiled up at me coyly. "You didn't plan on jumping me the second I got out of the shower?"

"I'm not saying that I didn't thoroughly enjoy it, but no, that wasn't my intention when I walked in here. I just can't help myself around you."

Taking a step closer to her, she backed away. "Uh uh, no way. Cassie is right outside that door." She pointed, still backing away from me.

I stalked towards her like a predator after its prey and she laughed as she took off running towards the door. She almost made it, but her long legs still weren't as long as mine, and I was able to grab her around the middle just before she reached the knob. Turning her in my arms, I backed her against the wall and sealed my mouth over hers one more time. The kiss started slow, searching but quickly became desperate and hungry. I had to break it off fast or I would end up fucking her against the wall with her friend just outside.

When I broke the kiss, we were both breathing hard. I put my forehead against hers and attempted to catch my breath. "I had some clothes brought up for you," I said and brushed a feather light kiss across her jaw. She moaned lightly and I smiled against her skin.

"Th-thank you," she stuttered and my smile grew even bigger.

"Can I see you tonight?" She just nodded, obviously not trusting her voice to answer me, and didn't that just harden a certain part of me again.

"Great. I'll pick you up at seven. Where are you staying?"

Before she got a chance to answer, there was a loud banging on the door and she flinched. "Are you two about done?" Cassie yelled through the door.

I looked at her and we both cracked up. Rissa walked to the door and threw it open dramatically. "What is it, Cassie?"

She looked between us and studied Rissa in nothing but a towel, her skin still flushed from our prior activities, and rolled her eyes.

"Hey forearm," she shot me a glare, "if you hurt my friend, I will cut your fucking balls off. Are we clear?"

The smirk fell from my face and I adjusted my towel like it would protect me from her assault at the same time Rissa yelled, "Cassie. What the heck?"

"I'm just making sure he understands," she said innocently enough, yet still glared at me.

"I have no intention of hurting her," I said honestly, still holding my hands near my crotch. I was a marine and did a tour in Afghanistan. Nothing scared me, but this little woman who was a foot shorter than me and a hundred pounds soaking wet terrified me.

"Good, do you have anything to eat here? I'm starving."

It was insane how fast she could change from terrifying to normal. It made my head spin. "No, but you can call down to room service and order anything you like."

I noticed she was wearing a T-shirt and nothing else. Thank God I had remembered to order up some things for her too. "I have a bag from the boutique downstairs with clothes for both of you on the couch in the living room," I offered.

Crazy Cassie gave me a megawatt smile, confirming my idea that my wife's best friend was nuts. "Thanks, I don't think it's a good idea for us to go downstairs in nothing but T-shirts. The paps would have a field day with that one."

"Maybe we should." Rissa laughed, then she looked at me curiously, having heard my growl, and shook her head.

I had no idea where it came—which really was bullshit, I knew exactly where that growl came from—but decided not to think about it as I walked over to my closet and started pulling a suit from the hanger.

"Hey Cass? Can you go get the bag and order me some food too? I need a shower," Rissa whispered to her friend.

"O-okay," she said slowly and left the room a bit confused as she looked at Riss with her wet hair and towel-clad body. Thank God she didn't say anything. I could feel her eyes burning a hole in the back of my head as I grabbed underwear and socks from a drawer.

"Sorry about her," Rissa said once she was gone.

"Don't worry about it. I'm glad you have a protective friend. Though, honestly she scares the shit out of me."

"She scares me sometimes too. You should have seen her the other night. I thought she was going to rip Maria's throat out."

"Maria? You mean…" I trailed off.

"Yeah, that Maria. My ex's current, who just happens to be

working on the same job I am now. She showed up at my house to gloat after she sent that video to my phone."

I flinched. My little brother had the worst taste in women and Maria sounded psychotic. Jake said that nothing happened in that video, but I didn't care. I was actually glad that it happened; it brought Rissa back to me.

"She your co-star?" I asked in confusion.

"Not for long, my manager is going to be taking care of that."

"Yeah?"

"Yeah. I'm going to have him tell the studio that if they don't remove her from the show then I'm walking. He already has about ten other parts lined up for me." She shook her head and muttered, "Everyone wants a piece of Hollywood's good girl."

"What do you girls have planned today?" I decided to change the subject. She looked conflicted with all that was happening. It couldn't be easy for her, being in the spotlight all the time.

The bright smile she gifted me was enough for me to realize I'd guessed correctly. "We're going shopping."

"Let me send Eric with you. You could use the security in case the vultures come after you."

"No, that's all right. I wouldn't want to impose. I'm sure you need him here."

"No," I replied with an edge to my tone that shouldn't have been there. "I want you to take him with you." She looked at me curiously and must have seen that I wasn't going to bend on this. She nodded. "Good girl."

"I really need to shower now," she said somewhat defiantly, trying I guess to get a piece of her own back.

"Do you want some company?" I asked suggestively, loving the blush that was beginning to cover her neck and face.

"You know we will never get clean if you come in there with me, and I have shopping to do today." She was walking backward away from me towards the bathroom door.

"Suit yourself." I smirked over my shoulder and walked out of the room, positive I heard her sigh as I closed the door behind me.

RISSA

That man was going to be the death of me. My body, hours later, still hummed from the things he did to me. I couldn't get him out of my head. I had never had an experience so unbelievably hot in my entire life. This new crazy me was enjoying the feeling.

"Earth to Riss?" Cassie snapped at me.

"What?"

She rolled her eyes. "What store are we going to?"

"Sorry." My cheeks heated in embarrassment; I'm sure they knew exactly where my mind was at. Eric chuckled, so I shot him a glare but he just laughed even harder.

We were walking down the strip, which was a bad idea. Cole had given me an old worn-out Red Sox baseball cap to wear. I cringed when he slapped it on my head. I had grabbed some oversized sunglasses at one of the boutiques in his hotel in the hopes that I wouldn't be recognized. My eyes were always a dead giveaway. Without them showing, I was just another blonde girl on the strip. "I'm not sure. You're the fashionable one, tell me where you think."

Cassie looked at me with an evil smile and I could see the glee in her eyes as she pulled me into a hotel on the strip. My stomach sank briefly, but I reminded myself that I had asked for this. I wanted to be a little crazy—if only for a week.

"Do you have my phone, Cass? I need to call Al."

"What for?"

"He needs to get Maria off the show before I get back, or I'm walking," I said confidently.

"That's the best idea you've had," she replied digging though her clutch and pulling the device out.

We walked into a little boutique with big fluffy couches and I sat down and waited for my phone to turn on. My notifications started pinging through almost immediately. When I opened it up to the home screen, I saw there were over a thousand Twitter notifications. I had no idea why I opened the app. I guess it was some sick desire to see what was happening back in LA or maybe I was trying to punish myself. I saw tweet after tweet of fans supporting me. Even with the pictures surfacing from last night they were still behind me. There was even a hashtag #BoycottDevilRising. I clicked it and saw over a hundred thousand tweets from fans who were disgusted by Jake and what he did. My heart swelled at the devotion I saw from my fans and a single tear slipped down my cheek.

"I knew I shouldn't have given you your phone back," Cassie snapped, walking back up to me. I shook my head and handed her my phone.

"Look."

A slow smile spread across her face as she read the tag and then saw the number of tweets. "That's right," she whooped. "I bet you ticket sales have tanked for the douche nuggets in Devils Rising. I wonder what they are saying about Maria's skanky ass now."
She read a few more tweets and laughed. "They are calling for her

to be removed from the show. No one wants to see her anymore either, look."

#FireThatSkank. I laughed out loud at that. I didn't swear at all, but when I read that tag, I couldn't help but feel lighter. I got out of the app and dialed Al.

"Honey, where have you been? Scratch that, I know where you are. What can I do for you babe?"

"I want her out."

"You and the rest of the world," he agreed.

"I'm serious, Al. I want you to tell the studio that if she is still there when I get back, I'm walking."

"I think that's the most unforgiving thing I have ever heard you say. I like it. Heartbreak looks good on you, kid."

"I'm not heartbroken. I'm mad and embarrassed. She did this out of spite, and I refuse to let her get away with it. She can have Jake Moore. I want nothing to do with him. I just don't want to have to put up with her every day, got it?"

"There's my ice queen. Your mother would be proud," he replied. That was not a reminder I needed—too many painful memories, but kept my mouth shut. "I will get on the phone with the studio and let you know before you get back, what their answer is. Remember, we still have all those roles to look over in case they say they are keeping her, but with everyone screaming for her head it would be suicide to keep her on and let you walk."

"Thanks Al." I hung up the phone and handed it back to Cassie. "Well?"

"He's gonna try to get her out by the end of the week." I smiled and she grinned back at me. Eric shook his head, looking a bit uncomfortable. I had no idea what his deal was, but I didn't care. Maria and Jake may not have ruined my life, but they had humiliated me and I wasn't going to let that go unpunished.

"I got one of the attendants to put some stuff in a dressing room that might help with your new look." Cassie grinned evilly.

"Awesome." I was feeling excited about what I had planned. I was done wallowing, done being the girl everyone else thought I should be. While I was here in Vegas I was going to do what I wanted, and I didn't care what anyone else thought.

The rest of the day was a blur of clothes and shoes that I never would have thought to wear before. The skirts were short and the heels were high. It was everything I wasn't and I loved every second of it.

Every once in a while I would see a camera phone out snapping pictures, but Eric was good at his job and made sure to remove the person from my presence whenever that happened. I was sure there were going to be pictures of me all over social media before the end of the day, but that didn't bother me.

By late afternoon, we were in some chic boutique off the strip, and Eric was loaded down with shopping bags that he insisted on carrying for us, when I heard a gasp from the front of the store. It was a sales lady. She was staring at me with her mouth open in shock, and I had a feeling that there was going to be trouble.

"Ms. Davies? Is there anything I can help you with?" she asked with a giddy smile.

I smiled back and shook my head. "We are just looking, thank you."

"If you need anything, anything at all don't hesitate to ask." She beamed at me.

"Discretion would be lovely."

She deflated. "Yes, ma'am."

"Come on." I grabbed Cassie and pulled her towards the racks. "I figure we have thirty minutes before every fangirl in the state descends upon this place."

"She said she would be discreet," Eric replied in confusion. Poor, sweet, guileless man has no clue.

"Look at this place," Cassie informed Eric. "No one shops off the strip. That woman is thinking about ways to get people in her store and will sell us out because everyone wants to shop where the great Honey Davies does." She actually used my name in air quotes. Geez.

I looked around for something to buy—might as well help the lady out. I could start a new trend and boost her sales for a bit—even if she was about to sell my location out. I found a gorgeous silk scarf that matched my eyes and took it up to the register. Her eyes lit up when she saw something in my hands, and she just stood there.

"I would like to pay now," I gently reminded her with a smile as she continued to gawk at me. That seemed to bring her out of her trance and she took the scarf from me ringing it up and swiping my credit card.

"Uh Riss?" Cassie said with trepidation. I turned and saw a crowd forming outside, complete with the dreaded paparazzi. The usual flash bulbs and some TV cameras were rapidly blinking, I turned an accusatory glare at the sales lady, who had the good sense to look ashamed of herself.

"I'm so sorry. Business has been bad lately and I was scared. When I saw you walk in, I couldn't help myself. I'm a horrible person," she cried.

"Look, you're fine." God, I really was too nice. "They have been on my tail since I got to Vegas. Next time a celebrity comes into your store, though, could you wait until after they leave to Tweet about it?"

"You really are a good person. I wasn't sure if it was just an image." She blushed bright red.

"There is a car waiting for us on the curb. Are you ready Ms. Davies?" Eric asked formally.

The chagrined woman handed me my bag and credit card, and I turned to look at the pandemonium outside. The crowd had grown in the time I was talking to the sales lady and I grimaced. "Ready as I'll ever be."

Eric walked ahead of us to keep the reporters and fans at bay. As soon as there was space between us and the door, the crowd surged around us, blocking us in from all sides.

"Honey! How are you feeling?"

"Is it true you are leaving the show?"

"Were you drugged at Voodoo last night?"

The questions were shouted from every direction, and I did my best not to react to them. The last question had me pausing and Eric grabbed me and put a protective arm around me. He had Cassie on the other side and he was pushing through the throng. I was grateful to Cole in that moment. Had I refused to bring Eric along, we would have been in some serious trouble. He helped me into the car and Cassie got in after me and I clutched her arm. Eric deposited our bags in next and shut the door before climbing into the front seat. I looked up and the look of concern on Cole's face had me blushing.

"Are you okay?" he asked before pulling away from the curb.

"I'm fine." I stared into his eyes through the rearview mirror. Eric nudged him with his elbow and the spell was broken and he turned to watch the road.

"Where am I taking you?" It was a loaded question. I knew where he wanted to take us, but I wasn't so sure Cassie would like that idea.

"The Bellagio," Cassie answered for me.

"The Bellagio is surrounded by photographers. I saw it on my way to pick you up."

"Shit, stupid ass clowns," she muttered and both men laughed loudly.

"I can get you a suite in my hotel for as long as you'd like," Cole offered.

Cassie and I looked at each other and shrugged. "How will we get our stuff?"

"I'll send someone to pick your belongings up."

"Okay," I said quietly and Cassie shot me a look. "What? The press have the hotel surrounded. Do you want to cut this short?"

"No!" Everyone yelled at once and I jumped back in my seat and looked at Eric curiously. I had a feeling he had a thing for my friend, but his vehement response to us leaving early caught me a little off guard. "I just figured you need more time to unwind before we go back to the madness," she added quickly, her face heating.

"Okay… we will stay in Cole's hotel then." I was surprised that the whoosh of air they all released didn't blow me out of the car.

"That's fine." Cassie waved a hand as if distracted, yet I noticed her little glances at Eric as we drove down the strip. I elbowed her giving her a little head nod in Eric's direction. She rolled her eyes at me and turned to look out the window.

"Let me call the hotel and have them set something up for you," he said messing with the Bluetooth in the car.

"Hello, Mr. Hillard. What can I do for you?" A perky voice said over the phone. I raised an eyebrow at him but he shook his head.

"Mindy, I need a suite set up for my… uh friend." He winced, then said with more conviction, "The best one we have for a Ms. Rissa Taylor."

"Sure thing Mr. Hillard," her voice deflated and I almost felt bad for the girl.

"Thank you, Mindy. We will need this in the next five minutes. We're on our way in through the VIP entrance."

"I will have Marco waiting with the keys. Can I do anything else for you?"

"No, and thank you Mindy," he replied with kindess before hanging up.

I sat back stunned. Even as gruff and demanding as I knew he could be, he was genuinely a respectful person. You can tell a lot about a person by the way they treat people—especially how they treat the people who work for them. Cole Hillard was an enigma, and I was wishing more than ever that we weren't leaving in a week.

We went into an underground parking garage, and I saw an older Latino man with salt and pepper hair waiting by a set of doors for us. Cole got out and shook hands with him before the man opened our door and grabbed our bags. "Rissa, this is Marco. He is the best concierge in the business. He will make sure you get to your room and get everything you need. I have some stuff I have to handle before dinner tonight," he said and kissed the side of my head.

"We're going to dinner tonight?" Cassie raised a perfect eyebrow at me.

"Yeah," Cole said not missing a beat. "I figured the four of us could have dinner in one of the private rooms in the restaurant tonight and then go to the club."

"Uhhh… I don't know if I want to go to the club again anytime soon," Cassie said looking a little green.

"Let's see how you feel after dinner," I said gently and lead her to the doors.

"Right this way Ms. D-Taylor," Marco stuttered.

I smiled at him reassuringly. "I know you know who I am, but can we keep it between us?"

"Sure thing Ms. Taylor."

"Thank you."

We took a private elevator to our floor and I looked around. "Is this Cole's floor?"

"Yes ma'am. Only the best suites are on the top floor. Mr. Hillard asked for the best, so here we are." He pointed at a set of double doors and handed me a key.

"Thank you, Marco." I dug through my purse, but he caught my arm and shook his head.

"That's not necessary. Just enjoy your stay." He set the bags inside the room and smiled at us before walking back to the private elevator.

"Marco?" He stopped and turned back to me. "Were you the one he sent to have my dress dry cleaned?"

"Yes ma'am, I will check on it for you."

Cassie was already walking into the room by the time I thanked Marco and crossed the threshold. The opulence was breathtaking, and the view across the desert, stunning. It was easy to see why Cole's hotel was as popular as it was. The room was exquisite and his staff was exceptional. Making my way down to put my bag in one of the bedrooms Cassie asked me suspiciously, "What are you doing?"

"Um… I'm going to look for something to wear. What does it look like?" I was confused by her question and more confused by her stance.

"No, Riss. I mean what are you doing with Cole?"

"What do you mean?" I asked innocently as I put my clothes in the dresser drawer, refusing to look up at her through the mirror.

"You know damn well what I mean. The two of you were in that room together… naked… for a long time this morning."

My face heated and the memories of what exactly we were doing that morning played in my mind. My body was humming again and I groaned in my head.

"Rissa," Cassie yelled, shocked.

Shit, did I groan out loud?

"What on earth are you doing with this guy?"

"Nothing, I'm leaving in a week, remember?"

"Yeah, I hope you remember that when the week is over," she said aghast. "I know you were hurt, babe-"

I cut her off. I didn't want her to think that this was about Jake and some type of rebound.

"This isn't about Jake. I'm not even hurt by him. You know how they say the opposite of love is hate?" I asked. "It's not. You have to love someone to hate them. Indifference is the opposite of love, and that is all I feel for Jake. Nothing. I hope he has a nice life."

"Wow, I never thought I would hear that," she replied thoughtfully.

"I realized that I never loved Jake, and I have no idea why I agreed to marry him."

"You really like the forearm, don't you?" She laughed and I rolled my eyes.

"Thanks for reminding me." I plopped down on the edge of the bed. Geez, this thing was comfortable, but before I could let my mind wander to places it definitely shouldn't go, I needed to stay focused. "How do you tell someone you think you could fall for... and fall for hard... that you need a divorce?"

Cassie took a running jump and landed on the bed beside me. "I don't know, babe, are you sure that's what you want now?"

"Of course it is." I knew from her reaction she could see the doubt written all over my face.

"Denial isn't a good look on you, chick. You need to decide." She flopped over on her back and proceeded to fluff the pillows under her head.

"What does it matter? We live in two different states."

"It's Vegas not New York, and you were willing to be somewhat long distance with Jake when he was on tour," she reminded me.

I crawled up the rest of the bed, and fluffed up my pillows as well, then turned and looked directly at my best friend. "True, but I don't know Cass. Let's just see how things go this week."

COLE

When I got to the office, I turned to Eric, who looked as anxious as I felt.

"Why did you include me in this dinner?" he asked me after a few minutes.

"You like her," I said simply.

"She's so far out of my league."

"I'm pretty sure she likes you too."

"Don't fuck with me," he replied angrily.

"I'm not, I swear."

"Fine, I will go to this damn dinner."

"Good, now I need you to go to the Bellagio and see to getting their stuff."

"You got it," he said and left my office. A moment later my phone rang and I groaned. My father had the worst timing.

"Hey Dad."

"Cole, how are things going?"

"They're great. What can I do for you?"

"Good, that's good. I'm in the process of acquiring a hotel in the Los Angeles area and I was wondering if you could manage it until I get someone new. It's going to be a big undertaking getting everything up to our standards and I don't trust anyone else to do it."

A slow smile spread across my face. My dad had no idea how amazing this opportunity was for me, and I found myself getting excited.

"I know you don't like the idea of being in the same city as your brother," he continued, "but I really need you to do this for me. I'm going to be retiring soon and I need to know that you can handle anything."

Shit I forgot about Jake.

"Absolutely Dad, I will do whatever you need me to."

"That's my boy. The sale won't be final for about a month. I will talk to you about it soon."

He hung up and I was left with a dilemma. If this happened, I would eventually have to tell Rissa who my brother was. Hell, if we continued on the path I sincerely hoped we'd be taking, she needed to find out, but I was hoping that day would come much later.

I toyed with the idea of just telling her now and getting it over with, since she would find out eventually. It was a pretty sure thing she would freak out, and I wasn't ready to lose her just yet. If I was honest with myself, even in the few hours I had spent with her, I knew I was never going to be ready to lose her. She was so much more than I'd imagined these past five years.

I plopped down in my chair and leaned back scrubbing my face. I was in some serious shit no matter how I looked at it. The longer I went without telling her the worse it would be. The image of her with her eyes filled with hurt and her face showing nothing but betrayal slammed into me unbidden and I had no idea where it came from, but it gutted me. The only thing I could do was prove to her that I was nothing like my brother *before* I broke the news. Hopefully then, she would be able to forgive me for omitting the truth. If not, misery was going to be my constant companion for the rest of my life.

My intercom beeped and Ruthie came over the line. "Mr. Hillard, I have a woman named Nikki on the line. She says she's a friend of Eric's and that you are expecting her call?"

"Yes, Ruthie. Put her through and sit tight. I may need you to fax an employment contract over to her." At least the day was looking up a little bit. Eric had said he didn't think she would call back until her trip was done. When the phone flashed I picked it up.

"This is Cole."

"Hello, Mr Hillard. Eric says you have a management job open in your club and were asking for me?"

"Yes, Nikki." I breathed out a sigh of relief. "When can you start?"

"Wow, I just got back into town—I flew in as soon as I got Eric's message. What happened to the old manager, may I ask?" I understood her curiosity. She needed to know why there was such a good position open so quickly and what she was walking into. Excellent signs of a quality employee. Looked like I was going to owe Eric.

"The old manager was breaking quite a few hotel policies and was fired immediately. My hope is that I won't ever see his face again."

"Understandable, though which ones, may I ask?" she questioned and I could hear the smile in her voice—she probably knew the answer before asking.

"As you can imagine, I have confidentiality policies in place, so I can't openly discuss that with you, but if you decide to accept the position, I am sure the rumor mill will let you in on all the sordid details."

Her knowing laughter filled the phone. "I'm sure they will. Eric has already filled me in on some of the specifics of the job. Were you interested in me starting tonight without a formal interview?"

"Yes, that would be perfect, thank you. Eric's approval and high praise of you is all I need. Would you be able to come in before five and fill out the employment contract as well?"

"If you don't mind me saying, Mr. Hillard, you have got to be the most polite club owner I have ever met. I'll be there at five."

"Excellent, and thank you, Nikki." Perfect, at least I wouldn't have to deal with Voodoo again tonight. My gut was telling me that Nikki was going to be an excellent hire, and with thoughts going to my night ahead, I knew I wasn't going to get anymore work done. As I was walking around to the front desk, making my way back up to my room, Mindy bounced over to me.

"Hi Mr. Hillard." She batted her eyelashes and I groaned internally.

"Hi Mindy, did you need something?"

"My shift is over," she said a little too suggestively and I swerved around her. "Did you maybe want to get a drink?"

"Sorry Mindy, and please remember, we have a strict no fraternizing policy, and I would very much appreciate you remember that," I said briskly and picked up my pace. I saw her face fall and the last thing I wanted to do was hurt the young girl's feelings, but I couldn't have my employees thinking I would break my own rules.

I was almost to the elevator when I remembered I didn't call the restaurant to make the reservations. Changing course, I headed towards the steakhouse on the other side of the casino, which took so much longer than it should have with the number of people asking for directions or needing help with operations. It was exhausting. By the time I made it to the restaurant I wanted to bellow in frustration, but the hostess perked up when she saw me, and I was glad I didn't have to go any farther to get help.

"Hello Mr. Hillard." She gave me a professional smile. "Is there something I can help you with?"

"I need my usual private table at seven," I replied warily, knowing my tone was going to be harsh, but it couldn't be helped. "I will have three guests joining me. It is imperative that the utmost discretion is used this evening. This guest is a VIP, and if I find out anyone does not respect her privacy they will be fired on the spot, understand?"

She nodded, eyes wide and wrote down the reservation, and I felt a little guilty for scaring the girl.

As I made my way back to my room, my phone started buzzing in my pocket. "Cole here," I answered without looking to see who was calling.

"I got their stuff, boss," Eric stated. "I'm on my way back now."

"Great, did you have any problems?"

"Someone had a camera last night and there are blurry pixelated photographs of us helping with Cassie. Add that to the pictures taken today of me with the girls at that boutique, and let's just say, I think I had at least one tail. I am pretty sure I lost them though."

"Shit. Maybe we should just skip dinner then."

"Do you honestly think these girls will stay cooped up in their hotel room?" he asked me in disbelief.

"No, you're right." I blew out a breath. "We will just have to make sure security is extra tight tonight. Oh, and I got that call from Nikki. You were right, she sounds perfect. I told her to come in early, but since it's her first day, call everyone else you got—I don't want anyone with a camera getting within fifty feet of Rissa."

"You got it, boss. I will start calling as soon as I get back."

"Thanks."

Walking to my coffee table, I picked up my laptop and googled her. The most recent pictures were of them at the boutique this afternoon. I scrolled through those and saw some horribly grainy cell phone pictures, which were so much worse than I thought. There was a picture from the dance floor when I ripped the guy off Riss and another of me leading her away. It was difficult to make out my face and the gossip blogs were speculating as to who I was.

That was the only solace I had, that, and the fact that they were calling me a hero. I chuckled at that thought. I was anything but a hero, and I needed to be careful to keep my identity hidden or this would be over before it began.

RISSA

"There is no way I am wearing this out in public," I yelled from the bathroom.

"Come on, it can't be that bad." Cassie huffed. "That outfit looked hot on you in the store."

"Yes, but we are going to dinner. You can't go to a fancy restaurant wearing torn-up shorts and a black crop top."

"You're Honey fucking Davies. You can wear a garbage bag and still look good," she bellowed back in frustration.

"Fine." I bluffed and walked out of the bathroom. There was a low whistle from Cassie.

"See? You look hot, but you're right. You can't wear that to dinner. Go put on that little black dress with the plunging neckline. Leave your hair down like that; it makes you look wild."

"Ugh, you can be so annoying sometimes," I groaned and trudged back into the bathroom.

I stripped out of the shirt and shorts, but left the fishnets on.

Slipping the dress over my head I looked in the mirror and smiled. This was the perfect dress. It was tight at the top and the neckline plunged between my breasts. I wouldn't be able to wear a bra with it, but that was fine I had gone braless many times. It flared out at the bottom and had a slit that nearly went to my hip. I looked back up in the mirror. My blonde hair was wild and my violet eyes popped with the smoky eye I had applied. I could totally see the wild and crazy vixen in my own eyes. *Cole is going to have a heart attack.*

Strutting out of the bathroom, I grabbed the sky-high stilettos that we decided to pair with the dress. They looked fabulous.

"Wait, the fishnets don't work with that outfit."

"You know, I think you're right," I agreed and started to strip them off. There was a knock on the door and Cassie jumped up. She wasn't dressed yet, still wearing the robe on from after her shower, and I watched from the hall as she strutted to the front door and flung it open only to freeze with a shocked look on her face.

"Cole... uh... he asked me to... um... bring your..." Eric's eyes smoldered and I thought he was going to devour my friend right then and there. I giggled and the spell broke. They each took a step back and he shook his head to clear it and I could see the blush coloring my Cassie's cheeks.

"Cole asked you to bring our stuff over?" I asked hoping to break the obvious tension.

"Yeah, he did." He was still staring at Cassie so I left them to it.

It was so nice to see my friend genuinely interested in someone. I liked Eric; he seemed like a nice guy. I hoped the two of them could get to know each other better over the next week.

A few minutes later the door shut and Cassie came in with a huff. "Why did you let me answer the door like this?"

"Me? You jumped up and ran out there before I could even say anything."

"You could have stopped me."

I laughed loudly at her. She shot me a disgruntled glare then stalked into the bathroom, slamming the door. My phone beeped, looking down at the screen, before hitting End, I groaned. I was not letting Jake ruin my vacation with his garbage.

"Who was that?" Cassie walked out of the bathroom in an electric blue maxi dress, looking hot. Poor Eric, he had no idea.

"Ugh. It was Jake… he won't leave me alone."

"It's an ego trip," she said offhandedly. "The only reason he keeps calling is because you bruised his ego when you dumped him."

"Yeah, that's probably it."

"He's an idiot and an egomaniac. You might want to answer the phone the next time he calls, or you may have an unwelcome surprise while you're here."

"Oh God, that's the last thing I need. Maybe, I should call him back?" She shrugged her shoulders and I picked up my phone.

"Why have you been ignoring me?" he slurred, answering on the second ring.

"My phone was off. What do you want?"

"What the fuck are you doing in Vegas? Are you trying to embarrass me?" He was getting angrier by the moment.

"Embarrass you? Don't you think you have embarrassed yourself enough with that little display of yours," I reminded him snidely.

"Your fans are ruining my life," he sighed out, the anger fading from his voice. "We've had three shows cancelled because of this little boycott. The band is thinking about kicking me out because I'm bad for business."

"You should have thought about that before you cheated on me." It was my turn to get pissed; my face was flushed and I wondered why the heck I even called him back. "Goodbye Jake."

"No wait. Please take me back. I need you."

"That's never going to happen," I replied and hung up the phone.

"What did he say?"

"His precious career is on the line. What do you think he said?"
I rolled my eyes.

"Really?" She laughed. "What an ass clown. He seriously
thought you would take him back? After the whole world saw that
video?"

"Yeah. He said my fans are ruining his life and they had to
cancel some shows."

I heard a knock on the door and looked down at my phone. *Five
til seven. Shoot.*

"I'll get it," I said as Cassie looked at me in horror. "Hurry up
and get your shoes on."

I walked out into the foyer and opened the door and was struck
dumb by what I saw. Cole was gorgeous in a suit, but the way he
wore dress pants with his crisp white button up and the sleeves
rolled up to his elbows was devastating. His forearms were
prominently displayed and I inwardly smirked. My eyes locked on
his and he smiled before leisurely perusing my body with his eyes.
My face flushed and I looked away shyly. His finger reached up
and turned me to face him before feathering the lightest touch of
his lips to mine.

"Hi," I said breathless.

"Hi." He knew good and well what he was doing to me. If I
swore, I would have had a few choice words for him.

A throat cleared behind him and I looked up at Eric. He looked
hot as usual and I couldn't wait for him to see Cassie.

"Cassie is almost ready and then we can go."

"I'm ready…" She paused and I could see it in her eyes just how
much she was digging Eric, who was looking at her with mirrored
appreciation—and I could swear I heard a soft groan leave his lips
as he stalked closer to her.

"You look amazing," Cole whispered in my ear. The hairs on
the back of neck stood up as I shuddered.

"Thank you, you don't look so bad yourself."

Cole offered me his arm and I looped my arm through his before heading out the door to the elevators. Cassie and Eric were standing awkwardly next to each other before realizing we were waiting for them.

The restaurant was busy, but as soon as the hostess saw us she walked directly over—there was recognition in her eyes when she saw me. I hoped this didn't become a spectacle. I really didn't want to have to be rushed out of the restaurant because over-eager fans or paps were looking for a story. When she led us around the back to a room, I breathed a sigh of relief. I should have known that Cole would have something like this planned. I smiled at him gratefully and he winked back at me.

"Here you are Mr. Hillard. Your server will be here shortly. Can I get you something to drink while you wait?" The hostess batted her eyes at him. Who could blame her? Cole had a damaging effect on the opposite sex. My own girly parts had been on overdrive since the moment we met.

"Can you get us a bottle of Dom, please?" She nodded her head. "Thank you, Kristy."

"Do you know everyone in this hotels name?"

"It wouldn't be good business if I didn't make an effort to know the people who work for me."

"You sound like a good boss," I said as he pulled out the chair for me. "You don't seem to have a superiority complex."

"What makes you say that?"

"You actually treat them like they are people. Most employers don't ask politely or thank an employee when they do what's asked of them. I'm trying really hard to find a flaw in you, Mr. Hillard."

Having him leaning over me while I was sitting down was doing wicked things to my body. He breathed in deeply and I heard a soft groan. "You smell heavenly."

"Thank you."

"I'm starting to wonder why they even brought us here," Cassie whispered to Eric, but loudly enough for us to hear. That snapped me from my daze.

"Yeah, me too." Eric was quick to agree.

Cole quickly pulled his own chair out before sitting down next to me. The table was rectangle, so we were able to sit two chairs next to each other. When Cole's thigh brushed mine, I nearly jumped and noticed his eyes sparkling as he laid a hand on my knee. He saw that I wasn't pushing him away, so his thumb started rubbing circles over my skin. I shivered. The devious smile he slid in my direction told me that he knew exactly what his touch was doing to me.

Cassie and Eric looked at us knowingly, but just before Cassie was about to open her mouth to comment, Kristy came in with a champagne bucket and four glasses. After pouring the champagne she gave us each a glass before handing us our menus. I smiled at her in thanks and she walked away without another word.

"The filet with sautéed mushrooms is to die for," Cole said once she was gone.

"I probably would die from it." He shot me a confused glance. "I'm deathly allergic to mushrooms."

"Do you have to ingest them for them to hurt you?"

"No, my reaction can be fatal—if they even touch my skin-"

"No mushrooms," he demanded and began looking at his menu. I had a feeling that I just ruined his dinner. "What about onions?"

"Sautéed onions are amazing."

"I need to go speak with the chef. Will you be all right for a minute?" He quickly excused himself, but leaned down and kissed my cheek before abruptly leaving.

"Sure…" I said blinking in confusion.

As soon as he was gone, Eric busted up laughing and I quirked a brow at him.

"You know what he's doing, don't you?" I shook my head. "He's going to tell the kitchen about your allergy, and will probably threaten to fire them if a mushroom gets within five feet of our food. I wouldn't be surprised if he had them banned from the

125

restaurant tonight." He was pushed back from the table, chuckling heartily now.

My heart melted at the thought. That was probably the sweetest thing anyone had ever done for me, and I continued to wonder, where was his flaw? No one was this perfect. There had to be a flaw somewhere and when I found it, I hoped that it wouldn't be a deal breaker.

When Cole came back he looked relieved. "There will be no mushrooms anywhere near your food tonight."

"What did I tell you?" Eric teased. "Did you threaten to fire the entire kitchen staff?"

Cole looked sheepish, which only made Eric grab the napkin from the table to cover his hysterics. I placed my hand on his knee and gave Cole a bright smile. "Ignore him. That was really sweet of you, thank you."

"It was nothing," he said, yet I could see the light pink shade creep up the side of his shirt collar.

Cassie was appraising him with new interest, and I knew she was thinking the same thing I was. Jake had been a jerk about my allergies—eating them right in front of me, and asking if I had my EpiPen. It was a behavior I'd come to expect, but when Cassie had seen him order mushrooms, she made sure to call him every name in the book and a couple that she just made up on the spot.

Cole was growing on my friend. She had never liked any of my boyfriends, so the fact that she was being civil was a surprise in itself. It appeared that Cole could find himself with a surprise supporter.

Dinner went much of the same. Cassie was quietly observing, while the rest of us chatted away. Cole told a couple funny stories about his and Eric's time in the Marines, all the while keeping his hand on my leg. As the night went on, I noticed it inch higher up my thigh until my body was as much on fire as our flambéed dessert. He wasn't doing anything overly sexy, just rubbing circles on my skin with his thumb, but I was practically sweating by the time dinner was over.

"You want to go to the club?" I asked Cassie.

"Not tonight." She shook her head vehemently. "I'm still feeling the after effects of last night."

"Okay, we can go back to the room and veg out and watch movies if you want?"

"No, you guys go out. I'm going to go lay down."

"I'll walk you back," Eric offered and Cassie shook her head.

"No, that's all right, I'll be fine."

"Honestly, I hate going to the club." He put his arm on the back of her chair, turning to face her. "You would be saving me from being stuck as the third wheel and making a fool of myself with my two left feet."

"If you're sure?" she asked shyly. *Where the heck did that come from?* I watched the whole exchange dumfounded, but they were so cute together.

"Well, we are going to Voodoo if you're sure?"

"I'll take care of her," Eric assured me and I hid my smirk. *Yes, I'm sure you will Eric.*

"If you need us, you have my number," Cole said shaking Eric's hand as the men stood up, while Cassie pushed back from the table. Eric nodded and pulled her chair out for her, and before I was about to get up myself, Cole sat back down after watching them leave.

Cole's hand slid higher up my thigh and I shuddered as he continued to move his hand until it was between my legs and they opened instinctively for him.

He leaned over and nuzzled my neck. "Do you have any idea how sexy you are? I have been dying to touch you like this all day." I shivered.

His finger slid up my skirt and he groaned when he didn't find a barrier—panties and my little black dress did not pair well. My head fell back against the chair as he swirled his finger around my oversensitive nub. My breath caught and I groaned when I watched him remove his finger and put it to his lips.

"Soon," he said with a wicked grin.

"Promise?" I reached under the table and grabbed him through his slacks. Turnabout was fair play and all. His eyes practically rolled to the back of his head as I squeezed him. He was hard as stone and completely ready.

"Are you sure you want to go to the club?" I asked him sweetly, enjoying this new bold me. This girl took what she wanted no questions asked—and it was freeing. I stroked him a couple times before I let go and slid my chair back. "Let's go dancing."

"Whatever you want, princess." I glared at him, and he chuckled getting out of his chair. Placing my arm over his, we walked out of the restaurant.

"Such a gentleman."

"That wasn't very gentlemanly back there," he snickered and wrapped his arm around my back instead. His hand kneaded my hip and I nearly combusted.

"One drink," I groaned leaning into him.

"One dance," he answered back.

I couldn't think of anything I would rather be doing with him in that moment. Well, that wasn't true. The heat of his hand was wearing into my hip and all sorts of dirty thoughts were racing through my head. Sadly, we made it into Voodoo before I could change my mind.

We went the same way to the VIP section that we did the night before, but this time it was different. The crowd seemed to part for us. There were hushed whispers and I swore I saw at least one smart phone out taking pictures of us.

"Maybe we should just leave." I cringed away from the flashes, whispering to Cole.

"Nope, you wanted a drink and a dance and that's what we are going to do." His tone brooked no arguments.

"But, they are taking pictures, Cole."

"Let them. You're not doing anything scandalous… yet." He

pulled my body flush against his.

I smiled up at him then because this was exactly what I wanted out of my vacation, a little crazy. *Who cares if the world sees me out with a hot man having a good time when I had just been so publicly humiliated? I'm sure they will understand.*

"You're right. Let's dance first." Grabbing his hand and pulling him to the dance floor, I ground my butt into him as we swayed to the music and his hands never stopped moving as he angled himself behind me, keeping himself barely within the respectful range.

One song turned into two until I couldn't remember how long we had been out there swaying to the music. Those hands traveled over the silky material of my dress and my arms were up around his neck playing with the hair at his nape.

"How about that drink, beautiful?" he whispered in my ear and kissed behind it. I nodded and let him guide me by my hips to the bar. I hadn't realized until then how thirsty I was.

"Yes please."

"Scotch on the rocks for me," he told the bartender and then looked at me expectantly.

"Cosmo, please."

We found a table in a corner and Cole helped me to sit before he slid into the booth next to me. Our legs were touching from hip to knee and I sipped my drink slowly waiting for him to say something.

"So, why Honey?" he asked out of the blue.

"Honey is sweet, and my agent thought it was funny because I'm such a good girl."

He laughed at my explanation, but I was totally serious. "So, Cole? What happened the first time we met?" I figured if he was going to ask surprise questions, the night was fair game.

"I found this gorgeous little spitfire in my bar who had just been cheated on," he started, then grabbed my hand in his. "I couldn't imagine why anyone wouldn't just fall at your feet and worship you. I had to get to know you better. We danced, we talked, we went skinny dipping in the hotel pool, and then when the night was getting ready to wind down, I panicked and asked you to marry me right here in Vegas—that very night. You said you wanted to be spontaneous, so we got married." He had a faraway look, smiling at secret memories and I couldn't help but feel guilty. He had these great memories of our wedding night, but I couldn't remember anything. The sadness must have shown on my face because he wrapped an arm around me and pulled me close.

"Hey, it's okay."

"I just feel bad that I can't remember anything. You're such a good guy, and I really want to remember everything we shared that night," I said softly.

"Let's do it," he said excitedly. I looked at him, confused. "Let's recreate the night we met."

"Really? I don't know." I was uncertain. There were two things on the list that if I were to do them, I could end up on a tabloid in either all my glory… or all my shame.

"Don't think about it. No one will know." His excitement was contagious. I could see the light burning in his eyes, and couldn't help my answering smile and nod.

Cole stood abruptly and reached for my hand. Trusting the moment, I took his hand and he pulled me to a hallway where he pushed my back up against the wall and pressed his lips to mine in a feverish kiss. There was no slow build up. It was carnal and passionate from the moment he pushed me until he broke the kiss moments later breathing hard. "This was where we first kissed, and I decided that hanging out with you for one night wasn't going to be enough." I grabbed his shirt collar and pulled his lips back to mine.

I have no idea how long we stayed there kissing and grinding against each other. My body was on fire with need for him and when he was finally able to break the kiss, he gave me a knowing smile and led me through the club and out into the casino. We walked into a room where VIPs and high rollers gambled and walked us up to the craps table like he owned the place (which he did). He looked at me expectantly, so I grabbed a hundred out of my clutch and threw it on the table. As soon as the dealer handed me chips I looked to Cole. "What did I bet on?"

"You bet on eight. You said it was a number close to your heart." He smiled down at me.

"Yes it is. I can't believe how you remember the littlest things that I said and did," I said before looking to the dealer. "One hundred on eight please."

The dealer smiled and put my bet on the eight. My mother's birthday was on the eighth—it was an important number growing up. I waited until the shooter rolled and when it hit I screamed in excitement.

"Oh my God. That was amazing."

Cole simply grinned as I jumped up and down like a little kid. I had no idea what he was thinking but when I suddenly stumbled he caught me before I hit the ground.

COLE

Watching her get so excited about winning at the craps table, it took all my restraint not to drag her caveman style to the nearest empty room and fuck her savagely. So glad I had the idea to relive our night together, I wanted to do other spontaneous things. "Come on, we have more to do." I grabbed her hand and dragged her away as she dumped her winnings in her bag.

"Okay! That was so much fun."

Her bright smile was all I needed to know I was doing the right thing. She looked sentimental earlier when I'd known about the number eight. I could never forget anything she told me, and it pissed me off to know that she couldn't remember anything—she hadn't even seemed that drunk that night.

Leading her to the bank of elevators, she looked at me warily. I knew she was worried about this next part; I could see it in her eyes. Skinny dipping wasn't something she would normally do, but that's why she needed to.

"Don't worry so much. It's completely deserted up there. No one will see you."

"Are there cameras up there?" she asked softly and I smacked myself in the head.

"I will make sure they are turned off. Do you trust me?"

She thought about it for a minute and then nodded. "Yeah, I trust you."

"Come on."

We got on the elevator and I hit the button for the roof. My brain kept going back to the fact that I was going to have her naked in that pool. I absentmindedly squeezed her hip, not even realizing I had put my hand there.

Everything was so natural with her, it was like breathing. She scooted closer to me and I couldn't stop from backing her up against the wall and kissing her. It took only a second for her to melt into me, and I felt my cock grow harder as she lifted one of her perfectly toned legs around my back and pulled me closer.

What was it about this girl that had me aching with the need to take her and to protect her from the world? I slid my hand up her thigh and around to her ass. Grinding my cock into her, I relished the sound of the needy moan I pulled from her lips as I reached between us and pressed a finger to her slit.

"You're so wet," I groaned into the kiss. "You want me to fuck you, don't you?"

"Yes," she whimpered.

"Right here in the elevator." I licked down her neck to the top of her breasts.

"Yes," she repeated breathless. I smiled against her skin and reached over to hit the stop button. Moving my hand back down to circle her clit, I felt her fingers slide through my hair. She was pushing and pulling it in every direction. The idea that I had her so hot that she didn't know whether she was coming or going, spurred me on.

Moving the flimsy fabric from her breast I smiled against her skin when I realized she wasn't wearing a bra either. *Fuck me.* I sucked her nipple into my mouth and watched as her violet eyes turned smoky.

"Oh my God," she moaned and held my head to her breast with a death grip on my hair, and I loved every bit of the pleasure and pain. I pumped my fingers in and out of her faster, curling them around so they hit her g-spot and felt as she shattered. My name on her lips as she came was the sexiest thing in the entire world, but I had no intention of taking her in the elevator.

When she came down from her haze, she looked at me quizzically but didn't comment. After adjusting her clothes back, I pushed the button to get the elevator moving again. Riss was breathing heavily and I smiled despite the pain in my cock. *Soon.* I promised myself. I would have all of her very soon.

"Was that something we did that night?" She giggled, obviously delighted with herself at the moment.

"No, baby, that was all tonight and you in that little dress tempting me beyond my restraint."

"What if I like tempting you?"

"Don't poke the bear, princess." I winked at her and she blushed. I loved the way she blushed—it told me everything I needed to know. Her innocence was sexy as hell and I was going to have so much fun corrupting the good little girl.

So caught up in my own thoughts, I almost didn't notice that she didn't berate me for calling her princess. *Baby steps,* I thought to myself. If she'd let me, I would show her all the ways she was my perfect princess and would worship every moment with her. I have no idea when I started thinking like that, but I knew deep down inside that I would do anything to make her happy. I just hoped when she found out the truth, she could find a way to forgive me.

RISSA

My body felt like I had just touched a live wire. I had never come that hard on someone's fingers before. It was exhilarating. As we stepped out of elevator I noticed a note of sadness on Cole's face. "I'm sorry."

He looked at me in confusion. "Why?"

I placed my hand up on his chest, smoothing down the non-existent wrinkles. "I know that you're upset that I can't remember what happened that night and I'm sorry."

"It's not the ideal situation," he said, putting his hand over mine, "but I'm not upset with you. Let's just have fun and see where this goes, yeah?"

His reply was so sweet I melted, but ruined the moment by blurting, "I'm leaving in a few days."

It was out there. The elephant in the room. It had been bothering me that whole afternoon. I really liked Cole—he was nearly perfect and I felt alive when I was with him. Like, nothing else in the world mattered, and I didn't want to leave.

That realization struck me in the chest. I hadn't entertained the idea of there being anything between us after this week was over. It hurt to think about what would happen when I left.

Removing my hands from his chest, and taking a step back, I waited for him to say something. He hesitated like he wanted to say something big, but instead he said, "LA isn't that far away." It seemed as though there was more that he wasn't saying and I wondered if I should drag the truth out of him, and decided against it.

I started to walk away, and he wrapped his arms around me from behind, lips traveling down my neck to my collarbone, and he nipped me softly. "If this is something you want, to get to know each other, we can make it work."

"The cameras," I groaned.

"What do you want, princess?"

"You."

He dropped his hand and moved away from me, the loss of his body next to mine, made me slump. The slight shake of his shoulders as he walked down the hall to unlock a door should have annoyed me. But, his cockiness seemed to suit him.

I followed him through the door leading to the rooftop pool, and a minute later he turned back toward me like a male model, undoing the buttons on his shirt, revealing the tanned expansive chest to my greedy eyes—I drank in the sight. When I finally lifted my gaze to his eyes they still seemed full of humor.

"Is something funny, Mr. Hillard?" I cooed, then started to strip my dress straps down my shoulders slowly. He stalked towards me and I backed up a few steps.

"Where are you going, Ms. Taylor?" he said silkily before pulling his shirt completely off and throwing it on a nearby lounger. His eyes never left mine as his belt came off next, my body growing warm and tingly as he slid it through the loops slowly and then dropped it with his shirt. With my knees about to give way, I reached out for the door when he unbuttoned his pants and I saw the outline of him stretched in his boxer briefs. He was huge. I began to salivate, thinking of putting his cock in my mouth. Oral sex wasn't something I'd ever been into or enjoyed. But, right then with Cole standing in front of me with the biggest tent happening that I had ever seen, my lips were moistening at the thought of wrapping around him.

"You're turn, princess," Cole's voice ripped me from my thoughts. My eyes came to rest on his smirking face and I felt hot again. Letting go of the fabric that was hanging from my shoulders, it fell and pooled at my feet. I was completely exposed to his hungry eyes. Giggling, I turned to run past him and my shoe got caught in the dress at my feet. Ungracefully, and not how I imagined the scenario in my mind, when I thought a naked game of chase could be fun, I started to fall to the ground. Like the hero he was turning out to be, Cole swooped in and cradled me in his arms before I hit the floor.

"Got you." He laughed. "You might want to lose the shoes."

That was the only warning I got to slip my shoes off before he started running, and I wasn't nearly ready for the rush of cool water on my skin. As I came back to the surface, I was sputtering and coughing, my hair matted all around blinding me with Cole's big booming laugh echoing off the building.

"Oh come on, don't be mad." He pushed my hair off my face to expose my pout. Turning my back to him, I folded my arms over my chest and waited for him to get close enough. Once the water was rippling around me and I felt the heat of his skin, I tangled my leg between his, knocking him off balance enough to push him backwards into the water.

Laughing, I dove into the water and swam as fast as I could to the other side of the pool. When I reached the other end, I turned around to laugh at him but he wasn't there.

Terror grabbed at my chest, and I looked around in the water frantically. *Did he not swim?* I had no idea. Getting ready to dive under the water, an arm snaked around my waist and pulled me in.

"That wasn't very nice, princess," he whispered huskily in my ear.

"I guess we're even, then."

"Not quite." He pulled me even closer and ground himself into my bottom. My ear tingled when he kissed behind it and a moan slipped free. "You see? Do you see how much I want you? That's not fair."

My whole body was wound up tight and I reached both hands over my head and threaded my fingers through his hair. My breasts pushed out and that was all the encouragement he needed to slide his hands up my waist and cover them with his hands.

"Do you want me to fuck you, princess?" he asked against my skin, and I moaned, nodding my head in encouragement. "Say it." I felt the smile against my neck and his tongue snaked out and licked all the way up.

"I want you inside me, Cole," I replied breathily. He chuckled softly but made no move to comply with my request.

"Uh uh uh, do you want me to fuck you, Rissa? If so, you're gonna have to say it."

Shoot, he's playing dirty. I started to shake my head but he tweaked one of my nipples and my head fell back against his shoulder. "Screw me, Cole."

"You're getting closer." His hand reached between my legs. *Oh my God, so was he.* My traitorous legs opened instinctively, again. "Say it. Say fuck me, Cole. It's just three words, and I will give you what you want."

"Oh God," I moaned as a finger slipped inside me at the same time he tweaked my nipple with the other hand. I was a puddle of goo in the pool, and the only reason I was staying upright was because he had me clutched to him. Another nip at my ear, and I nearly came undone. "Fuck me, Cole," I whispered softly.

"I'm sorry, I didn't hear that."

The laughter in his deep voice, rumbled through me. "You're so mean."

"Why am I mean?" he asked and ground himself into me again. I had no idea when he took his underwear off, but I felt his skin against mine and couldn't help but arch against him. "Say it louder, Riss."

"Fuck me, Cole," I nearly yelled as he bit down my shoulder. I had no idea what happened, but suddenly I felt full. Cole's fingers were still rubbing my clit as he pounded into me savagely from behind.

"You're so fucking sexy, Riss. I have to consciously stop myself from ripping your clothes off every time you're in my presence." Cole groaned into my neck and suddenly, he pulled out, turning me around to face him. His smile was devilish as he grabbed me under the knees and hiked my legs up around his waist before thrusting himself into me hard and fast.

"Oh my God, Cole," I screamed.

"What is it, princess? You like that," he grunted into my neck. "You're so sexy, I don't know if I'm going to last."

I pulled his hair until his eyes met my own and kissed him hard. Circling my hips, I felt him tense before he pulled out, forgetting for a second we were in the pool. "I'm sorry," he panted and lifted me up so my butt was on the edge of the pool.

"What are you doing?" I asked confused.

He didn't answer, instead he pushed me back so I was resting on my elbows. He dove in—and it wasn't the water—without another word, I was lost. My elbows gave out and all I could do is squeeze my eyes shut and arch my back as his tongue plunged into my folds. He licked, sucked, and nipped me until I was screaming his name to the empty roof.

"Much better." Putting his arms on the side of the pool, he easily lifted his naked body out and bent down on to the concrete next to me. I was still panting as he wrapped his arm around my shoulder and kissed my forehead tenderly.

"Did we do that on our wedding night?" I giggled once I caught my breath.

"No," he chuckled with me. "The only thing left is going to the chapel." When I made a disgusted face, he replied sounding hurt, "Hey now, I'm not a bad guy."

"No." I placed my hand against his check, cradling it. "You're taking that wrong. I just can't have the gossip rags see me go anywhere near an all-night wedding chapel. Could you imagine the scandal? It's always surprised me that they never found out the first time."

He was grinning now, and I wondered if he silently loved the fact that he and I shared our own private secret from the world. "I knew you would say that. I have Jacuzzi tub in my room. Would you like to go back there and soak with me?"

That sounded divine, so I nodded and he jumped to his feet, holding out his hand to help me up, before going to get my dress and shoes that were thrown all over the place.

After we were dressed, he left to turn the cameras back on and walked back to wrap an arm around my back. We walked to the elevator arm in arm, and I rested my head on his shoulder in contentment. I had never felt more at peace than I did when Cole had his arms around me. I didn't want to analyze why that was. It was important to just keep thinking that we were having fun, that this was all temporary. An evil little voice inside my head taunted me. *If this is temporary, why haven't you asked him for a divorce yet?* I told that little voice to be quiet and tried to enjoy the time we had together. My track record with men was not good, and inside my head, the war waged the whole ride down to Cole's room. By the time we finally made it inside, I was so mentally exhausted from my own thoughts I didn't even want to hang out in the hot tub anymore.

"Are you all right?" he asked sweetly.

"Yes, I'm just tired."

"Let's go to bed then." I looked at him warily. "I promise no funny business. I'll just hold you all night."

This man continued to surprise me. He was fine just holding me while I slept? I had never had a guy like that before. He walked us straight to his bedroom and handed me a shirt. After stripping out of my dress and shoes while he walked into his closet, I hopped into his big cozy bed. Cole came back a few minutes later wearing nothing but his boxer briefs and snuggled into the bed behind me. "I want to go zip-lining," I said groggily as he spooned me from behind.

"You got it, princess. We'll go tomorrow. For now, just sleep." I couldn't help but listen to his command. In a matter of minutes, I was sleeping with Cole's body wrapped snugly around mine.

COLE

I awoke to the incessant ringing of my phone. It was annoying, but it only took a second of feeling her soft body next to mine to remember the events of the night before. I got up gingerly so I wouldn't wake her and answered the call.

"Hello," I whispered as I walked out of the bedroom.

"She's been seen at Voodoo two nights in a row," Jake said by way of greeting. "With some random guy that no one can identify."

"What are you talking about?" I asked, pissed that he woke me up for this crap.

"Honey, she's in Vegas and hanging out with some loser who is taking advantage of her."

My stomach dropped at the words. "What makes you think he's using her?" I asked carefully.

"Come on, Cole. She's too trusting and innocent. I need you to watch out for her. She won't answer my calls. Well, she called me back today, but she stuck to her ice queen attitude and wouldn't give me the time of day."

"Good, that means she smart enough to see through your bullshit."

"You don't understand," he bellowed. "I need her. My career is in the toilet. My band is about to kick me the fuck out because we keep having to cancel shows because we've been boycotted. Some asshole is trying to take advantage of her and my own brother won't help me to protect her."

"That was a lot of self-absorbed bullshit I just heard, Jake. The only asshole trying to take advantage of her here is you," I replied fuming. I was glad he hadn't realized who she'd been seen with yet.

"Come on, Cole. You're my brother. You're the protective one. I don't know how to do the knight in shining armor shit. That's always been you. Can you just keep an eye out for her, please?"

"You are so all over the place right now. Why do you even care?" I was confused by his up and down behavior towards her. "You're just using her to further your career. Why even bother asking me to protect her?"

"I do care about her," he admitted. "When she threw that ring in my face something in me clicked and I realized how bad I felt about hurting her. I haven't been able to sleep since. The whole thing is ruining my life."

"Fine, I will take care of her." I thought about what I was saying and shook my head in disgust. This whole situation was getting more fucked up by the minute. "But, I'm not letting you use her. Stay away from her, Jake. I mean it. Your brand of crazy isn't something a sweet girl like her needs."

"Wait a minute, have you met her? Three days ago you didn't give a fuck. What's changed?"

"Yeah, I met her and I spoke with her and her friend. She's a nice girl, you need to leave her alone. That bitch Maria did a number on her. Plus, her friend Cassie may just cut your balls off."

I snickered at the image.

"Ugh." The sound of his shudder went right through the phone. "She's crazier than me. She has always hated me."

"She probably saw right through you. Look, I have to go. I have shit to do. Like get another couple hours of sleep. I don't know why you insist on calling me early as fuck all the time."

"What are you talking about? It's nine."

"You're in Miami, dickhead. It's only six here." I shook my head and hung up. When I turned around, I nearly jumped out of my skin. Riss was standing in the doorway with a sheet wrapped around her.

"Hey beautiful, I'm sorry I woke you up."

"That's okay. Who were you talking to?" she asked yawning.

"Nobody important. My little brother. He's an idiot."

"You have a brother? I didn't know that."

"Yup he's my half-brother. My dad is somewhat of a philanderer. I'm actually surprised he doesn't have more kids." I cringed.

She just smiled, and it was so bright it almost struck me dumb. No wonder she was the hottest thing in Hollywood. That smile alone could make a man forget his name.

"Come on, I need another couple hours of sleep." I yawned and pulled her back to the bedroom; she shot me a coy look, but I wasn't talking about sex. We laid down and I pulled her body into mine and listened to her breathing. My mind was still stuck on the phone call with Jake. I needed to tell her. It was only a matter of time before she found out and she left me for good.

"You want to go zip lining today?" I asked into her neck. She flipped around and looked at me excitedly.

"Really?" I nodded smiling at her wide-eyed innocence. "Yes, I have always wanted to do that."

I pulled her close again and nuzzled her neck. "Good, we will go in a couple hours. Let's get a bit more sleep first."

I fell back to sleep holding her in my arms with a content smile on my lips. *This is something I could get used to.*

I had no clue how long I had been asleep but my very sexy dreams woke me up on a moan. Something was happening to my cock, but I couldn't register what it was until I felt the soft skin of her fingers cupping my balls. Looking down, the sight of her red lips stretched around my cock nearly had me coming down her throat right then.

She noticed my movements and looked up into my eyes as she bobbed her head up and down. When she swirled her tongue around the crown, I'd had it. The need to be inside her, and not her hot little mouth that was doing wicked things to me, but her soaking wet pussy. She was dripping wet—for me—I could see how turned on she was just by looking into her eyes. The usual violet color seemed darker. I reached down and lifted her under her arms and threw her on the bed beside me.

"You're turning into a very bad girl," I said huskily and she smiled wickedly.

"You going to fuck me now, Cole?"

Just those words coming out of that sweet mouth was like music to my ears. I didn't even have to pry it out of her this time. "No Princess, I'm feeling a bit hungry myself."

"Oh God," she sighed and I kissed and sucked my way down her belly to her core. Putting two fingers inside her, I pulled a moan from her lips. My tongue swirled its way to her clit and she nearly shattered on the spot. A gush of hot liquid coated my fingers as I pumped in and out of her, still sucking on that little bundle of nerves. Then, I nipped it with my teeth.

"Oh fuck," she screamed and arched into me, and I couldn't take anymore. Crawling up her body, I licked and sucked my way to her lips. Her legs fell open in perfect position for my hips between hers.

As soon as I thrust into her tight pussy, something was different. The primal, gut feeling that I was home surged through me and nearly brought me to my knees. I knew then and there that she was it and that I would do anything to stay right there for the rest of my life.

"You got a dirty mouth, princess. Is this what you wanted when you woke me up to those pretty lips wrapped around my cock?" I teased her.

"Yes. Oh God, yes, Cole," she yelled and I grinned in triumph.

"Say it. Tell me what you wanted."

"I wanted your cock. I wanted you to fuck me." The way her innocent sounding voice said those words had me near collapse.

"Good girl," I replied silkily and pumped into her harder and faster. Her back arched off the bed and put her pretty tits right in my face. I couldn't resist sucking one pink nipple into my mouth and nipping it with my teeth. Another orgasm ripped through her and I smirked against her skin. "How many times do you think I can make you come before I do? I'm thinking five."

"What?" she asked in shock. "I don't think I can handle another one. It's too much."

"You can handle it," I demanded before moving my mouth to her other breast and giving it the same attention while circling her clit again. I knew I couldn't really drag five orgasms out of her before I came, since I was hanging precariously over the edge at that very moment. When I pinched her clit between my fingers, she broke apart in my arms and she pulled my orgasm along with hers.

I collapsed on top of her and then rolled to my side, pulling her heaving body in next to mine and cuddling her close. The feel of her warm soft body next to mine as I smelled her honey scented shampoo mingled in with the musk of sex clung to my nostrils, and the thought of her leaving came unbidden. But I pushed it away. Rissa would forgive me for not telling her about Jake—she *had* to because I was quickly getting attached to this sweet innocent girl, and I wasn't going to do a damn thing to stop it.

RISSA

After Cole gave me the most fantastic orgasms of my life, I put one of his shirts on and decided to slink my way back to my hotel room before Cassie woke up. She wasn't an early riser like me, so I shouldn't have a problem sneaking in before nine. I kissed Cole quickly and made a dash for my hotel room before anyone could see me. The walk of shame never felt so good. I could feel his eyes on me as made my way down the hall to my room. As I rounded the corner, I stopped dead in my tracks. Eric was standing there quietly pulling the door to my hotel room shut behind him.

"Are you sneaking away from my friend?" I asked angrily and he jumped.

"Riss? Where did you come from?" He gave me a knowing look, staring me up and down.

"Answer my question, Eric." I glared at him.

"No, I'm not sneaking out on your friend, if you must know... she kicked me out." He sighed dramatically, which looked funny coming from the enormous man in front of me. "She said she doesn't do relationships, especially long-distance ones and then she asked me to leave."

"She what?"

He shushed me and waved a hand at my T-shirt clad body. "Do you want people to see you out here like this?"

I immediately looked around but didn't see anyone and was able to relax marginally.

"Don't worry about it, Riss. I'm a big boy I can handle it." His smile was sad and I instantly felt bad for the guy. He seemed to really like Cassie and I knew she really liked him too, but she was closed off to everyone but me. Time for my friend to step up and change.

"Don't give up on her, Eric," I pleaded. "Everyone does. If you really like her, don't stop trying. I promise it's not you. I can tell she likes you... she's just guarded, okay?"

He smiled at me then and nodded his head. "Thanks Riss. I will keep trying."

"You're welcome. Now, I gotta get in there before someone sees me and starts snapping pictures."

I stormed into the room, mad at my friend for what she did to that poor guy. Eric seemed like a genuinely good guy, who didn't deserve her tantrum.

"Get in here, bitch," I yelled.

Cassie came in with her mouth gaping, which would have been comical if I hadn't been so mad.

"You just cursed at me." She actually had the audacity to look at me aghast. "And you're wearing Cole's clothes again."

"That's not the point!"

"What is the point, Riss?"

"I just ran into Eric in the hall," I said raising my eyebrow at her.

"So?"

"He looked crushed, Cass. He really likes you, so what's the problem?"

"Not everyone can live their lives in this happy little bubble." She sneered at me and I took a step back in shock.

"What the heck is going on, Cassie? Where is this coming from?"

"Some of us have real problems. We don't have time to get caught up in one romance after another."

"Is that what you really think?" I asked as my world was turning blurry with the tears I was trying to hide, then I saw it. Saw the look I knew too well. I marched closer, right up in her face. "Go ahead Cassie push everyone away. Did Eric get too close? Is that why you're lashing out at everyone? You're scared," I accused. "I know you're MO. Where are you going to run away to this time? Huh? How long are you going to stay away?"

She took a step back, but I could see my words got to her. "I don't need this bullshit from you, Riss. I thought you had my back just like I always have yours. I guess I was wrong."

"I do have your back, you moron," I said, toning down my anger and seeing that she really was affected by whatever happened last night between her and Eric. "That man out there likes you—a lot—and I think the two of you could have something if you just got out of your head and let him get to know you. A best friend always has your back even if she has to save you from yourself. So, go ahead and run." I smiled at her despite the tense situation. "I'll be waiting for you when you get back." Cassie huffed and slammed the door to her room.

Walking to my own room, I got dressed for the day thinking about my friend. She said some really hateful things to me, and I knew she didn't mean them—she was lashing out at me out of fear from last night and it terrified her, but that knowledge didn't make her words hurt any less.

I was putting my make-up on when the front door to the suite slammed shut, and I knew she was gone. *She really left me here.*

There was a knock at the door and I pushed the stray tears away before opening it. Cole stood there looking gorgeous in a pair of stone washed jeans and a black T-shirt, holding a bouquet of white lilies.

"Hey beautiful, what's wrong?" he said, handing them to me, and pushing his way into the room

"Cassie and I had a fight and she left."

"What? She just left you here?" I could feel the scowl in his voice, against my neck as he crushed me and the flowers to him.

"I know she was just picking a fight with me so that she wouldn't feel bad about leaving. Something happened between her and Eric, and she freaked and bolted like she always does. There's no telling where she went or when she's coming back."

"It'll be okay." He pulled away a little but kept his hand running up and down my back.

"You are still planning on staying until you have to go back, right? How about you stay with me until then?"

"Really? I was thinking about just going home."

"Don't do that, we can have a good time."

"I came here to hide and relax." My voice sniffled into his shirt. "But, the press knows where I am and there is no hiding. The person who always knew how to help me relax is gone."

"I can help you relax," he whispered huskily. "You promised to go on the zip line with me, remember? Let's go have some fun. We can forget all about the paps and just have fun."

I looked up at him. His eyes were bright with sympathy and something else that I couldn't name. "All right."

"You'll stay with me?" The hope in his voice was nearly my undoing—the insecurity made him look boyish, and I loved seeing the smile that lit up his face when I nodded. He swung me around in a circle and I giggled. "Come on, let's go ziplining."

COLE

Zip lining had been a blast. I loved watching Rissa's expressions when she came down the line—it was priceless. Despite the way the day started, we had a great time, and Riss was able to relax and enjoy herself. I tried to call Eric that morning to see how he was but he wouldn't answer.

As we walked along the strip hand in hand, Riss pulled her phone out, but she just rolled her eyes and hit Ignore. I had a feeling I knew exactly who was calling and I cringed.

"If you need to take a call you can, I don't mind."

"No, it was just Jake for the millionth time." She smiled reassuringly. "I don't want to talk to him."

"Are you still upset about what happened?"

She looked at me curiously. I had no idea why the next words out of her mouth were so important to me, but they were. I felt like my entire future hung in the balance. If she said yes I would back off and let them figure their shit out even if it would literally feel like my heart was being ripped out, but I would do it.

"You know, surprisingly I'm not. I realized that I never really loved him." Her words brought me out of my thoughts. "I mean I'm mad because that was humiliating. But, do I care that he cheated on me? Not so much."

My smile was automatic. Squeezing her hand, I pulled her into the nearest door which just so happened to be Ben and Jerry's. "Do you want some ice cream?"

"That sounds amazing."

People were giving her curious looks because she kept her oversized sunglasses on and her hair was tucked into the old Red Sox cap I gave her. She looked so cute in that red and blue cap. I remember the way she scrunched her nose up in disgust when I handed it to her.

"What's wrong?" I had asked, chuckling.

"It's the Red Sox," she replied like it was obvious.

"Yeah? I happen to like the Red Sox."

"Cole, honey? I grew up in New York. Liking the Red Sox is practically against my religion." Her voice was dripping with derision and I looked at her in mock horror.

"You mean you're not a good little catholic girl?" I teased and she blushed ten different shades of red.

"No, and what does that have to do with hating the Red Sox?" She laughed and took the hat from me and stuffed it on her pretty blond head.

"Now, no one will ever think it's you because no diehard Yankees fan would be caught dead in a Red Sox hat," I said, patting her on the head. "In fact, I may have to burn it when you're done."

"Hey!" She mock-pouted and then stuck her tongue out. "Who says I'm giving it back?" she said over her shoulder with a wink and then skipped to the door. "I wonder when the next time they play each other is? I would love to go watch a game and watch my Yankees kick some Red Sox butt."

"It's a date." I grinned. "They play in Boston next month."

"I don't know." Her face suddenly fell. "The studio hasn't called me back yet about Maria."

"What about her?"

"I gave them an ultimatum. Her or me. I don't want her anywhere near me."

"What does that have to do with going to Boston with me?"

"I took a week off already to deal with this mess with Jake. If the studio decides to keep me, I may not get much time off since we are behind schedule now," she explained.

Her buzzing phone brought me out of my thoughts. "It's important, I have to answer it." She gave me an apologetic look and walked to the back of the shop.

I had no idea who it was, but she didn't look like she was happy about it. I paid for the ice cream and walked to the booth she sat in, waving her hands wildly, while trying to keep her voice down.

"They realize that I'm done, right? I can get a job anywhere." She paused. "Al, what do I do? I can't work with that woman."

Her look of utter frustration and hurt was painful, and although I didn't exactly know what was going on, I knew that if she left the show Maria would win.

"Babe, you have to finish out your contract," I whispered to her, interrupting her call.

"What?" She looked up at me in shock. "Cole, you don't understand, that woman is horrible."

"If you quit, she wins. She gets everything she wanted. Do you want her to be walking around smug thinking she beat Hollywood's good girl?"

She thought for a minute and then hung her head. "Al, I will call you back in a minute. No. Don't do anything until I call you back. Okay, bye."

"I'm sorry I just don't think you will be happy if you give this up. I know women like her, and she wants you to fail because you have everything she wants. Don't let her have it." I grabbed her hands in mine, squeezing them tightly. "Your fans will skewer her soon enough."

After a minute of thought, she looked to the ceiling and groaned, "You're right. I guess I need to call Al back."

While she made her call, I sat there quietly eating my ice cream, and checking my texts. I had several from Jake. I froze as I read them.

Jake: 12:37 Where are you? Have you seen her?

Jake: 1:15 I thought you were going to watch out for her? WTF?

Jake 1:37 Fuck this! I'm on the next plane out there.

Shit! No! He can't come out here.

I looked at the time and realized that last text had only come in five minutes before. Excusing myself I walked outside into the oppressive Vegas heat. He answered on the first ring.

"There are pictures of her zip lining! What kind of idiot takes a megastar to do something like that? Especially, when she could get seriously injured? I thought you were looking out for her?"

"Are you serious? What did you expect? Am I supposed to just have one of my security guys follow her around? Get a grip, bro."

He continued as though I hadn't even spoken. "She's ignoring my calls and I keep seeing pictures of her living it up in Vegas, while I'm out here miserable and on the verge of losing everything." Could my brother be anymore self-absorbed? I started getting pissed—no, change that, I was already pissed. Pissed at this whole situation. Pissed that Rissa was my wife, yet here I was hiding and keeping secrets from her because of my asshole brother.

"So, stop looking at the rags. You know better than anyone that they post half-truths and rumors. Don't be selfish, asshole." I was breathing hard, trying for calm, and battling the fact that Rissa would realize that I was being just as much a selfish jerk as Jake. "If she wanted to answer your calls, she would. Stay where you are and let her cool down before you come out here acting like a caveman."

I felt a hand reach around me from behind. I froze, except for sliding my thumb against the End button, and hoping to hell my brother was going to stay put.

"What's wrong?" she asked as I pulled her against me and wrapped my arm around her shoulders.

"Nothing. Let's start heading back." I needed to finish this day with her and spend as much time with her as she was willing to give me.

"I have a problem." She looked up at me with trepidation. "The studio is mad about the money they are losing, and they said if I'm not back in forty-eight hours ready to work, they are going to let me go."

"Damn, that sucks. I was hoping to keep you in my bed for a couple more days." I winked at her and relaxed when I saw her blush. "You have to do it. This is your job and even if it wasn't I can tell how much you love it."

"What are *we* gonna do, though?" She motioned her hand between us.

Yes, I mentally fist pumped. "I would like to keep seeing you, and honestly we don't live that far away from each other."

"You're right. I just really don't want to leave tomorrow."

"We'll make the best of the time we've got." Pulling up the brim of the baseball cap, I kissed her temple then put my arm around her as we walked back to the hotel.

We brought her stuff over to my suite late in the afternoon, and I ordered a bottle of wine to help her unwind while she got ready. I had a surprise for her and I hoped she liked it. I was getting more and more excited as the day went on and by seven I was practically jumping out of my skin.

"Are you ready, Riss? We are going to be late."

She walked out of the bathroom in a sparkly silver dress. It was definitely a club dress, strapless and short enough that I wanted to run my fingers under the hem to see what I discover. Her golden blonde hair hung around her shoulders in soft waves. I was mesmerized.

"You gonna answer that?" She laughed softly and brought me from my daze.

"What?"

"Your phone is ringing."

"Shit. Yeah, sorry." I answered and swiped my finger across the screen. "This is Cole."

"Hey," Eric said, his voice rough.

"What's going on? I have been trying to call you," I said and mouthed *it's Eric.*

Rissa's face fell slightly and she walked into the other room to give me privacy.

"I just needed to clear my head. Listen, I need to take a night off. Nikki is already doing a great job. Do you think everything will be all right if I don't come in tonight? My heads all fucked up."

"Sure buddy, take all the time you need."

"Thanks Cole, I appreciate it." He blew out a breath, but before I got a chance to ask him any questions the line clicked.

Walking out into the living room, I spied Rissa sipping on a glass of wine and staring out the window at the Las Vegas skyline. She was a vision standing there with the sun beginning to set in the distance.

"How's Eric?" she asked quietly.

"He's okay, I guess. He's taking the night off to clear his head."

She huffed and I looked up just in time to see her shaking her head. "I don't know what Cassie's problem is. She totally likes him and I have no idea what went down for her to just take off."

"Hey, it's our last night here together. Let's leave the unpleasant thoughts for tomorrow." I walked up behind her and wrapped her in my arms. "Come on, I have a surprise for you."

She turned in my arms and beamed at me. It was the most brilliant thing I had ever seen. "Do you now?"

"Yup, and if we don't get going we are going to be late."

"We definitely wouldn't want that." She angled up to kiss my chin, and I captured her lips with my own in a searing kiss that I felt all the way to my bones. "I thought we were late?" She teased and slipped from my grasp.

"We are, let's go, but you're going to pay for that later."

She batted her eyelashes at me and strutted to the door, shaking her ass the whole way. I followed her like a lost puppy out into the hall and to the elevator.

"Are you staring at my butt?"

"Absolutely, *wife.*" My grin was wolfish and the desire in my eyes evident. Her breath caught. We stared at each other for long minutes before the elevator doors opened with a ding and broke the spell. I prowled towards her and backed her up against the wall inside the elevator. The doors slid shut and I reached back to jab the button for the lobby never taking my eyes off of her.

"You're so beautiful," I said then mashed my lips against hers. A strangled whimper left her throat, but I muffled it with my mouth. The kiss was heated and deep, and by the time the elevator stopped, we reluctantly pulled apart, breathless. She looked down and smirked at my obvious reaction to her as I adjusted myself straining against the zipper of my pants.

She sashayed her way out into the lobby.

God, this girl was going to kill me!

RISSA

I loved torturing him. We got along so well, but there was a black cloud hanging over us with my being forced to leave in the morning. I hated the idea that this would all be over tomorrow. It wasn't fair. Why couldn't he live in LA?

I smiled sadly as he opened the back door to a limo for me. He really was the sweetest guy ever, so different from the guys back home. Cole was genuine and kind, and even though he was busy, he gave me his time which was more than Jake had ever done—he just showered me with expensive gifts, which I was learning was not the way to express love.

Staring out the window, looking over the desert landscape, deep in thought, I realized that I was being stupid. If I'd been willing to be a rockstar's wife—being left alone while he was out touring all over the world—then why couldn't Cole and I make it work? He was right, Vegas wasn't that far from LA. A small weight lifted from my chest at that realization.

"Sorry, what?" I said, turning to the sound of a throat clearing next to me.

"I said..." Cole smiled. "...what's on your mind, princess?"

"Tomorrow." I sighed and shook my head. "I hate that our time got cut short."

His shoulder brushed up against mine and he reached down to squeeze my hand. "Let's leave tomorrow where it is and just focus on tonight."

The trill of my phone—for the millionth time that day—ruined the moment. I lost it.

"Leave me alone, Jake!"

"Wait, don't hang up."

"Why?"

"Who's this guy you have been traipsing around Vegas with?" How dare he ask this? He, who was cheating with a woman who posted a video of them in *my* house.

Not willing to stoop to his level, I kept my voice as professional and distant as possible. "I'm not discussing this with you. My life is no longer any of your business."

"It is my business," he screamed into the phone. "You're my fiancé!"

"No Jake, I'm not. You said yourself that you don't even like me. That right there pretty much sealed the fate of our relationship, not to mention your cheating." I hung up the phone and huffed in frustration. Cole looked uncomfortable and my mistake dawned on me suddenly. Letting my emotions get the better of me I answered the phone right in front of Cole, but I was so tired of the jerk calling every five minutes.

When did my life get so messed up?

"Hey, what's wrong?" Cole asked gently and reached over and lifted my chin so that I would look at him.

"I'm sorry. I shouldn't have answered his call. It's just that my emotions seem to be all over the place."

He shifted a little and pulled back. "I'm sorry that he made you feel bad."

"I'm not upset about him. I'm upset because I made *you* uncomfortable by answering his call."

He shook his head and smiled. "You don't have to worry about me. I'm fine. I was trying to keep from punching something—that asshole keeps calling and making you sad."

My heart melted at the growl in his words. Reaching up, I kissed him softly. "So, where are we going?"

I wasn't sure if it was asking him what we were doing, or my soft kiss, but one of them broke the tension and he smirked. "If I tell you, it won't be a surprise."

I huffed with a mock-pout, willing to do just about anything to keep that smile on his face.

"Come on, princess, you'll find out soon enough."
***

We pulled up to the MGM Grand and I looked at him in confusion. "What are we doing here?"

"This is the surprise." He winked at me before stepping out of the car, holding his hand to help me from the back seat. Looking around I realized that we weren't in front of the hotel, but in an empty lot at some sort of back entrance. There was a huge man with an earpiece and a clipboard standing outside an unmarked door. I couldn't tell if he was watching us, but I felt his eyes trained on me. He nodded as we approached and opened the door without a word.

"What's going on?" We were walking in what looked to be backstage of an arena. Cole had an excited look on his handsome face that was contagious. I couldn't help but feel a little bit excited despite having no idea what was going on.

When we got to a door with a star on it, he knocked and waited. A second later, it swung open and again I was hit with shock and confusion.

"Cole," the woman yelled excitedly. "How's my favorite hotel manager?"

She had a soft twang to her tone and I stood there struck dumb. Apparently, I was slapping Cole's arm excitedly because he winced grabbing the offending arm and putting my hand in his. When I finally got my voice back I made a fool of myself. "Is that? Are you?"

"Sure am, sugar. And, you are Honey Davies. It is a pleasure to meet you."

"You know who I am?" It was a stupid question. *Most* everyone knew who I was, except Cole; he didn't even own a television.

"Sure, I watch your show all the time. I was so sorry to hear about your co-star and fiancé. I hope they do something about that awful business."

I smiled, uncomfortable with the way the conversation was turning. Cole must have picked up on my mood because he jumped in quickly. "Honey here is a huge fan of yours."

"Really? Isn't that nice? I hope y'all are staying for the show?" She looked between me and Cole.

"Yes, that's the plan," Cole reached down and squeezed my hand.

She looked at us funny, but she didn't comment which I was happy about. I didn't think I could explain all the crazy that had gone down in the last few days.

"You can stand in the wings and watch if you'd like."

"Thank you, that would be amazing!" I answered like a young girl crushing on her favorite pop star.

"Great, well I need to go get ready, sugar. I'll see y'all after the show." She finger waved at us and sashayed back into her dressing room.

"Cole, how do you know her?" I whisper-shouted, so no one would hear me crushing on one of Country music's biggest star.

"She's stayed at the hotel a few times. I helped her with a paparazzi problem once." He shrugged nonchalantly.

"You're a regular knight in shining armor." I playfully slapped him in the arm, and he quickly turned, grabbing me around the waist and I squealed when he lifted me up. "Put me down psycho."

"I like being *your* knight in shining armor," he whispered, then kissed me behind the ear. "Come on, let's go get a good spot to watch the show."

He set me back on my feet and wrapped his arm around my waist as we walked toward the wings of the stage.

The concert when on like that. She came out and played some of her hits, and Cole's hand never left my hip.

About the time she was about to play the last song, she stopped and addressed the audience, "Hey y'all havin' a good time tonight?" The crowd screamed and she chuckled into the mic. "I have a special request tonight from a new friend. Would y'all like to meet her?"

The crowd went crazy again and I froze. *She can't be talking about me, can she?*

"I think ya know her already, but let's bring her out… shall we?" The crowd screamed even louder than before we heard. "Come on out, Honey!"

Cole looked about as sick as I felt, but I had to put on a brave face and a bright smile—the Hollywood smile. The one I reserved for fans and people I didn't necessarily know or like, but had to put up with.

"Hey sugar," she drawled into the mic. It was so hot under all the lights that I had no idea how she managed to still look fresh after running and singing on that stage the past two hours. "Our mutual friend tells me there is a particular song of mine that you enjoy. Ya' wanna help me sing it?"

"Sure," I laughed, walking out to join her at the head of the stage. Having had vocal training as a kid, I knew I could hold a tune, but it just wasn't my favorite thing in the world to do— especially since keeping a low profile had been my original goal coming out here, but clearly I had blown that door wide open.

"What do you think? Should we sing 'I Don't Even Know'?" The crowd went wild.

I froze and looked over at Cole, who still looked green. How did he know that was one of my favorite songs? It was the song Cassie referred to all those years ago when I woke up married to a complete stranger.

As the crowd was going completely crazy waiting for her to sing one of her break-out songs, I looked back at Cole and smiled—and evil one. It spoke of vengeance and he paled a bit. Whether he orchestrated this whole thing, or he just happened to tell her this was my favorite song, I had no idea. But I knew one thing.

I want him to be scared. I'm so going to get him back for this.

COLE

The look she shot me, spoke of destruction and pain, and I couldn't help but smirk. She could try, but I knew she would enjoy getting up on stage. The song I picked was fitting, and seriously, my acting job of looking shocked should have won me an award.

"Hey everyone, how are you doing tonight?" Rissa asked the crowd of cheering fans. "You don't really wanna hear me sing do ya?" I chuckled when the crowd of fans chanted yes. She shook her head in resignation and smiled at the crowd. "Fine" giving them a dramatic sigh into the mic, playing up the actress she obviously was.

The music started up as if on cue. I was in awe. She was a born performer. The crowd totally believed that she didn't want to sing and not only that, they ate it up. She flew across the stage gracefully dancing with the country superstar. It was a sight to behold. I was suddenly so glad that I had thought this up and was hoping it would be the perfect ending to our time here and the beginning of something much brighter.

I hadn't told her anything about the new hotel in LA that was going to be opening next month, not knowing what she would think about that. So absorbed watching her strut her sexy stuff on stage, that when the black cloud hanging over any kind of relationship we might have was currently calling my cell, I sent it to voicemail. The needy selfish child would probably blow up my phone all night, but I didn't care. Jake had tainted enough in the last couple days, I would be damned if he was going to ruin this too.

"Thank you Las Vegas," she boomed into the microphone and blew them air kisses. The crowd went insane, and then the two performers hugged and Rissa stepped off stage wiping the sweat from her forehead smiling brightly. This wasn't the plastic looking fake smile she had for the rest of the world. This smile was genuine and her eyes danced with excitement. "I don't know how she does it. I was only up there for one song and I'm exhausted."

"You looked amazing out there. Did you have fun?" I asked as I wrapped an arm around her.

"I was going to make you pay for putting me on the spot like that." She looked at me her expression stern, but couldn't hold back her obvious joy. "But, that was so much fun!"

"I'm glad."

"How did you know that song was one of my favorites?"

"It came on in the car when we were driving to the chapel the night we got married, and you blasted it through the speakers and started singing. It was actually pretty comical considering where we were and what we were getting ready to do."

She giggled at that. The irony had never been lost on me, especially the next morning when I woke up and she was gone. I kissed her softly and looked into her eyes, hoping beyond hope that we could see where this mindless attraction we had for each other would go. We were technically married. Though, that subject and whether we were going to stay married or not hadn't come up, and it was one I didn't want to talk about because I didn't want to know the answer—it had the ability to make or break me. As I sat there, completely inside my own head, my phone rang again.

"Shit, it's the club. I have to take this. I'm sorry," I said to her before answering. "This is Cole."

"Cole, its Nikki. Larry, your ex-manager, is here starting to cause a scene and I can't get a hold of Eric."

"Fuck. Larry's a moron. I will be right there. Eric is off tonight for personal reasons. Don't call him, okay?"

"You got it. How longs it gonna take for you to get here? I have busted some balls in my life, but this guy looks like he's on something." I heard her shudder over the phone.

"Where is the rest of security?"

"I haven't been able to get ahold of any of them on their earpieces. It's like they are ignoring me." Something wasn't right. I grabbed Rissa's hand and pulled her towards the exit as Nikki continued, "I know it's not my place, but these three guys we have in here are useless without Eric to lead them."

"I will take care of it as soon as their shifts are over. They won't be working security again."

"Good, can you hurry please? I can usually handle this type of situation, but the Larry guy is freaking out."

"We are at the MGM and will be to the car in ten seconds."

"Don't take the car. I was in that traffic half an hour ago and it was hell. You'll get here a lot faster if you run."

"Call LVPD and get them over there. Larry has been blacklisted from the hotel. He threatened when I fired him, but I didn't take him seriously." I heard her intake of breath, knowing she suddenly realized why Larry was probably so off the wall. "Tell the police that he is trespassing and getting out of hand. They will get there as soon as possible. I am running down the strip right now. See you in five."

I hung up the phone and pulled Riss along. I couldn't let anything happen to all the people in that club or my hotel.

When we finally got to the hotel, I ran through the open door and looked to the check-in desk. "Get me every security guard you have down to Voodoo. Now!" I ordered the girl behind the counter. My head was too fuzzy to remember her name at that moment. All I could think about were the possible scenarios when I walked into that club.

The masses of people fleeing the scene pushing and shoving each other to get out of the way weren't helping. I watched in horror as a young blonde girl in sky high heels got trampled by the crowd and not one person stopped to see if she was okay. I rushed Rissa over to a wall out of the line of fire. "Stay here. I need to go help that girl and find out what's going on in my club."

She shook her head and grabbed on to my arm. "I'm not letting you go in there alone."

"You saw that girl get trampled. I'm not letting anything like that happen to you."

"Everyone is running away." I could see the tears forming in her eyes. The damn was about to break and there was nothing I could do about it. "Let's just wait for the police, please?" she begged me.

"I can't, this is my club. I have to make sure no one gets hurt." I grabbed her hand that was still clutching my arm and pried it away, putting it to my lips and kissing her softly. "I promise I will be back. Stay here."

As I made my way back to the mob, I noticed three hotel security guards running towards me. "Chris, I left Honey over there. Go stay with her. You two come with me."

We took off in the direction of the girl who'd been trampled. By the time we got there, two men were stopping the traffic and shoving people away from the girl who was lying injured on the floor. Pushing our way through the crowd of fleeing patrons, I turned to the two remaining security guards. "Get her out of here and call for an ambulance. I'm sure there are more people injured."

"Do you want one of us to go with you inside? These guys are doing a pretty good job of protecting her."

"Alex, come with me. Dave, get the girl and the names of the guys who protected her. There may be some new positions to fill in security tomorrow." They nodded, then did as told. These were Eric's top guys, they knew how to follow orders.

Alex and I pushed our way through the screaming crowd to the empty bar. Looking around, I didn't see a single bartender until I looked over the counter and saw three of our scantily clad cocktail waitresses huddled next to the bar.

Leaning over the bar, I shouted, "Do any of you know where Larry is?"

"He's in the VIP section. The new manager Nikki is trying to talk him down. He is waving a gun and insisting she get you in here to..." She gulped and looked away. "... to face him."

"It's all right Kimmy, we are going to handle it. I want all of you to go and lock yourselves back in the store room. Call 9-1-1 and find out what the hell is taking the cops so long." She, along with the others, nodded and scooched their way through the back door. I was thankful there weren't more people who had stayed behind. If Larry was really waving a gun around, then less people meant less chances to take a hostage.

The main section of the bar was finally emptying out and quieting down. Alex and I started heading toward the VIP area, and I hoped like hell there were even fewer people in there.

"Boss, what's the plan?" Alex asked as we peered around the corner into the VIP area.

"I don't know yet. Let's see what's going on first." I didn't see Larry, but I could hear him yelling. Thank God the VIP section was empty except for two bartenders standing with their hands in the air and Nikki, the new club manager, trying to coax him into putting the gun down. Larry, the lunatic that he was, did have a gun and was waving it around like he had never held a firearm in his entire life. I shook my head in dismay. Just the careless way he was holding that gun was going to get someone hurt.

Taking in the situation, and hearing Larry riling up even more as his yelling became uncontrolled screaming, it was clear there would be no stealthy way to do this.

Pulling Alex back from around the corner, to hide from Larry seeing us, I told him the plan. "Alex, see the door, back over on the other side? I'm going to go through that entrance behind him, then rush him and knock the gun out of his hand. As soon as it skids away I need you to grab it."

The look he gave me would have made me laugh if we weren't actually dealing with a gunman. "Boss? Are you sure that's the best idea?"

"No," I agreed. "But, it's the only one I have. Look at him, he's completely unstable, and the best way to get through this without anyone getting hurt is to disarm him as soon as possible before he actually pulls the trigger, even accidentally."

Alex nodded his head. Sneaking around back to the door opposite the bar, which thankfully was opened. Alex and I snuck in while Larry continued his rant. Holding up three fingers, I counted down and then took off.

Barreling into his left side, he made an oof sound as he hit the floor, his right arm letting go of the gun with a thud as it skittered across the floor. It only took him a second for the shock to wear off and he started swinging wildly in to my back and kidneys as I tried to straddle him and hold him pinned to the ground, but a woman's scream distracted me.

Rissa. The next thing I knew, there was a meaty fist flying towards my face and then everything went black.

RISSA

When Cole left me standing there alone in the corner, I felt useless and afraid, but there was no way I'd be the damsel in distress, the one that needed watching over.

The crowd was thinning out, but there was still a mad rush for the exit of the main bar, like Black Friday at the local mega-store. I watched in horror as another girl went down to her hands and knees and she couldn't get back up as the mass of bodies stepped and kicked over her.

Making a decision I knew Cole wasn't going to like, I removed my shoes and rushed towards the crowd and came up short when a big burly security guard stepped in my path. What was with all the huge and imposing security guards in this place? And how the hell did that Larry guy get past them all?

"I'm sorry Miss Davies, I have orders to keep you here," he said in his deep baritone. *Of course! I should have known Cole would send someone to watch me.*

"Another girl went down over there. Someone needs to help her. I'm not going to just stand around watching that poor girl get trampled!" I screamed at him. He turned his head to look where I was pointing, and I darted around his other side and into the throng of people, desperately trying to shove them out of my way in an attempt to make it over to the girl before she was seriously injured. I heard the guard cursing from behind me but I made it—barely— to her in one piece and reached down to help her up off the floor. The girl was in hysterics, bloody nose, clutching her side from the myriad of kicks and shoves she received. She looked at me in a haze as I took her arm gingerly to put it over my shoulder to guide her back. The security guard caught up to us and in seconds lifted her into his arms as if she weighed nothing.

"Gun," she mumbled. "He had a gun."

I blanched hearing her words and just as I was getting ready to bolt into the club against the swarm of fleeing patrons, someone recognized me. "Honey Davies!" a man shouted.

Fuuuckkkkkk. If I was going to start cursing, now would be the time, and I might as well start with the king of them all.

The crowd, like a swarm of bees intent on a new object, seemed to change direction mid-escape, as if they hadn't just been fleeing a madman with a gun. In seconds I was surrounded, people pushing and shoving. The mob mentality changed its focus from fleeing to getting a piece of me. The screams of my name rang out along with questions about Jake, Maria, and the mystery man.

The security guard, holding the injured woman, tried his best to protect me, but it was no use. Everyone closest to me was being pushed into me. One giant surge of people later and I was on the ground huddled in a ball, hands over my head, barely able to get a breath in, while people were getting jostled around me. I mentally tried to calm myself and get in quick breaths, when the next thing I knew, I was being lifted into big strong arms up and over the mass of people.

Shouts, cries, and questions filled the ears, but my face was planted into a muscular wall, which I assumed was a security guard's chest.

"You're okay, now. I've got you." I heard as cool air and the beautiful sound of silence blanketed me.

Opening my eyes, I looked up into pained green ones. "Thank you." I patted his chest and released the death grip I had on his shoulders. "I'm all right, Eric. You can put me down now."

"Not a chance, Riss. They were after blood. Probably not intentionally, but you would've been crushed if I hadn't gotten you out of there."

He set me on a counter in what looked to be a storage room and looked me over. I was sure I looked a hot mess after what had just happened, but I felt fine. Nothing hurt except maybe a couple places on my head where my hair had been ripped out.

"Are you okay?"

Eric looked over at the small group peeking out of a cracked open doorway. "She's fine," he answered for me, "but you all need to get to out of here and head to the front reception and wait. Now that I have her out of the bar, it should be close to cleared out. Go. Use the door to the main section."

"We called 9-1-1," a young cocktail waitress offered helpfully.

"Thanks Kimmy, but right now, I need you all to get yourselves out of here."

Doing as he instructed, the group let themselves out through the door we had just come in from.

"Eric, Cole's in the VIP area. The girl, who I went in that mess to help, said that Larry guy came in here with a gun. We have to go help Cole," I finished just as we heard a loud thundering crash from the VIP area.

"No." He pointed at me. "*We* don't have to do anything. *You* stay here. Cole will kill me if something happens to you," he replied sternly and sprinted out the second door that connected to the VIP side of the bar.

Yeah, like that's gonna stop me.

I noticed a broken barstool sitting on its side and picked it up. The bottom half of the legs had broken off and the only thing left was the round cushion and round metal foot rest. It would be perfect for what I had planned.

Jogging with my weapon of choice into the VIP area, I screamed when I saw the man punching Cole in the back. When he turned to look at me, the man took his chance at Cole's moment of distraction, and punched him on the side of the head. I watched in horror as Cole slumped forward on top of the man, who shoved him off to the side. Thankfully, Larry was slow trying to get himself up, and I reacted on instinct. I ran at him with the barstool held high and swung it at the man's head. He ducked the first swing but couldn't get out of the way fast enough to miss it coming back the other way. The metal footstool clanged against his head and his eyes rolled back and he slumped to the floor.

Eric was there a second later, relieving me of the barstool and wrapping his arm around my waist to pull me away. Depositing my butt ungracefully on top of the bar, he looked over at an extremely beautiful Latina woman, who was looking at me with something akin to awe in her eyes. "Nikki, keep an eye on her. I'm starting to think she's dangerous." Eric smirked and then walked over to the man and checked his pulse.

"That has to be the coolest thing I have ever seen." Nikki chuckled, holding out her hand to me. "I'm Nikki, the bar manager. Nice to meet you, killer. You look like you could use a drink." She nodded at one of the shocked bartenders.

"I'm-"

"I know who you are," she cut me off.

The bartender brought over a top shelf bottle of tequila and two shot glasses. "Miss Davies," He smiled as he poured, "that was amazing. You really should do some action movies—you'd be great!"

I laughed, so inappropriate considering the situation, but the adrenaline dump was still going. As I grabbed the shot, my hand shot out... *Cole!*

I turned abruptly to see Cole sitting up and shaking his head, and jumped up to go over to him but Nikki grabbed my arm. "Leave him be for a moment. He just got his clock cleaned. His ego is probably bruised especially since it looks like Eric is telling him what you did. Best to give him a minute."

"But..." She shook her head. I couldn't understand why she didn't want me to go over to check on Cole, but she seemed like a woman who commanded any situation, so I nodded, sat back on the stool, and lifted the shot to my lips. I normally didn't like tequila, but my nerves were frayed around the edges—this whole scene was going to be in every tabloid before the morning.

"To a crazy fucking white girl," Nikki laughed as we clinked our glasses together and took the shots. The alcohol burned going down, but I relished it. I was glad for the pain because it stopped the numbness I had felt circling me since I hit that man with the chair.

"Who is he?" I pointed to the man I took out, still laying passed out on the floor and now surrounded by a few EMTs.

"That's Larry." I nodded, having heard Cole mention his name when we were on our way back here from the MGM Grand. God, that felt like days ago, instead of an hour or so.

"Rumor around here is that he was fired the day you first came to the club." She eyed me as she delivered the news.

"What? Why was he fired?"

"He's a sleaze and was banging one of the cocktail waitresses, and..." the bartender interrupted then paused for dramatic effect, "gave her confidential information about a certain superstar who was going to be joining us in the VIP area that night."

"Wait, so he was fired because of me?" They both nodded.

The bartender laid a hand on my arm. "Don't worry, sugar, it had been a long time coming. He was bringing all kinds of nasty stuff into the club. Everyone was too afraid to tell Cole because they were afraid Larry would hear about it and fire them like he did his assistant."

"Wow," I said softly and noticed Cole was on his feet heading toward me.

"Where's Chris?" he barked at me, while holding both his hands on his back by his kidneys.

"Who? Oh, you mean the security guy? He had to help another girl that got trampled," I replied making a note in my head to thank Chris for his help later. Cole shook his head and muttered something I couldn't hear under his breath.

"Don't you dare fire him." Putting my drink down on the bar, I turned on the stool and pointed a finger directly at him. "It was my choice, Cole, besides, I didn't give him much chance when I distracted him and ran the other way."

"You should definitely be in a spy flick, ya total badass." The bartender interrupted us with a laugh.

"A bunch of people are getting fired tomorrow. Do you want be on that list?" Cole shot him a shut-the-hell-up-if-you-want-to-keep-your-job look. Smart bartender, just shook his head. "Then keep your comments to yourself."

"Hey, be nice." I grabbed his arms and dragged him a little closer. "He was just trying to lighten the mood a little. Are you all right? I saw you get knocked out. I'm sorry."

"Yeah and then you went all WWE on him and hit him with a chair."

"Barstool."

"Whatever."

"Well, half a barstool actually," I started rambling and he shut me up by slanting his lips over mine, clearly not caring that his employees were all around us. As I kissed him back, the realization struck me in the gut—I was totally falling for him. It'd only been a week, and yet the thought of him being hurt and never seeing him again, was no longer acceptable. I didn't want to live without him. Deep down, somewhere that I didn't have the energy to examine at the moment, I was definitely and irrevocably falling in love with

Cole Hillard.

A throat cleared behind us, and I turned my head to see Eric standing there grinning like a fool. "Sorry to break this up but the cops finally arrived and want to talk to you."

"Sure," Cole said and turned to leave.

"No, boss. They want to talk to the Incredible Hulk."

"It wasn't even a whole barstool!" I swatted at his massive arm. "Just the seat and the footrest thingy. Honestly, you all act like I lifted a Volkswagen." I hopped off the stool to a chorus of loud laughter behind me.

COLE

I watched her ass as she sashayed away, and for the first time since she re-entered my life, I wasn't thinking about what it felt like in my hands. I was thinking about how fucking terrified I was when I heard her scream. How nervous I was when I woke up and didn't see her anywhere, the thought of losing her a knife to my chest.

"Your girl just clubbed Larry with a chair." Eric smirked and offered me a hand.

"How did you know what was going on?"

"Nikki. She left about a dozen messages. I walked in and Katie told me you ordered all the security to Voodoo. I sprinted over and saw the mob scene, but I didn't realize Larry was behind it." He pointed over to the bar where Rissa was sitting with Nikki. "I got her out relatively unharmed-"

I cut him off. "What do you mean relatively?"

He chuckled. "I mean she has a bit less hair on that pretty head of hers, but she's good."

"Not funny, dude." I would have punched him if I didn't need my hands supporting my back. Damn, Larry gave me some solid kidney shots. "She could have been seriously injured. What was she thinking?"

"The same thing you were, bro. People were getting hurt and she tried to stop it. I never heard of a Hollywood superstar taking people out with chairs, though. She's what? One hundred pounds? There was enough power behind that hit to knock Larry out." We both looked down to where the EMTs were lifting Larry onto a gurney.

Shaking our heads in mutual awe, all I could think was that she was amazing. No matter what she did, she surprised me constantly.

"Cole? Cole."

"You've got it bad." Eric laughed as I made my way to the bar to join Rissa and Nikki.

"Yup."

There was no point in denying it. Nothing I could do about it, I was falling hard and fast. Every little thing she did, drew me in more and more.

If I was completely honest, I would admit that I'd thought and maybe even hoped that once I found her, the novelty would wear off, and I would be able to divorce her without it tearing my insides out, but finding her had only made it worse. Once she figured out what I was hiding, she would leave and take my heart with her—could I live like that? Probably, but I'd be a cold empty bastard.

I'd just given my statement to the cops and Rissa was now walking over to give hers. Eric tapped my shoulder. "Hey, Earth to Cole?"

"What?"

"I asked who was on duty in the club tonight?"

"Wait, you don't know?" I asked, confused.

"Not off the top of my head, no. I have the schedule in my

office."

"I have to wait for Riss. Go grab it and bring it back. Those guys are getting fired in the morning. Nikki? Can you go check and make sure the EMTs are also dealing with the girls who were trampled and they aren't out there bleeding in the lobby?" They both nodded and left me to sit there and watch Rissa as she spoke animatedly to the detective, whose face mirrored the majority of people that came into contact with her. My girl was charisma from head to toe—she oozed it. A throat clearing behind me had me turning.

"You let that tiny woman distract you?" I asked Chris, the security guard, who was supposed to be keeping Rissa safe.

He looked like he was going to be sick, standing there under my heated glare. "A girl was getting trampled, sir."

"Your one order was to watch *my* girl. You failed. She broke a barstool over Larry's head after Eric had to rescue her from a mob." When the color of green took over his face, I decided to put him out of his misery. "Look, you messed up and let her get away from you, but you chased after her into a mob and got a wounded girl out of it... so I'm not going to fire you. *But,*" I warned, "next time you don't follow my direct order you *will* be."

"Yes, sir." The relief in his voice was palpable and I smiled a bit. "She really broke a barstool over Larry's head?"

"It was already broken, actually." We heard her voice from behind. "I may have dented it a bit though." I spun around and grabbed her around the waist.

"You ready to go, princess? Or should I now call you warrior princess?"

"Yes, please." She ignored my joke and dropped her head to my chest, looking as if all the energy had drained from her body. Dipping my head down, I kissed the side of her neck then grabbed her hand and led her to the front doors.

Eric and Nikki approached us just as we were leaving. "I got the list of guys who were supposed to be working security at the club tonight. I will call them all in tomorrow and fire them," Eric started.

"Good. I was thinking we need more vets in here working security. Not only would it give us the type of trust I'm looking for, it would be good for PR for the hotel as well." Eric nodded in full agreement. "Talk to Dave too. There were a couple guys that helped rescue a girl after she was trampled. He was supposed to get their information to see if they wanted a job."

"The two girls that got trampled are at the hospital, no serious injuries, but one has a broken rib."

"Thank you. Have a bouquet of flowers sent to each of them and have hospitality send over a comp package—week free at the hotel, all inclusive. I want them taken care of. Understand?" She nodded and walked towards the front. "Oh, and Nikki." She turned back around. "The club is going to be closed down for the weekend—take the weekend off. Good job tonight getting Larry herded into the VIP area where there were less people."

"Thanks, and sounds good, boss."

Riss was beaming up at me. I didn't know why, but I loved that I put a smile on her tired face. "What?"

"Nothing. You have got to be the sweetest man ever."

I pulled her back against my chest and whispered into her neck. "Maybe I don't want to be sweet. Maybe I want to be dirty and sexy."

Her ass brushed my cock and it instantly stood at attention. She moaned under her breath and I didn't know if it was from my words or if she felt what she did to me. It was probably a little bit of both.

"Oh, you're those things to," she whispered softly.

"Let's go back to the room so I can show you just how dirty I can be." I nipped her neck where it met her shoulder and goosebumps prickled over her skin.

Without a second's hesitation, she grabbed my hand, chirped a quick goodbye to Eric and Nikki, and dragged me across the front reception to the elevators, laughter following us all the way.

Rissa then did the craziest sexiest thing. Shoving me against the wall, she ripped my shirt and the buttons went flying everywhere as she dragged it down my arms, nearly holding me hostage. I'd let her be in control for a bit, and honestly, at the moment, I was too shocked to do anything but let her kiss the hell out of me while she wrapped one long leg around my thigh and tilted her hips so her pussy was grinding against my painful erection. This was so out of character for her, and I didn't care—I needed the friction she was causing between us.

When she wrapped her arms around my shoulders to balance herself with her leg wrapped around me, I untangled my now destroyed shirt then slid my hands up her thighs to her nice round ass and groaned when I realized she wasn't wearing any panties. God this woman was driving me to the brink. Grabbing her other leg, I wrapped both of them around my waist as I drove up with my still clothed cock. Her muffled moan told me how close she was. Flipping us around, so her back was against the wall, I slammed my palm against the elevator panel.

No one was interrupting this.

Bringing my hand down between us to find that little button, I groaned into her mouth finding she was slick, and dripping-fucking-wet. There was no stopping me. I circled her clit and drove up with my hips simultaneously. The high pitched keening sound hit me like a shot to the balls, and I had to forcibly stop myself from coming on the spot as a gush of wetness coated my fingers. *Oh, I was so having a taste of that.* Removing my hand from her clit, and licking it clean, her eyes rolled in the back of her head briefly before she looked at me and one word left her lips. "More."

Oh hell yeah.

RISSA

I had no idea where this wanton creature came from. The throaty way I said "more" probably took me more by surprise than it did Cole, but all I knew was that I needed him inside me, now. The ding of the elevator announced our arrival and he carried me into the suite. Had we even stopped the elevator? I was so totally gone in that moment with him, the thing could have gone up and down, letting people on and off, and I wouldn't have even realized.

We barely made it past the door before I was tugging futilely at his belt because the sensual kisses he was placing on my neck were making it hard to concentrate. Finally, after what felt like an eternity, I got the belt and button undone and reached into his pants, wrapping my fingers around his huge cock, and began pumping it.

"You're wearing too many clothes." I felt his smile against my neck. Removing one hand from my ass he pulled the zipper to my dress down inch by inch, taking far too long. I swear he was trying to torture me. My body was on fire, igniting like a live wire and every touch amping me up more. Especially the whisper of his calloused fingers down my spine as he moved agonizingly slow.

When the zipper was all the way down, he released me and my feet hit the floor. His gaze ate up my body and I flushed harder. He lifted my hands against the wall.

"Don't move them," he said in a domineering tone that I hadn't heard from him before. Pulling the dress down further, he licked and sucked on every inch that had just been hidden from his gaze. My breasts popped free and a strangled grunt left his lips right before he attached them to one and pinched the other between his fingers. I gasped and started to move my arms until I remembered his demand and left them where they were against the wall.

He didn't stop there, following my sequined dress with his tongue as it made it way closer to my hips. I thought—no I hoped—that he would find my center and extinguish the fire burning me inside. But, nooo, he licked a path down my outer thighs to my ankles and back up to my inner thighs, my dress now a puddle on the floor.

"Cole," I cried out. "Please."

He smiled lasciviously and looked up at me from his knees. "Please what, princess?"

"Please, I need you."

"Where?"

"You know where," I nearly screamed.

"What do you want?" he repeated huskily. "You know what I want to hear."

"Fuck..." all words were cut off when his tongue finally made it to my center and I whimpered, nearly buckling over top of him. He was like an animal licking me up and down driving his tongue inside me, igniting that flame higher and higher. At some point I forgot all about his command and threaded my fingers through his hair and tugged.

"More, Cole. I need you to fuck me, now." I screamed, but he didn't stop, if anything, he was more ravenous. When he nipped my clit with his teeth the biggest orgasm I ever had slammed into me. It started in my core and a white flame enveloped my whole body in a wash of electricity. I was more than a live wire. I was the power grid, a lightning strike. I was made of energy burning in every direction.

When he came up for air, I was writhing with no clue how my legs were holding me upright. A quick look down assured me that I wasn't. My legs were thrown over his shoulders, and he was holding me up with his big hands clamped on my butt. As he started to stand, my jello-legs slid off his shoulders, but before my feet could touch the ground, he wrapped them around his waist and thrust.

Oh my God.

When he thrust in to the hilt, my eyes rolled back in my head. Was I chanting obscenities? No clue. I had no control over the words that were coming out of my mouth. Each powerful thrust brought me closer and closer to a climax that was building up to be even stronger than the one before. On the last hard thrust, I was gone, and bit into his shoulder, hard. He came on a roar so loud I was sure they could hear it in the casino. "Fuck! Oh my fucking God. You're so fucking beautiful. So fucking perfect. So fucking… *mine.*"

He started walking down the hall. I was still wrapped around him like a spider monkey as entered his bedroom. I have no idea how in the heck he was still standing, let alone walking.

"Let's take a bath."

"That sounds like heaven," I sighed into his mouth as he laid me down boneless on the bed. He chuckled as he made his way to the bathroom, but I couldn't hold my eyes open any longer and drifted off to sleep.

COLE

I was in the bathroom for less than five minutes. After dropping some bath salts and smelly oils into the water, I walked back out to grab my princess. Never had I felt more possessive of something or someone than I did of her. The path we were flying down only led to destruction... *my* destruction. I couldn't help it though. When I said those words to her—mine—I never felt so certain of anything in my entire life. She *was* mine and I was irrevocably hers. It had been that way since she walked into my club five years ago and turned my whole world upside down in one night.

I walked back into the bedroom and chuckled at the sight. She was laying completely naked half on the bed, exactly where I left her and snoring softly. The only thing left on her were her heels that I had forgotten to take off in my haste. I rather enjoyed the pain of the spiked heels digging in my back and mixing with the pleasure of being balls deep inside my girl. That errant thought had my cock hardening again and I shook my head at myself. "Down boy," I muttered under my breath. The sweet satisfied sigh that left her lips didn't help any. Walking over, I scooped her up and cradled her in my arms. She stirred and snuggled in closer. "Are you going to carry me to the bath?" she asked groggily.

"No, I'm putting you to bed." I smiled when she huffed out a breath in indignation.

"Don't wanna to go to bed," she said yawning. I laughed softly and laid her down and crawled in behind her. Wrapping my arms around her, peace flowed through me. *This was what I'd been missing these past five years*, I thought as the dreams took me.

When I opened my eyes, I thought I was still dreaming at the sight of bubbles floating in my bathroom. I shook my head to clear it and blinked. *Nope. Still there.* It dawned on me and I cursed loudly.

"What's wrong?" Rissa looked over at me and busted up laughing. "You forgot to turn the water off?"

I have no idea how long we were sleeping, but when I got up, bubbles had covered the bathroom floor from the sink to the tub, which was virtually invisible. Riss was cackling from her spot on the bed, and I couldn't help but crack a smile as well, even though there was sure to be some damage to the room.

Rissa walked up behind me still laughing like a hyena.

"You drive me to distraction, woman." Before she realized what was happening, I had her around the waist and was striding into the suds with her in my arms. We slid and she squealed as I fell on my ass right next to the tub. *Found it!*

I dumped her in unceremoniously, and she sputtered when she came to the surface looking like the most adorable drowned rat I had ever seen. Laughing, I searched around for the tap. It was difficult to find through all the lavender scented bubbles, but I was finally able to turn it off. So focused on the task at hand, I hadn't even heard Riss get out of the tub and sneak up behind me until a handful of bubbles were slapped in my face. Unable to see, I slipped, falling into the tub face first. Figuring it would be fun to scare her a bit, I stayed under a few moments longer than necessary before jumping up out of the water. She squeaked when I grabbed her, yanking her back in with me. When her head shot up, she spit a mouthful of water right in my face. "Truce," I laughed. "Give me one second or we're gonna flood the whole place."

She smiled and batted her eyes at me. I wasn't sure if I trusted her, but I needed to drain some of the water out so it would stop overflowing the sides onto the bathroom floor. After ducking down under the water to release the plug, a wave hit me square in the face and Rissa grinned. I sunk below the surface again and snagged her around the waist and dunked her back under.

"You're a jerk," she sputtered spitting water out, but she was smiling.

"You love it and you know it." I laughed, harder than I had in a long time.

"Don't be so sure of yourself." She crawled on her knees over to me and rubbed her naked breasts against my chest. She shot me a flirty smile and then turned to get out of the tub.

Reaching out, I hooked my arm around her and smiled at the disgruntled sound she made as I pulled her back into me.

"We really need to clean this up," she said, but she was breathless and her ass was grinding down on me.

"Fine, but I want to do something first." Grabbing her hand, I led her out of the tub to lay down in a pile of bubbles still covering the floor.

She looked at me as if I were crazy.

"Come on, snow angels!" Reaching my arm up, she reluctantly grabbed it and laid down next to me. The laugh that left her lips was like music to my ears.

"I have never done this before."

"What lay on a bathroom floor, covered in water and bubbles in a fancy hotel?" she asked with a mocking shocked voice.

"Funny, princess. No, I grew up in Miami and even though I

have been to some of the best ski resorts in the world," I looked over at her and watched as she moved her arms playfully above her head, "I never got a chance to just play in the snow."

"That's kind of sad," she said softly. "I grew up on the East Coast. Mom wasn't too fond of regular playtime just for fun you know? Everything needed to have a purpose. I used to sneak out and play with the neighbor kids in the snow. We made snow angels and had snow ball fights."

She had a wistful look on her face, and I'd never seen her look so beautiful. Reaching up, I pushed a lock of hair behind her ear. "You're so beautiful."

Smiling, she jumped up and lobbed a handful of bubbles at me and I laughed loudly. Slinging to my feet, I tried to run after her and slid halfway across the floor. She squealed as I caught her and I pulled her in for a searing kiss.

"Let's get this mess cleaned up and go back to bed," I said, and smacked her ass for good measure.

"Mmm, sounds good."

"I'm going to go call housekeeping and get some more towels. I'll be lucky if the rooms below us haven't already called the front desk about a leak in the ceiling." I couldn't actually believe myself. I was laughing about this, laughing with her. It was a moment that I knew I'd never forget.

I got dressed in a pair of gym shorts and walked into the living room to use the phone, when I noticed my cell was lit up. *Who would be texting me at four in the morning?* I flinched.

Jake 4:13 a.m. **Have you been online? You're everywhere, bro. You and Honey are everywhere. What the FUCK is going on?**

Shit! This was extremely bad. Grabbing my laptop, I logged into my seldom used Twitter account, which to my chagrin was set-up by our public relations department. There were over a thousand notifications, and videos… oh God, the videos! Clear ones of me and Rissa when I left her in the corner, another one of

THERE'S SOMETHING ABOUT VEGAS

her and Chris rescuing the girl and then her getting mobbed right after. Somehow, or rather someone—who was going to be fired if they weren't already—leaked surveillance tape to a rag showing Rissa beating Larry with a barstool and us kissing. It was a fucking wake-up call.

"Riss? Babe? You may want to look at this," I said into the quiet room.

"What?" She walked in completely naked. I looked up to the ceiling hoping for strength. This was kind of an emergency, and if I looked at her for two minutes more I wouldn't be able to concentrate.

"Princess, put something on please," I groaned. "I can't concentrate when you're all naked and wet."

She giggled and walked back into the master bedroom to put a shirt on when a knock at the door startled me.

"Hold on," I yelled at whoever was on the other side of the door then opened it abruptly. "Who are you?"

"Oh my God, honey, the question is Who Are You? My Rissa has been holding out on me." The man said in a distinctly flamboyant voice.

"Names Cole Hillard. And, you still haven't said who you are." He didn't look like anyone who planned anything scandalous, but with Rissa, I was taking no chances.

"I'm Cliff. Cassie and Rissa's resident designer and BGF."

"Do I wanna know what BGF means?"

"Best Gay Friend," he sassed and rolled his eyes as he put his hand on my chest to try and push me out of the way and let him through. He looked at me pointedly then raised his hand and he rolled his wrist like "get on with it."

"Come in?"

"Don't worry honey, you are delicious, but I don't poach my girls' men." He winked and sauntered past me and made himself at home.

"What can I do for you, Cliff?"

189

"Cassie called me and said they got into a fight and she left her here. So, I came to the rescue."

"Cliff?" Rissa squealed and rushed him. "Oh my God. What are you doing here?" She wrapped her arms around him in a huge hug.

"I have been watching your fine ass in the rags for the last couple days and thought I would come crash the party. Babe, *you* have been holding out on me," he said suggestively to which Riss giggled and I cleared my throat.

"We kind of have a crisis on our hands."

"What?" Her face immediately drained of color. "What crisis, Cole?"

"There are videos all over Twitter. The club incident. Clear videos of us kissing. You beating Larry with a chair. You getting mobbed by fans."

"Oh, and don't forget the fab performance with that country superstar," Cliff interjected as if this was all fun and games. "I'm so jealous, babe. Was it absolutely divine being up on stage with her? You must tell me everything."

"Cliff. Focus." I snapped.

"Videos? Of me and you?" I hated the dread in her voice. I hated that I had put it there. She had been so happy a second ago, but we had a real problem. Someone in my hotel had leaked some of those videos, and while I needed to find out who, more than that, we needed to come up with some sort of game plan to protect her.

"Yeah," I admitted. "I had a thousand notifications on my Twitter feed, including tons of videos including surveillance footage that no one should have had access to."

"I saw how you hit that awful excuse for a human being with that barstool. You looked like a warrior princess." Cliff cut in gleefully. "I bet you have ten new offers for action movies by the end of the week. It was fan-ta-bulous," he sang out the last word.

I shook my head in defeat and had to laugh because he was right. I saw the video, and she looked like some avenging angel in her silver sequin dress and wild blonde hair. It was one of the sexiest things I had ever seen.

Her phone rang and she looked down at it like it was a dangerous animal. "Fifteen hundred notifications… and that doesn't even include the text messages from my manager and my publicist. There are ten from Jake alone."

"You're a star, darling. When people see that move or the gorgeous hunk of man candy you're locking lips with, they want a piece of it."

"It will be okay Riss." I walked over to her and grabbed her hands in mine. "Once you get home and get back to filming this will all blow over."

"Wait, you're leaving? When?" Cliff asked.

"In a couple hours. The studio said they needed me back immediately." Hand still in mine, she walked us both over to the couch and dropped herself in it.

"Cassie said you were going to be a couple more days."

"Cassie called you? Did she tell you she ditched me here? Where is she?"

"Um, yeah, girl. That's why I'm here." Cliff was looking at her with a little sorrow, before he reverted back to his usual over-the-top self. "She's off to some art conference in Paris or Milan or some equally fabulous place."

"That is just like her." Riss sounded disgusted with her friend. "Run off every time something that could be great stares her in the face."

"Spill, what or should I ask who, was staring her in the face?" he asked just as there was another knock on the door.

"Who the hell else is here at four in the morning?" Launching myself up off the sofa, ready to rip someone a new one, I cut myself off when I saw the disheveled face in front of me. "Were your ears burning?"

"What?"

"Nothing, never mind." I opened the door wider to let him in the entryway, but he didn't move. "What's going on?"

"I don't want to tell you this, man, but there's a shitload of paparazzi surrounding the hotel. They know who you are."

"Shit. Fuck. Shit."

"And as soon as they find out who your brother is… you're toast."

Running my hand through my hair, half in and out of the suite, I sighed in resignation. "I know. What am I gonna do? This is gonna kill her and the headlines are going chew her up and spit her out."

"What the actual fuck, Cole?" The voice that came from behind Eric was the last one I wanted to hear right then and I cringed.

"What are you doing here, Jake?"

RISSA

Telling Cliff about Cassie's life and what I felt was the worst mistake she could have made, was freeing… almost. He sat there and listened carefully while I told the whole sordid tale.

"That little idiot," was his blunt reply. "I love her, I really do, but she is going to regret her reaction for the rest of her life. I can't believe she is flying all the way around the world to hide from this man."

"Yeah, I know. He's so perfect for her, and I can tell he likes her-" my speech was cut-off when I heard yelling coming from the foyer. A ball of dread filled me when I heard one of the angry voices. Jake.

I rushed to the foyer with Cliff on my heels.

I was right. Jake was standing there, his eyes angry and dark circles around them. His clothes were rumpled and his light blonde hair looked almost greasy.

"How could you? You're my brother!" He was shouting at Cole

and when I gasped, they all snapped their gazes to me. Cole came out of the haze first and moved towards me, but I shook my head and held my hand up in a stop motion. "What is he talking about, Cole?"

My throat clogged, the heat in the back of my eyes was beginning to burn. The dam was about to break.

"Riss, he's telling the truth. I was going to tell you. I swear... I just wanted to prove to you that I wasn't like him, first."

Cliff's gentle hand on my back in support couldn't suppress the humorless laugh that bubbled up out of me. "Nothing like him?" I whispered venomously. "By not telling me that you are related to him, you have shown me that you are *exactly like him.*"

He flinched and the hurt I saw in his eyes nearly broke me in two. A stupid errant tear slid down my cheek. Jake stood stock still looking between the two of us completely confused.

"Who is Riss?" he asked angrily. "I want to know what the fuck you think you are doing with my fiancé. She's wearing one of your shirts for Christ's sake."

"You." I directed all of my anger at Jake. "You have no right to come barging into my life anymore. You are no longer a part of my life. I. Am. Not. Your. Anything. Do you understand?" It was impossible for me to process the shocked look on his face while I raged then hit my finger dead center in his chest. "You will not call me." Hit. "You will not text me." Hit. "If you see me at a club or walking down the street you will turn around and walk the other way." Hit. "Or I will slap your *ass* with a restraining order." Hit. I pulled back. "Do you understand me, now?

There was a collective gasp as we all stood there in and out of the suite doorway, and Cliff looked at me as if I sprouted another head. "Well said, darling. And, I do believe that's the first time I have ever heard you swear."

I was drained. I was exhausted. I just wanted to go home. I should have known what Cole and I had was too good to be true.

"One last thing before I leave." Looking now directly at Cole, I asked, yet he heard the demand in my voice. "Can you get divorce papers filed quietly so that no one will know? I don't want your money. I just want to be done and not destroy my reputation even more than I already have."

"Wait!" Jake looked at Cole with shock in his eyes. "She's the girl?" He pointed at me in question. "The girl you married and have been pining for all these years?"

Cole nodded.

This was too much. The resigned look in his eyes nearly killed me, so I turned to Eric and on a broken voice asked, "Can you get us out of here without anyone knowing, please?"

"Sure Riss, no problem."

I nodded robotically and turned towards the master suite with Cliff following close behind.

He gasped when he saw the mess in the bathroom, which had already started to seep into the plush carpet in the bedroom. "What in the world happened in here?"

As the memory assaulted me, the walls I'd erected finally broke. "Shhh, it's going to be okay. I'm sorry I asked. Let's get you home. I have a surprise for you."

Taking deep breaths, I attempted to pull myself together. "Sorry, I don't know what came over me."

"You really care about him don't you?" Cliff asked quietly. I nodded because I was afraid if I tried to speak, I would burst into tears all over again. "Maybe you should talk to him then."

"No, I can't. Have to be the ice queen—never let people see you cry. They will see it as a weakness and use it against you."

"Who the hell taught you that garbage?" Cliff reared back and barked out. "Babe, you cry if you need to. It's okay to feel things. Never ever let anyone tell you otherwise." After the mini-lecture, he pulled me back in and a fresh wave of tears overtook me. I sobbed until all the tears were gone—minutes, hours, I had no idea. My heart was splitting in two and I didn't know how to stop the pain.

Someone knocked and I swiped at my eyes angrily, turning my back away from the bedroom door. "Can I talk to you, please?" Cole's voice was soft, threaded with layers of guilt.

Squaring up my shoulders, glad for the years of training I'd received, I turned around, face determined. "No. I'm leaving. You let me go on about my ex-fiancé knowing good and well that it was your brother. You think I'm an actress, well, you are the best actor. Kudos. Lying to me all while doing the sweetest things at the same time."

"Riss, let me explain."

I shook my head, grabbing my bag and tossing the few things I had together, all while swallowing a million times with my head ducked, knowing the tears were welling up. I had to get out of there. In seconds it would be impossible not to break. "No. Just no. I'm done with you, Cole. Have your lawyers contact mine about the divorce, so I can finally move on with my life."

The traitorous bitches—tears came pouring down my face as I picked up my bag and shoved past him into the hall. "Goodbye Cole." My voice broke on those final words. My mind knew I was doing the right thing. Too bad my heart wasn't getting the memo.

"You ready, Eric?" I brushed past Jake, who was opening and closing his mouth like a fish out of water. If my whole world hadn't felt like it was falling apart, I would have laughed at how ridiculous this scene was.

I paused when I saw my purse on the little table in the foyer, remembering how it felt like home, the first time I walked in here and saw it there. A gut-wrenching sob left my throat as Eric wrapped an arm around me and led me out the door with Cliff right behind me, who I knew was probably staring at Eric's butt as he walked us to the elevators.

"He's been looking for you a long time, Riss," Eric said squeezing me close. "Can you blame him for not wanting to ruin it before it ever got started?"

"He should have told me from the beginning, Eric. He should

have been honest with me."

"Would you have given him a chance if he had?"

"Maybe…"

"Bullshit," both men said in unison, and I looked from one to the other, startled.

"Babe, don't lie to us. You may be able to lie to yourself, but I have known you long enough that this last week would have been a lot different if he had been straight with you." Cliff's surprisingly serious tone was startling. The over-the-top gay man was suddenly gone, replaced by a man, I'd never seen before. "You would have bolted faster than Cassie did."

Eric flinched briefly and Cliff realized his mistake a moment later and looked over at him. "Sorry sugar," and boom, there he was back in all his sass again, "but Cassie has more walls than a prison yard. That girl is sealed up tighter than Fort Knox. You're gonna need more than a fine ass and a pretty smile to break those walls down."

"I figured that out when I slept with her and she bolted like a scared little mouse," Eric replied grimly, as I looked up to see the hurt etched across his features. "I'll be okay Riss. The question is will you be?"

"I don't have another option. I have to look my best and be on set first thing tomorrow morning."

The ride down in the elevator was quiet. I was trying to steel myself to the inevitable lonely existence—looked like spinsterhood would be my future after all. What a lonely existence I would have as the ice queen.

So, I did what I always did—rebuilt the walls that Cole had torn down and locked all my emotions inside. This would be my life. I told myself as long as I had my career, nothing else mattered, so why couldn't I make myself believe it was true?

COLE

When Rissa walked out that door without looking back, she took my fucking heart with her. There was a hollow chasm where it used to sit in my chest, and I almost broke down in my living room. My little brother was sitting on my couch with his head in his hands and his elbows rested on his knees. "We really fucked up, didn't we?"

"We?" I asked, incredulous. "God Jake, you just ruined the best thing I ever had, just to try to save your career."

"I know, and if there was something I thought I could do to fix it, I would." He finally looked up at me and the expression on his face was tortured. I could see it in his eyes that he regretted everything.

"Why? Why couldn't you just leave well enough alone?"

"I don't know. When I saw you kissing her in that video, I thought you had betrayed me. I never guessed that it was the other way around. Cole," his voice hitched, "I'm sorry."

He meant it. In that moment, I realized he and I could move past this, but it was at the cost of what I valued the most. "We both screwed up with the greatest woman in the world." My laugh was self-deprecating, hollow, and cold.

"I don't think she will even talk to me, but I will try. I'll tell her about the idiotic things I did and let her know what a good man you really are. It's the least I can do for ruining everything."

"It's just as much my fault as it is yours." I plopped down heavily on the couch next to him. "I should have told her about you from the beginning."

"Nah bro, I may not have dated her for long, but I know one thing. There never would have been a good time to tell her. It would have ended the same no matter what. At least this way, you have some good memories out of it. "

"Yeah, I really do." The snow angels came to mind and I winced. "Shit, I flooded my bathroom and never got a chance to clean it."

"You what?" Jake laughed. "How the hell did that happen?"

"You really don't want to know." Making my way down to the master bedroom, I chuckled, "Let's just say we had an amazing bubble fight and made snow angels."

"Seriously? She did something goofy and carefree with you? We never did anything like that. You know she's called the ice queen?"

"I don't understand why people keep saying that. She was anything but an ice queen with me. I wouldn't say that she wore her heart on her sleeve, but she showed her emotions with me readily."

"That's funny because the first time I ever saw her let her emotions out in three months was the night we broke up. A single tear, that's it. And then she threw that god-awful ring, hit me in the face with it. After she dropped my bottle of cologne in the box and broke it all over everything. That shit stinks to high hell." He grabbed a handful of towels and handed them to me as we got on our hands and knees in an attempt to clean up the mess. "What I'm trying to say is, she's different with you—obviously if she's opening up to you within a week. I never got that from her."

"What are you going to do now?"

"I'll figure something out. I always do. If the record label and my band both drop me, I'll start over." He shrugged and this time, it looked as if he really didn't care.

"What about Maria?"

"I kicked that crazy bitch to the curb as soon as she pulled that shit on Honey. Did you know that she actually went back to her house and confronted her after I kicked her out? What kind of self-important sociopath does that to someone?" He sighed. "I'm reevaluating my whole life. This shit has to stop sometime, you know?"

"Yeah, I was wondering when you would finally get your act together." We finished mopping up and drying the best we could, but I'd need to get a professional service in to see if the carpets were salvageable.

Making our way back into the living room, Jake put his hand across my shoulder. I tried to smile but I couldn't. The cold cavern where my heart used to be wouldn't let me. I was literally dying inside and she had only walked out that door minutes ago.

Once we made it back in the room, and I dumped myself unceremoniously on the couch. Jake walked over to the bar and grabbed a thousand-dollar bottle of Maccallan's along with two glasses.

"You know what that is don't you?" I balked.

"What better reason then having your heart ripped out to down a thousand-dollar bottle of booze?" He laughed lightly. I thought about it and he was right… I couldn't think of a better reason.

"You've got a point there, crack that bad boy open."

We stopped talking about deep shit, just sitting there for long minutes drinking and stewing about the mess our lives were.

A knock sounded on the door, just before Eric walked in. I was feeling the burn of the alcohol down my throat and the buzzing in my head was a nice change, dulling the pain just slightly.

"It's six in the morning. What the fuck are you assholes doing?"

"Having a drink. Want one?" Jake slurred.

"You drank an entire bottle of scotch between the two of you? In an hour?" He picked up the bottle looking closely and then cursed.

"It stopped hurting, didn't it?" I looked at them both as if they could answer my own question.

"I don't know, Cole. Did it? Because you look like shit, man."

Dropping my head, which seriously felt like it was floating away, back on the couch, I said, "Yeah well I don't give a fuck. I just want to be numb for a little while, asshole."

"You're not even going to try to go after her?" Shit, the man was really starting to get angry. "I thought you were a fucking Marine, not some pussy that lets what he wants walk away. What happened to failure is not an option?" He was leaning down over me at this point. I heard him but whatever he was saying wasn't registering through the haze of alcohol.

Had I failed? If so, then it was the first time that I could ever remember failing at anything. As that thought started to sink in through the haze, I cursed. "You're right."

"Well? What the fuck are you gonna do about it?"

"I don't know, okay? She doesn't want to see me. She said I was just like him." I pointed to my brother who was barely conscious.

"Hey. Fuck you." Ah well, I guess he still understood what was going on. "I'm trying to get my life…" he passed out mid-sentence.

"Can you get me some water? I need to clear my head."

"Sure man, and when you sober up, we're making a plan."

RISSA

Cliff was hovering. I had been home for a few hours and he was watching over me like a mother hen. It was cute but annoying at the same time.

When I got home from Vegas I walked in like a zombie, barely noticing the new bed before I flopped on it. The pillows that I buried my face in smelled fresh and clean, thank God. Cliff walked in behind me with my bags—such a sweet man—and with my voice muffled by the pillow I asked, "You did get rid of the mattress, right?"

"No, darling. Was I supposed to?"

I jumped up from the bed without a second's hesitation. Stupid Cliff started cackling like the wicked witch and I about punched him. "I'm kidding. Of course I got rid of it."

"You scared me. I thought you let me lay on the same as... ugh..." I shuddered not even able to say her name.

"Never. Now, you go have a bath and I will run to the store and stock up on snacks and ice cream. We, Missy, are having a girl's night." He nearly squealed in delight, which would have been contagious if I thought I could ever smile again. "Now, Miss doom and gloom, go get in the bath. I'm going to Redbox some rom-com and stock your fridge with junk. And darling, don't cry. I'm sure it will work out, that man of yours, Mr. hot-as-hell Cole, will not be giving up on you that easily." He kissed my forehead and sashayed from the room.

I thought about what he said while I soaked in the whirlpool tub surrounded by candles and new towels that Cassie must have asked him to buy for me. Did I want Cole to give up on me? If I was completely honest with myself the answer was heck no. My heart wanted to believe Cole was a good guy, but my head kept telling me that if he was able to lie so easily to me, he would eventually cheat on me, too, like the rest of them. Deep in my thoughts, I never heard him come in.

"Look at this," Cliff exclaimed excitedly. He was carrying an enormous vase full of yellow roses. There had to be at least two dozen there and my eyes started to water again.

"Get them out of here, please?" I sniffled. Cliff glared at me. "Oh no, darling, you need to hear him out. This isn't the end of the world."

"Don't you get it, Cliff? This is already going to ruin my reputation. Once the gossip rags figure out their relationship, I am going to be the "Slut who is keeping it in the family.'" I air quoted at the headline. It was about to get so bad—the studio might cut me from the show with all the bad press.

Cliff looked like he was going to be sick and then after a second his face morphed to just plain pissed. "That's the reason that you refuse to give him a chance? Because your *reputation* has been ruined? Girl, you need to get your priorities straight. Many superstars have done far more scandalous things than get involved with brothers. If that's your only reason for ditching that hot hunk of man, then you need to get over it and call him." He fluffed the flowers and left them right there on the bathroom counter and stormed from the room.

It was disarming how right he was. There were plenty of stars that had done way worse things, but I was Honey Davies, the good girl, the ice queen, but deep down, I knew that wasn't the real reason. The pain of his loss was going to break me. I'd made it through Wes and Jake, but Cole had my whole heart.

I got out of the tub and wrapped the nice new fluffy white bathrobe around me and padded over to the flowers and inhaled their sweet scent. Most would find it surprising, but no man I ever cared for had ever bought me flowers. It was a lonely existence when your mother was the queen of old Hollywood and expected nothing less than perfection, setting her adult daughter up to follow in her footsteps, yet dying before she witnessed her break out. At least I had those years of peace, before I got my first part.

My boyfriends since had all been liars and cheaters, all wanting what I could do for their careers, never really wanting me, except Cole; he was the only one who had ever wanted me for me. But, I couldn't think about that now. I *had* to get my crazy emotions under control. Backing away from the bathroom and the small smile those flowers brought to my face, I padded into my room and noticed it looked like a beach. The carpet was the color of sand and the whole room was done in bright blues and greens. It was beautiful.

The dresser was inlaid with sea shells of all types. There was huge sand dollar and some clam shells and abalone. The vanity mirror looked like something Ariel in the little mermaid would have. Cliff had definitely out done himself on this one. It was absolutely perfect, just enough over the top to make me smile. I heard the sound of shuffling feet behind me and turned. Cliff was standing there with two tubs of ice cream and two spoons looking at me expectantly. "It's perfect."

He blew out a breath and walked further into the room. Thinking he'd left after our fight, I was sure I was going to be binge eating and crying alone while watching romantic comedies all night. My phone rang where I had thrown it on the bed earlier. Why did a pang of disappointment strike me in the chest when I saw it was Al and not Cole?

"Hello," I said as bright as possible.

"Honey, how are you holding up?"

"I would be a lot better if I didn't have to see that crazy woman tomorrow and her smug smile that I want to punch off her stupid face," I replied angrily.

"It's only for a little while. The studio just called with a new script. I'm having it sent to you by courier as we speak. She's out. Two more episodes and she is going to die some very public heinous death or something. They didn't give me all the details." I smiled, relieved. "Your fans have been sending in hate mail and posting on Twitter. They want her gone. The studio is finally listening. Some focus group skewered her and now they want nothing to do with her. She may never work in this town again."

"Oh my God. I know it sounds horrible, but that is great news, Al." I looked over at Cliff and sliced my finger across my neck mouthing "Maria" and he squealed. "Do I still have my call time tomorrow or are they going to let me learn the new lines first?"

"What was that noise in the background?"

"Oh, nothing. Just Cliff."

"No babe, they're giving you tomorrow and the weekend off to memorize the new lines. I'm glad everything's working out for you, Honey."

That one phrase drained all the happiness out of me. Everything was not working out for me. The one thing I wanted was gone. He lied to me and I was wondering if life would ever be the same. "Thanks Al, everything is great now."

I didn't know if I sounded convincing, but from the pitying look on Cliff's face I was guessing that would be a no.

"I know something went down in Vegas other than what we've seen in the media, but you don't have time to lose your shit, Honey.

You have to be on set Monday morning ready to work."

"I know, Al. I'll be there," I said stabbing the disconnect button with my finger repeatedly.

"Well, at least one thing is going right." Cliff had a hopeful smile. I figured he was just hoping I didn't burst into tears again, which was very possible, but they had to stop because my eyes would be all red and puffy when it came time to shoot on Monday.

"Come on, I got that Ryan Reynolds movie that we love cued up on the big screen." Cliff handed me the tub of ice cream and lead me out of the room and down the stairs to the movie room.

It was my favorite room in the house, but one I hardly ever got to hang out in. Mom had the theater style seats put in when I was a kid and when I got home from boarding school, we'd sit mindlessly watching movie after movie.

The rest of the weekend was more of the same. I got up, showered, and memorized my lines; every movement was robotic. Each day a new bouquet of flowers arrived and each day they came without a card. When that first bouquet arrived, I'd assumed it was from Cole, but now it left me wondering… did he neglect the card because he thought I would throw them out if I knew who they were from? Was it even Cole?

When I got to the studio on Monday, there was a huge bouquet of lilies waiting for me, but this one had a card.
Knock' em dead!
J

What kind of sick twisted game was he playing? He sends me flowers when I screamed in his face to leave me alone? I hadn't heard anything from any of them since I left Vegas a few days ago—to my complete and utter disappointment. Every time my phone rang or I got a notification I jumped, hoping it wasn't Cole but then when it wasn't him, I was even more devastated.

The morning passed by in a blur, going through the motions on autopilot just like I had all weekend. At least the producers were really good about keeping Maria away from me, but on my lunch break that all changed. I was looking down at my phone as I was walking to my trailer and got a boney shoulder to the chest.

"Watch where you're going, bitch." I heard just before I looked up and saw Maria sneering at me.

"Seriously? I don't have time for you and your petty games, so why don't you go bother somebody else?"

"That's it?" she asked incredulously.

"Yes, Maria. That's it. Just go away." As I went to walk past her, she grabbed my arm.

"You ruined my life, you stupid whore. And that is all you have to say to me?"

"Maria?" I was exasperated with it all. "You ruined your own life. I didn't push record on your little sex tape, did I? I didn't push the button to upload it to social media. Everything that's wrong in your life is your own doing, so let me go and get the hell out of my way."

The audible gasps from everyone around me reminded me that we were not alone. Maria smirked and shoved a tabloid that I hadn't realized she was holding in to my chest and walked away. The dread started immediately and I almost threw it in a nearby trash can without even looking.

"Oh, how the mighty have fallen," she tossed over her shoulder as she walked away.

When I looked down at the paper in my hands, I cringed. There was a shot of me and Cole kissing. It was a cruel joke to put this in front of me after everything I had been through the last couple days, but it didn't surprise me that it was Maria who showed it to me. I have no idea how I put one foot in front of the other and made it to my trailer without running into anyone.

I was in a haze looking at the headline. "Mystery man confirmed to be rocker Jake Moore's half-brother." I didn't care about the headline. They could say whatever they wanted to about me, and as long as they never found out about the marriage, I was fine. The haze was more about the grainy cell phone picture than anything.

"I have something to tell you."

I shrieked, nearly knocking back the sofa I was sitting on, I was so surprised. "What the heck, Jake? What are you doing here?" My heart was beating a mile a minute and my breathing was shallow.

"I need to talk you."

"Jake, there isn't anything you can say to change my mind about us," I said vehemently. My breathing was returning to normal and I was starting to get angry.

"Not me, Rissa. Cole. I'm here for my brother."

"What?" I whispered. I didn't think I could control my voice. His words were a shock.

"He's a mess. A real mess. I was selfish and I did some things I'm not proud of to save my image." He laughed a hollow self-deprecating sound.

"What?" I repeated. This conversation had reduced my vocabulary to one syllable words.

"You're going to make me spell it out for you? Yeah, I guess I deserve that," he said and loomed over, looking at me with an intensity that reminded me of his brother. "I got with you because the label was getting tired of my bad boy crazy ways and I had to clean up my act. I thought if I dated the good girl then they would get off my back. They just wanted more, so I proposed, but honestly, I never meant to hurt you. I didn't know about you and my brother or I *never* would have done it." He hesitantly sat down on the couch next to me. "Honey, Cole is the responsible one—the war hero. Obviously, nothing like me." I could hear the truth and pain emanating from him. "I have never seen him like this. He's lost. The day you left, he sat there and drank an entire bottle of Macallan's with me. He's never done anything that crazy. I know you don't have to, but you really have to give him another chance."

I sat there, numb. I didn't know what to say. Even if I did, I'd lost complete control of my voice. Clearing my throat and wiping my eyes, I looked over at him. "It's over, Jake," I said shoving the rag magazine at him.

"Where did you get this?"

He looked angry, and I had no idea why.

"Your girlfriend shoved it in my face after she told me that I ruined her life."

"That fucking crazy bitch. Don't worry Riss." *Huh, I guess we were on a real first name basis now?* Didn't matter, I was done with them both. "I'll deal with her. She comes at you again with this bullshit, you call me. Got it?"

I nodded even though I knew I wouldn't. He had better things to do with his time then worry about me and some school yard bully. "It's fine Jake. She has two more episodes and then she's gone."

"No, Maria's crazy. She won't stop until she thinks she's evened the score. Let me handle this, okay? It's the least I can do after everything I put you through."

"Wow." I tapped him none too softly on the arm. "I think Jake Moore has finally grown up."

"It's all thanks to you, Rissa Taylor." He winked.

"I forgive you, Jake. I even forgive Cole." He started to speak but I shushed him. "I just need to work on me for a while though, you know? My life is here and his life is in Vegas. It probably wouldn't work out anyway."

Jake jumped up from the couch and leaned over and kissed my cheek. "I wouldn't be so sure about that." He was humming as he made his way to the door.

"What do you mean by that?" I yelled after him and heard his chuckle just outside my trailer.

COLE

"It's done," Jake said over the phone on Monday afternoon. "How did she look?"

"She was all done up for work, but I could see it in the way she held herself that this has been hard on her."

I hated that. I didn't want her to be feeling the way I was—the crushing sense of loss was killing me. "Thanks Jake."

"I'm not done yet. That vindictive bitch Maria made it worse by giving Rissa one of the rags. She didn't even realize I was there until I accidentally scared the shit out of her. They figured out who we are, bro. You're going to be getting a lot of publicity very soon."

"Shit, the publicity doesn't bother me, her being hurt is what does."

"Stay the course, man. I'm sure it will all work out in the end. She said she forgives you, but she needs time."

"Thanks Jake, and I mean that. I'm not sure what I'd do without you. Keep an eye on her for me?"

There was a beat of silence before my brother got out, "Of course" before hanging up the phone. It seemed that instead of Rissa pulling us apart, she'd fixed me and my brother.

I was pacing around my apartment when I hung up the phone. It wasn't anything new. After the call with Jake, I continued pacing my suite, as I'd been doing since she left, and figured there was one more phone call I could make. The only thing she asked of me, and it killed me to do it.

Every second that I waited for someone to answer, I thought about hanging up flying down to LA and dragging her ass back here. I couldn't do that though. She needed to see that I would do anything for her, even if it meant tearing my own heart out in the process. Anything in my power to give for her to be happy, I'd do it.

"Hello Mr. Hillard," the slick voice on the other end of the phone brought me out of my musings.

"Hey Jack, I need some paperwork filed."

"Sure thing, Cole. What kind of paperwork are we talking?"

"The personal kind."

"Ahh I see. So, you found the woman you married all those years ago?"

"Yes, and this needs to stay quiet. She is a big deal in Hollywood and I don't want it getting to the press."

"Cole, you know I take anonymity very seriously. No one from my office will leak a thing. I can't, however, speak for the county clerk's office," he replied, his voice gruff.

"I know Jack. Can we just get it done? The quicker the better."

"You know she will have to come here to sign papers?"

"I'm counting on it. I want her to have half of everything I own," I said out of nowhere. An idea was forming in my mind and I knew she would be outraged at the idea. An evil grin spread across my features as Jack sputtered on the other end of the line.

"Cole, you can't be serious," he yelled.

211

"I'm dead serious, Jack. Don't worry, she won't take it. Can you have someone from your office deliver the papers in Beverly Hills? I will pay for everything. I'll even send them in the company plane."

"Yes of course. But, again I must advise against this Cole."

"It's all right, Jack. Trust me, she won't take it." I smiled and hung up the phone.

Dialing one more number, I waited. I didn't want to make this call either but it was what she told Jake she wanted. The Beverly Hills florist picked up on the second ring.

"Thank you for calling The Tilted Tulip. This is Amy. How can I help you?"

"Hi Amy, this is Cole Hillard. I have an order on open account for flowers to go to an address in Beverly Hills every day for the foreseeable future. I need you to cancel the ongoing order. I have something on the way to you now, which will arrive to you by tomorrow, and I'd like you to include it in a bouquet."

"Of course, sir. What kinds of flowers would you like?"

"Anything you have that's red, white, and blue."

"Absolutely. And you said to cancel the rest?"

"Yes, please."

"All right as soon as the package arrives we will send the bouquet out. Is there anything else I can help you with, Mr. Hillard?"

"No, that's all, Amy. Thank you."

"You're welcome Mr. Hillard. Have a nice day," she chirped.

"You too."

RISSA

Two weeks. It had been two weeks since I left Vegas and nothing seemed to be getting better. Sleep was a thing of the past—I had bags that had bags. My clothes no longer fit properly, which made sense since food was totally and completely unappealing. But, the one thing that was going really well was that we'd just finished shooting Maria's final episode, and outside of looking and feeling awful, I couldn't have been happier.

Random tabloids kept popping up in my trailer every day; pictures of Cole were everywhere. New ones of him out running errands or whatever, old ones of the two of us at the club. It was getting annoying and I was so glad Maria and her sneer were gone.

I hadn't heard anything from Cole since the day after Jake's visit. Late afternoon that next day the doorbell rang, and I may or may not have run to the door hoping it was Cole. When I saw the monstrously gorgeous bouquet of red, white, and blue flowers the tiny girl was juggling, I laughed out loud, knowing immediately who they were from. Cole and I had a long-standing feud about which baseball team was better. He was a devoted Red Sox fan and I knew these were a joke, but I loved them anyway. I quickly took the vase from the girl.

I looked down at her name tag. "Thank you, Amy." She looked at me star-struck.

"Um, uh, can you sign for those please?" she stuttered and I grabbed the pen and signed.

"Have a nice day." I smiled sweetly and the girl just stared as I closed the door.

The flowers smelled heavenly. I inhaled deeply as I took them into my stainless steel kitchen and set the vase on the marble counter top. There was something different about these flowers... finally... an envelope. I reached for it hesitantly, not knowing what it contained. What if he said he was done with me? What if he decided that space was what he needed too. I know it's what I said I wanted—the divorce—but in that moment, I realized how wrong I had been. I didn't want space. I wanted someone to fight for me.

Opening the card, my eyes got misty when I reached in and pulled out the two tickets. They were tickets to the game we had talked about going to together. It seemed like a million years ago when in fact it was only a matter of days. I'm not too proud to admit that I sat down at the kitchen island and cried. I never felt lonelier then I did in that moment. Cassie was gone. My mom was gone, and Cliff had a hot date that night. I knew that if I called him, he would cancel it, but I didn't want to do that to him. He had his own life. Not knowing what else to do, I called the one person I knew would give it to me straight. The phone rang and rang until the voice mail picked up.

"Hey this is Eric. I can't get to the phone right now. Leave a message and I'll call you back."

I hung up the phone without a word and laid my head down on the counter and cried. Guess the crying hadn't stopped after all.

As I sat there thinking about that day and the crushing

loneliness, my doorbell rang and startled me from my pity party. I moved slowly toward the door not caring who was there or what they wanted. A man in a cheap rumpled suit and thinning grey hair greeted me.

"Are you Miss Rissa Taylor?" I nodded. "Could you sign this for me please?" he asked handing me a thick envelope.

"What's this about?"

"I just need your signature that you received the papers," he stated emotionlessly.

A tiny voice in my head taunted me. *You know what this is. You asked for this You couldn't expect him to stay married to you when you asked for divorce, now can you?* I signed the paper and closed the door.

Ripping the packet open, my heart shattered and then pieced itself back together as I rifled through the papers. One page stuck out at me—the divorce settlement. It said that he was giving me half a billion dollars. The crushing loss I had felt a moment before was replaced with anger. I dialed the first person I could think of.

"What the hell was he thinking?"

Jake's laughter resounded through the line. "What are you talking about, Honey?"

"Half a billion dollars!" I shrieked. "He can't give me half of everything he owns. What the fuck?" That was how angry I was. He'd reduced me to cursing, and I didn't care. Jake's gasp on the other end of the phone told me everything I needed to know.

"Riss, he's trying to get a rise out of you and you know it. Breathe for me babe."

"Don't babe me Jake. This is the most asinine thing anyone has ever done in the history of forever."

"Or maybe it's a romantic gesture—a show of good faith that all he cares about is your happiness whether you want to be with him or not," he said in all sincerity, then added, "He wants to take care of you."

That took all the wind out of my sails. "Why would he do this,

Jake? We knew each other for a week."

"There's no timeframe on this kind of thing. I never believed in love at first sight. Even five years ago when I watched my brother pine for a girl he had spent one magical night with, I'd never gotten the appeal. But, I saw the utter heart break in your eyes and his when I showed up and announced that Cole was my brother. That's when I realized that maybe it does exist. Let me ask you something. Were you utterly devastated about us?"

I couldn't respond to his question. Anything I said would be hurtful, and while he had hurt me, he really hurt my pride more than anything. Neither one of us really ever touched each other's hearts.

"Your silence speaks volumes."

"I'm sorry, Jake." I was resigned, numb by it all.

"No, Rissa. I'm sorry. I was a giant prick to you. I'm actually glad that I didn't break your heart—I'd have been a much bigger asshole then. You taught me something by showing me that there are more important things than my career. You and Cole need to work shit out, so I can strive to have something as amazing as what you have." He chuckled softly. "You just need to get out of your own way."

This phone call was not going as I expected. Turns out, maybe I didn't pick such a jerk after all. While he wasn't the brother for me, Jake was actually a good guy, who obviously cared a lot for his brother. "He's giving me what I asked for, Jake, he's done." I blew out a breath.

"Come on, Riss. I know you're not that stupid. He's giving you what you want—not because he's done with you, but because he's hoping that's the way he'll get you back."

"What do I do, Jake?"

"You're asking the emotionally stunted guy with the maturity level of a twelve-year-old?"

"Yeah, I guess I am that desperate," I laughed.

After a few moments, he said, "I don't know Riss. I do know

you care about him. I bet you've been just going through the motions the past two weeks, but not really living. You haven't even mentioned the awards. Do you even know it's award season? Did you even care that everyone's been buzzing about your possible Golden Globe nomination?"

"Wait? What? I hadn't heard anything about that."

"They are saying best new actress, best actress in a drama. Best new series, drama. Hell, they will probably make up some new categories just to give you more."

"No way." I was starting to forget my anger, my disappointment at how my life was going. I knew I had to fix this because the only person that I wanted beside me when I went to these award shows was Cole. The thought chilled me that I might be too late.

"When is the court date?" he asked completely flipping the subject. I looked through the information he sent.

"It's in freaking three days?" I shot up from my spot on the couch, practically knocking over any piece of furniture in my path. "How did he know we would be done filming then?"

"I don't know, Riss. It looks like you're going back to Vegas though. Want some company?"

"No, I think this is something I have to do on my own." Looking out the window over the pretty flowers dotting my back yard, I said, "Thanks though, you've turned into a really good friend, Jake."

"Speaking of friends… where has Crazy Cassie been? Why haven't you been calling her?"

"We had a fight in Vegas. She hit it and quit it with Eric and I got mad. I saw how upset he was when she kicked him out. I just wish she would let someone in once in a while. She took off to Europe or something. That's Cassie's typical MO."

"Damn, I'm not playing cupid for them too. My match making skills are limited to immediate family only," he chuckled, and I laughed right along with him.

"Thanks, I needed that. I'll talk to you when I get back, okay?"

"All right Riss, talk to you soon. Give him hell, yeah?"
"You know it."

COLE

The last two weeks were pure torture. I had been away from her more than twice as long as I'd actually known her. No girl had ever tied me in knots as much as Rissa did. The second I looked in those bright violet eyes I was a goner, but after getting to know her I realized I was falling. Giving her the divorce she wanted had crushed my spirit. I was a shell, not even caring about myself, work, anything other than her. I'd expected something after sending those flowers, or hell, after having the divorce papers sent... some text, phone call, irate woman stomping in my hotel.

Nothing.

"Hey fucker, you need to snap out of it," Eric said walking into the living room and handing me a beer.

"What? How can I possibly snap out of it?" I snarled at him and immediately felt guilty. "Sorry man, my heads all over the place. What if she doesn't come? What if she just sends her lawyer?"

"She won't do that, bro."

My phone rang in my pocket and I fished it out slowly, and then

I smiled and popped it on speaker phone.

"What's going on, Jake?"

"You're a crazy bastard, you know that?" *Yes, fist pump! Maybe my plan had worked.* "What were you thinking?" he said with a chuckle.

A smile, my first one in two weeks, crossed my face and actually reached my heart. "I don't know what you're talking about."

"Half of everything?" His booming laughter resounded through the suite. Eric was looking between the phone and me, trying to figure out what the hell was happening.

"Go big or go home, brother."

"You definitely went big. She called me spitting mad."

"I knew she would be pissed. But, is she coming?"

"Do you even have to ask?" he asked astonished. At my stupidity or my brilliance? I didn't know. All I knew was that she was coming back to Vegas and I had my shot to get her back. Eric walked over to me, gave me a high five before heading to the bar to grab us a few beers. I was totally down with a small celebratory drink, or five.

"When is she coming?"

"Tomorrow. Are you sure you know what you're doing, Cole?"

"Absolutely. We will be back together by the end of the week." I clinked bottles with Eric, who sat back down, popped his feet up on the coffee table and looked more relaxed than I'd seen him in weeks.

"I hope so, brother. She has been a mess the last few weeks."

"Trust me. I have a plan. Do you know where she is staying?"

"Nah, she called me as soon as the papers showed up at her door."

"Shit, well I know some people. I can work it out." My smile was sinister and Eric looked at me a bit scared.

"What are you planning?" they asked in unison.

"A total blackout of all hotels on the strip. If I have to reserve every suite on the strip, I will."

"Nah, I know a guy who can hack in and do that for you. I'll call him now," Eric offered laughing, obviously enjoying my scheme.

"You're going to sabotage her so she has to stay in your hotel?" Jake marveled at me over the phone. "What if she reserves a room there, anyway?"

"Then I won't have to lift a finger, but if I know her, she's going to stay some place like the Bellagio just to spite me."

"You're probably right. I'm so glad I don't have to deal with this shit, bro."

"Just wait, one day you're going to fall in love and do the exact same thing. Only yours will probably be crazier."

"No way, bro. No one is going to lock down the great Jake Moore." I shook my head as I listened to my younger brother. I used to think the same way until I met Rissa. Now I know that my life wasn't worth living unless she was in it.

"You will one day, trust me on this. And when you mess up, I will help you get her back," I said honestly.

"Whatever you say Cole."

"I have shit to do. Let me know if you find anything else out, yeah?"

"Of course. Check you later, bro."

"Later."

I turned to Eric who was typing away on his phone. "Already? I knew you were good, but damn." He muttered as though talking to the phone.

I looked at him curiously, and he responded, "My guy hacked her phone already. You were right, she already booked a suite at the Bellagio for tonight."

"Tonight? Shit. Is he going to be able to fix it in time?"

Picking up the phone to place the call directly, he said, "Tony? Yeah man it's me. Can you cancel her reservation and block her from booking anywhere else?" My knee was bouncing like crazy, waiting to hear Eric's half of the conversation. I was nervous as hell.

"He said he can make it look like everywhere is booked... it'll last for an hour after she arrives, so she'll have no choice but to stay here." Eric had a devilish grin on his face and I blew out a breath.

"Can he make sure the blackout happens after she tries to check in at the Bellagio? There is no telling how bad traffic is going to be."

"Oh come on, man. You can't just do it for love?" Eric laughed. I looked at him like he was crazy. "He says he wants Laker tickets. Courtside to be precise."

"Done. I will even put him up in the new hotel I'm going to be managing down there."

"Deal, he will track her phone and let us know when she's leaving the Bellagio... with no room."

I rubbed my hands together like an evil mastermind and jumped off the couch. There were a lot of things to do before she got here, and since she was coming sooner than I planned I had no choice but to bump up my time line.

"Time to get to work." I smiled and strolled from the room to the sound of Eric's big booming laugh.

CHAPTER 41

RISSA

"Cliff? Sorry, I have so much to do. I have to go back to Vegas. Cole is being crazy and trying to give me half of everything he owns."

"What? Rissa, darling. You realize this is a set-up, right?"

"Of course it's a set-up." I laughed. It was the first joyful sound I had heard come from my mouth in a while and it felt good. "I have no idea what game he's playing, but I have a plan too."

"Whoever started calling you Hollywood's good girl has never seen your devious streak." He giggled into the phone. "Would you like some help?"

"No thanks, hun. I got this."

"What is this insanely devious plan you've hatched?"

"You'll find out soon enough. The whole world will."

"You're not? Tell me you're not gonna do what I think you're gonna do."

"You'll see. I have to go now. I have a plane to catch."

"Rissa, Rissa! I think this is a very bad-" I cut him off by hanging up the phone and grabbed my suitcases.

I had a car waiting to take me to the airport. The driver placed them in the trunk after opening the door for me. I was nervous. I had no idea what he had planned or whether my own plan was going to work, but I had to try something.

After spending the best days of my life with Cole and then coming back to my lonely existence, I realized something. I didn't care who he was related to or what the press said about my relationship with him. At some point during that week I had grown to feel more for him than I had for anyone else, ever. He was sweet, funny, caring, and attentive. He was everything I could ever want and I couldn't live without him. The only way to show him was to go public. I would do it too. My only regret was that my best friend wasn't there to cheer me on, was my thought right before my phone started ringing.

"What the hell are you doing? Tell me I don't have to fly half way around the world to come knock some sense into you," Cassie's voice scolded through the phone, as though she hadn't ignored me for two weeks.

"Nope, I have never been more clear headed in my life."

"That's not what Cliff says. He called me in a panic saying you had lost your mind. That you were going to leak information about yourself to the press."

"Well, yeah. That's the idea. I have to prove that I don't care what the press thinks. He's prepared to let me go because he knows as well as I do what they are saying about me. He served me with divorce papers, Cassie," I said on a sigh. "He's doing everything I asked him to. He just wants me to be happy, but I was so, so stupid. I love him and I am going to prove it, and this is the only way I know how."

I was waiting for the argument, for all the reasons I shouldn't be doing what I was, but it never came. "Okay, as long as you know what you're doing."

"I really wish you were here," I said honestly.

"Me too, but I couldn't refuse the offer I got to work with one of the best artists living today. I was going to tell you before we went to Vegas, but all hell broke loose and I didn't want to dump that on you too. This is the opportunity of a lifetime for me, and I just couldn't pass it up."

"When are you going to be back?"

"Six months. Venice is a dream. You should totally get the forearm to bring you here for your honeymoon," she giggled.

"What about Eric?" I asked cautiously

"What about him? We had one night. It was great and then it was over. He lives in Vegas and for now I live on the other side of the world. It never would have worked out anyway."

"If you're sure?"

"Yup, totally positive."

There was something about this conversation that just didn't sit right with me, that wasn't really ringing true, but being on the phone with her in Europe was not the best time to argue with her. Instead I said, "I'm so glad you called. I'm just about to the airport, so wish me luck and have a fabulous time in Italy. Don't do anything I wouldn't do."

"That doesn't leave me with a whole lot to do, at this point!"

"You would be surprised my friend. I'll call you and fill you in on all the dirty details—we can have virtual girls' night over sushi and wine when I get back."

"Deal. Bye babe."

"Talk to you later, hun."

The entire one hour flight to Vegas was a blur. I was freaking out in my first-class seat. One woman in particular kept staring from across the aisle.

"Excuse me? Are you…"

"Yes." I smiled.

"Oh my God, Rissa Taylor. It is you!" she exclaimed.

"I'm sorry?"

"Oh! I'm sorry dear. My name is Marguerite and I was very close with your mother."

"Marguerite Nelson? Yes, my mother spoke very fondly of you."

"Oh come now, darling. We both know that was a lie. Your mother was a right hag when she wanted to be," she chuckled. "But, she was one of my dearest friends."

I laughed out loud at that. My mother could be a mega beast when she wanted. I was glad that the majority of my childhood was spent in boarding school across the country.

My mother was old-time Hollywood royalty and people practically fell at her feet, but Marguerite was royalty as well. "I have noticed some things in the tabloids, dear. Don't let them get you down. One thing your dear mother never understood was love. I sincerely hope that you didn't learn that particular er... flaw from her. I saw it in those pictures you know—not the ones of you with the boy who cheated. Nasty business that was. But, the new ones with his brother? It was obvious even from the photos the love in both of your eyes. Can I be inquisitive... are you on your way to see him?"

"I am," I said quietly, leaving out important details of the situation, not wanting anyone else on the plane to overhear.

"Your mother," Marguerite confessed, "she never forgave me for falling in love with husband number three."

"Is that why you stopped talking? She never said."

"Yes it was. While I dearly loved her, she didn't truly understand the concept of love. Me and my dear Ronald, God rest his soul, were together for fifteen years before the cancer took him. I never did forgive myself for not contacting your mother sooner to put our differences to rest, but by the time I got out of my own stubborn head, she was gone." She gave me a watery smile, but one that resonated her sorrow.

"I'm sorry," I said, reaching over the aisle to pat her hand.

"Don't live with regrets, darling. It's not worth it."

"I'm working on that." Squeezing her hand, I told her, "If it makes you feel any better, I think she did forgive you. She never spoke ill of you. There was only ever a fondness or a deep sadness whenever she mentioned stories of the two of you—friendship was important to her."

"Thank you." She squeezed my hand back before releasing it. "You have made an old woman very happy."

I scribbled down my phone number and handed to her. "Please, if you ever feel like talking or reminiscing about mom, don't hesitate to call me. I would love to hear more about who my mother really was. She left me way too young."

"Absolutely. I would like very much to get to know you as well. There is so much of her in you. You're talent and beauty. You are a remarkable young woman."

As the plane descended on Vegas, I smiled, looking out the window over the desert canvas. My heart felt lighter than it had in a while. I finally understood a little more about my mother and where I came from. It was then that I truly felt like everything was going to work out for the best.

    **

But, I was so wrong. "What do you mean I have no reservation? You know who I am right?" Throwing my Hollywood status weight around, wasn't really my thing, but desperation and all that.

"Yes, ma'am, and I'm sorry but there aren't any rooms available anywhere in the hotel."

"What about any of your affiliate hotels? Are there any rooms at any of them?"

"No ma'am. I'm not finding any rooms at any of our hotels. I'm so sorry. I don't know what happened."

Tempering my annoyance, since clearly it wasn't the clerk's

fault, and I so didn't need to be labeled with more bad press, I smiled and replied, "It's okay. I guess I'll just find another hotel."

Sitting in the lobby of the Bellagio, I called one hotel after another down the strip. It took me nearly an hour, but they all had the same answer—booked. Something was definitely not right in Kansas... and that's when the idea struck me like a bolt of lightning. That sneaky, sneaky man.

"Do you have any rooms available?" I asked when the receptionist answered to the dead-last hotel I wanted to stay at.

"Yes ma'am. Let me check for you." She typed a few keys and said exactly what I knew she would. "Yes, but we only have a penthouse suite on the top floor available. Will that suit your needs?"

I groaned as I gave her my information. There was no way every room was booked in all of Vegas on the one night I happen to be in town. This was all Cole's doing, but I had a plan to formulate, and he was ruining everything.

"Would you like me to send a car for you Ms. Davies?" she chirped, happily.

"Yes, please. I'm at the Bellagio."

"Right away. I have a car in route as we speak. Will that be all for you?"

I grumbled out a "Yes, thank you," before hanging up the phone.

It was less than three minutes before a limo pulled up and I rolled my eyes. Once we were back together I was going to kick his butt for trying to force my hand like that. Although, if I were completely honest with myself—which I wasn't about to give him at the moment—I was preening inside with the knowledge that he was chasing after me.

The car pulled us into the same underground garage it did the last time and Marco was standing there at attention waiting for me. He opened my door and helped me out of the car.

"Hey Marco."

"Miss Taylor. It is so good to see you back so soon," he said, then lowered his voice conspiratorially. "If I may say, Mr. Hillard has been unusually grumpy since you've been away."

"He put you up to this, didn't he?"

"I know nothing, Miss." He winked at me.

Expletives ran through my head on a loop. We were both trying to prove ourselves to each other, like that old Christmas story where the couple sells their prize possession to get the other something perfect only to find out that the presents are now useless. I needed to step up a new timeline. Two could play at this game, I thought as I followed Marco up to the penthouse... the exact same one I stayed in with Cassie the last time I was there.

"Thank you," I said to Marco as he set my bags down in the master bedroom.

"Don't be so hard on Mr. Hillard. He's trying, ma'am" was his parting shot before leaving me alone in the huge suite.

I slumped down on to the couch and called Joanie. "We have to step it up. How soon can you leak that information I sent you?"

"Well hello to you to, Honey," she chuckled in greeting.

"Sorry, but this man is frustrating me. I don't know how he did it or why, but he managed to block out rooms at every hotel on the strip, so I would have to stay at here. At his hotel! And, worse, I have no idea what he's planning." I huffed an exaggerated breath, annoyed he was beating me at my own game.

"I will have it on every major blog and tabloid website within the hour, but I need you to know that once this is out it isn't going away, Honey."

"That's the point, Joanie. It's my show of good faith. My way to tell him by my actions that he means more to me than my career."

"Okay then, hun. I hope he's worth it."

"He is, and even though at the moment I'm annoyed with him, if there is one thing I know for certain, it's that Cole is everything to me.

COLE

It was a goddamn clusterfuck. Even though she made it to my hotel—I'm sure wondering what the hell I was up to—someone (I'd kill them later) leaked the divorce papers. I didn't pay attention to the tabloids, so when Jake called me five times in a row, I knew something was up.

"What's going on, Jake?" I answered the phone a ball of dread eating at my stomach.

"I don't know how they did it, but check out TMZ."

Opening up my laptop, I cursed at TMZ's website and their *Breaking News*. My divorce papers were splashed across the screen. The headlines read "What happens in Vegas?" I cringed when I saw the date of marriage had been circled in red for all to see, and I knew they would skewer her in the press for this. Her career may very well be over, and it was all my fault.

"Shit. How did they get all this?"

"I don't know, Cole, but, it's everywhere. It doesn't look like someone sold the story. It looks like it was leaked."

I couldn't sit still behind my desk. I had to pace. "Who could have done this?" Whoever leaked this information, ruined all of my plans.

"I don't know, but the best way to deal with this is head on. Release a statement through your PR department, and let everyone know what happened so she doesn't look bad because. I got to tell you, this makes her look really bad." We both sighed out. My plan, my perfect plan was going to shit. Nope, strike that, was already shit. "I will release a statement too. Maybe we can maneuver this so she doesn't lose her entire reputation."

"That's probably the best solution. I gotta call my lawyer and find out if this was from his office, then I need to call my PR people. Thanks Jake. I don't know what I would have done these last few weeks without you."

"Don't go getting all mushy on me. Go make your calls. I have some calls to make as well." He hung up the phone and I continued pacing, thinking things through and calming myself the hell down before calling the lawyer's office.

Not two minutes later someone was pounding on the door and I had a feeling I knew who it was. I didn't want to see her like this. Throwing the door open, I was startled to see Eric standing there breathing heavy, hands holding himself up on the doorframe.

"There is a media circus outside the hotel," he panted out as if he'd run a marathon. "I have security holding them back and we are erecting barriers as we speak to keep them out. What the hell is going on?"

"Someone leaked the divorce papers!" I was pissed.

"What?" Eric looked like he was about to be sick. "Have you talked to Rissa? Is she okay?"

"I just found out five minutes ago. Jake called me." I could feel the rage bubbling up inside me. This was such a violation it was unreal. Walking to the nearest wall, I reared back and punched it. The wall gave way and my fist went through, but it didn't lessen the anger running through me at all.

"What are you going to do?"

"First, I'm calling Jack, my lawyer, and letting him know that he's fired unless he finds out who leaked the papers. Then, I'm doing the only thing I can do, I'll make a public statement letting everyone know that this is not her fault and that we were basically separated for five years."

"You realize there is no good way to spin this, right? No matter how you look at it she is going to look bad. Two brothers, Cole-"

"I know," I cut him off. "That's why I'm talking to the PR department. If they can't figure something out that minimizes the danger to her career then what the hell am I paying them for?"

"Good plan. Do you want me to go check on Riss? She might need a friend."

"Actually, I think Jake was calling her as soon as he got off the phone with me. Seems they've patched up their relationship, which funny enough, makes me feel better. Three weeks ago, I was ready to kill my brother." I was rambling, the anger dissipating the more I tried to focus on the task at hand. "Get the head of PR up here. I don't want to go downstairs just yet, in case security hasn't cleared out all the press."

My phone vibrated in my hand. I looked down as notifications started scrolling through one after the other. "I'm going to have to turn off my damn notifications; this is ridiculous."

Eric laughed and I glared, which of course made him laugh harder. Ignoring the giant asshole, I unlocked my phone and dialed Jack. The anger was still simmering under my skin. It was like a living breathing thing. Jack finally picked up the phone when I was beginning to think he was ignoring me.

"I'm on it, Cole. I have no idea how those papers got leaked, but I *promise* you that if anyone in my office did it, they will be dealt with. They all sign iron-clad NDAs and I will not go easy on them."

"Good, I'm counting on you to find out what the hell this is all about. Her career is at stake here. Everything she has worked for her entire life is on the line. I will not let this ruin her life. Do you hear me?" This was such a violation of her privacy. I didn't care much about my own—you don't go through the military without developing a thick skin. She was all that I cared about. I let out a shaky breath and most of the anger deflated out of me. "Just fix it, Jack."

After hanging up with him, I flopped on the couch and tilted my head back. *What the fuck am I going to do now? How will she ever forgive me after this?*

RISSA

I had no idea how long I laid on the couch before my phone started buzzing in my hand. *Jake.* I sat up and looked at the phone curiously before answering. "What's going on, Jake?"

"Have you looked at the rags?"

"No, why?" I said cautiously.

"Ummm, you may not want to Riss, and I'm serious here. They got some information on you—you're everywhere. They even know where you are right now."

"What?" I screeched. "How? Jake, what's going on?" I swear I deserved that Golden Globe. They had no idea how good my acting skills really were.

"The divorce papers were released to the press." *Wait, what? That wasn't the plan! What the hell is Joanie doing?*

"They what?" I yelled for real this time. That was not acting. That was me being seriously freaked out. Joanie was supposed to leak the marriage license along with my real name. Not the divorce papers. "Tell me that they didn't leak the settlement page. Please

235

Jake. Tell me that I don't look like a gold-digging whore."

"Hey, watch your damn mouth. No one talks shit about you. Even you. Cole and I are figuring out a way to fix this."

"Cole? Why would he try to fix this? It isn't his fault."

"You can be seriously dense sometimes, you know that? Everything that guy has done in the last three weeks has been for you. Hell, most of the stuff he's done over the last five years has been to find you. The last thing he wants is to be the one that caused of the end of your career."

"Shit."

"What? Did you just say shit? That has to be the first sign of the apocalypse or something," he chuckled. "Wait why did you say shit?"

"I just realized that I may have caused this whole mess."

"How?" he asked with deadly calm.

"I should have known they would dig deeper." I muttered to myself and jumped up. "What am I gonna do now? My big grand gesture just blew up in my face." I continued to talk but I wasn't really paying attention.

"Rissa? Rissa! What the fuck are you talking about?"

Uh oh, I blanched, totally forgetting I was still on the phone with Jake.

"This is all my fault," I began. Time for total honesty. "I just wanted to show him that my career wasn't as important to me as he was. After all of those horrible things I said to him when I left, I just wanted to show him that I didn't care what people said about me... about us."

"You're not making any sense. You need to tell me what you did, so we can try to fix this." The worry in Jake's voice was apparent.

"Included with the divorce papers was a copy of the actual marriage license. I gave it to my publicist and told her to leak it," I rushed out the rest and waited for him to explode. He didn't explode, though, he started laughing hysterically. "Jake. This isn't funny. I ruined everything."

"It is kinda funny, Riss." He took a moment to get himself back under control. Glad someone found my life amusing. "He has been working so hard to make sure your reputation is intact, and then you went and blew it all out of the water. He is probably devising a plan with his PR firm to take all the blame himself."

A burst of laughter bubbled up inside of me. I couldn't help it. We were the biggest idiots ever. "Oh my God. I need to go talk to him," I wheezed out.

"Yeah, you better go do that before he decides to give a public statement or something."

"Oh God. Why would he do something like that?"

"He thinks it's the only way to give you what you want. The divorce, your career-"

"I gotta go." I hung up without another word and dialed Joanie.

"Honey, before you get upset, let me assure you that I had nothing to do with the divorce papers. I already called my contact at TMZ and chewed his ass. I will never leak anything to them again after what they did. He said all it took was a call to the county clerk's office and he had all the information faxed to him. Honey, your life is a matter of public record. They just had to know what they were looking for. I'm sorry but we kind of gave them everything they needed to dig deeper."

"I should have thought of that. But it's time to fix this. I need you to put out a statement. Cole is working with his PR people in an attempt to lessen the blow to my career, but I need to beat him to it."

"What did you have in mind?"

I told her my plan and she listened intently. "Okay, if that's how you want to play it, I will get a statement written up and sent out to all the major news outlets."

"Thank you, Joanie. I'll talk to you soon."

I had stalled going to see Cole as much as I could. Looking in the mirror by the front entry door, the circles under my eyes were like bruises. I looked like crap, but I needed to go see him before he did something insane like take all the blame for our "quote unquote" marriage.

Banging the door to his room, not caring who else heard me, I yelled, "Come on, Cole. Answer the door."

I was muttering to myself bouncing up and down, feeling uncomfortable in my own skin, when the door flew open. "Where is he?" Eric looked shocked but quickly shut the door behind him. I would have thought that strange if my mind had been working right.

"Riss, you need to calm down. He's going to fix this. It's okay," Eric said taking my agitation to mean I was pissed at Cole. "He's downstairs holding a press conference right now."

"What? Where? You have to take me there."

"Why? He's fixing it."

"No, he's really not! My publicist is drafting a statement as we speak. TMZ screwed me over and I have to fix it."

"Slow down. He's in one of the conference rooms. It's going to be hard as hell to protect you on the casino floor though. There are paps and fans everywhere."

"I don't care, Eric." I huffed and stomped my foot like a two-year-old. "I need to get down there. *Now.*"

COLE

"Are you sure this is the route you want to go?" Leslie from public relations asked over the phone after I explained the situation.

"Yes, that's the only way." God, I was frustrated. She had asked me that five times in the last fifteen minutes.

"I understand that you want to protect her, sir. But, it's my job to protect you and the hotel from bad press."

"This is how I want you to do your job, or should I find someone else to do what I ask?" I replied angrily. I wouldn't actually fire her, probably. I just needed her to see that I was serious. I couldn't have Rissa hurt by this.

"No, sir."

"Good, I need that statement as soon as possible. And, schedule a press conference in whichever conference room is available for one hour from now."

"Is that going to be enough time to get everyone here?"

"Have you seen what it looks like outside? They're all already here," I said exasperated. "One hour Leslie and not a minute more."

I hung up without another word and dialed the concierge desk.

"Marco, I need a conference room outfitted for a press conference. Call hospitality and tell them to drop everything and get it done immediately."

"Yes, sir," he replied and hung up. That was one of the things I liked about Marco; he never asked questions and followed orders without so much as a word of explanation. Some of my other employees could definitely take some pointers from him.

Stomping toward my bedroom get out of my jeans and T-shirt and into a crisp power suit—I hated the damn things, but the situation called for professionalism—I needed to show my best self, even if I was about to tell the world what a useless hap I really was, since losing the only girl I ever really loved because I lied to her.

I passed her suite on my way to the conference room and had to restrain myself from knocking on her door and pulling her into my arms. Salvaging the career she loved was the only way I knew to get her back. To prove to her that her career and her life back in LA were just as important to me as they were to her—that *she* was the most important to me.

When I got down to the casino floor, it was bustling with activity. It was impossible not to notice the few sideways glances and hushed whispers as I walked through the hotel and to the conference room. The staff was running around prepping the room as I made my way over to Leslie.

"You have the statement?" I asked and she hesitated before nodding. "Are you going to give it to me?"

"Are you sure I can't talk you out of this, sir?" She flinched briefly when I glared down at her.

"No," I growled and instantly felt guilty and softened my tone. "No, I need to do this. It's the only way."

Handing me the statement, I looked down to see an extremely

short statement with none of the things I asked for it to say. My irritation at the meddling woman was growing, and I had to walk away before I lost my head.

As I stood there looking at the statement, trying to come up with the best way to modify it, Eric walked up. "Cole, you need to calm down buddy."

"Can you go back to my suite and make sure that you stall her? If I know her, she will be looking for me, and soon. Keep her away as long as you can. I don't want her interrupting the press conference. This is something I have to do."

"Okay, I'll go back and wait for her," he sighed. "Are you sure this a good idea? They could turn your words around so it sounds bad. Then what good will it do? It won't help her career."

"Yes." I said staunchly. "This is what I have to do. These people love her. She's the most beloved celebrity in Hollywood right now, and if they understand what happened, she'll get to stay that way."

"Whatever you say bro." He clapped my back and walked away.

The crowd of reporters started filing in minutes after Eric walked out the door. I was a reasonably confident man, but even I started to sweat when I realized how many people I was going to divulge my personal life to. My phone rang and I wiped my sweaty palm on my pants before reaching in and pulling it out. "Hello?" My voice was rough with nerves and Jake heard it right away.

"Cole, you need to call this thing off. Right. Now."

"No, Jake." I refused to let him continue. "I'm not stopping this. I am going to make this right. It's my fault she's being dragged through the mud in the first place. I gotta go. We are getting ready to start."

"Cole-" I hung up and shoved the phone back in my pocket. I couldn't deal with everyone telling me not to do what I knew in my gut was the right thing. I didn't care if I looked like a predator, as long as Rissa came out of this with her reputation intact.

Rubbing my sweaty hands on my pants again, I stood behind the official looking podium and waited for everyone to take their seats. It was a packed house. I looked down at the paper Leslie had given me and shook my head. *Guess I'm gonna have to wing it.*

Clearing my throat, I started, "Thank you all for coming. By now you know who I am. So, I'll just start at the beginning with a question for you. Have any of you ever done something impulsive? Spontaneous? When I went into a club five years ago, I didn't go with the idea my life would change. I went to have a drink and unwind from the week, but Honey Davies captured my attention immediately and I wanted more. Long before she was a star playing a role, and long before she was even on your radar, that woman captivated me. It was the best night of my life, and when it started to come to a close, I panicked. I didn't want it to end." I was speaking to the room with confidence, but I was looking without seeing anything. So, when the doors flew open and the reporters began murmuring to themselves, I looked up.

Rissa was stomping her way to the front of the room. I braced myself for the onslaught. Her violet eyes flashed with anger and I swallowed the lump in my throat.

"What are you doing, Cole?" she whispered once she got close enough to me.

Holding my hand over the microphone, I whispered back. "I'm fixing this." I could read the irritation in her eyes so, when she smiled at me it threw me off.

"This is my fault, Cole," she said softly, placing her hand on mine to cover the microphone even more. "I did this. And, you standing here talking to these vultures isn't going to help matters. Come on. We need to talk." She looked at me amid all the flash bulbs pulsing in our faces. I could barely hear all the reporters screaming questions over one another through the blood rushing in my ears.

"This press conference is over," I said robotically, and awkwardly followed Rissa out of the room.

RISSA

It was weird, walking next to Cole without touching him. He was so close. Even though I was mad at him and still felt betrayed, I had dreamed of being close to him for the past couple weeks. I still wanted him. Now, though, it was awkward, since I didn't know where we stood. He kept looking over at me probably trying to gauge my mood, which was going to be impossible, considering I didn't know where I stood. His look of terror when I said those four little words was almost comical. Guys everywhere hated the phrase "We need to talk" as it almost never meant anything good, and in this case I wasn't exactly sure myself.

The awkward silence in the elevator was oppressive. I hated it, but I kept my mouth shut until we made it to his penthouse. Even though I was here earlier, pounding the door down, I never even noticed… the boxes. His suite looked empty and cold with the couch sitting alone in the middle of the large room. "Where is everything?"

"It's all been boxed up. The moving guys will be here tomorrow to take everything to the new hotel." He replied off-handed not even looking at me.

"What new hotel? Where?" I was beginning to panic. This was so far from how I imagined things to be for us when I started this scheme.

"I thought you wanted to talk. I know this wasn't what you meant, so let's just get it all out in the open." I flinched at his words, like I had been slapped. "How is this all your fault?"

I deserved it. I was the reason that his entire life was broadcast to the world. It shouldn't be a surprise to me that he was avoiding telling me what had happened to all his stuff and where he was relocating to, but it hurt nonetheless.

"I released the marriage certificate to the press," I rushed out before I lost my nerve. His head finally swiveled in my direction.

"You what? Why would you do that?"

"I'm not even sure now. I thought I was proving something to you. Now, I'm not so sure because as soon as they saw the marriage certificate they went digging and everything blew up in my face." I sat down on the lonely couch in the middle of the wide-open space and covered my face with my hands, unable to face him.

I could literally hear him pacing the empty living room and feel his eyes burning holes into my covered face, willing me to look. But, I couldn't bear it. Anger I could handle, since I was angry enough with myself, but hatred, disappointment, maybe even disgust? Those were things I couldn't stand to see cross his handsome face.

"Look at me, Riss," he demanded and I shook my head in my hands. "Damn it, Riss. Why would you think you had anything to prove? Ruining your career? The thing you love to do… that was just plain idiotic."

That stung and I flinched back further on the couch. He was right, I knew, but I also knew that he was wrong. I pushed up to my feet, looked up, and mustered the frustration, anger, and hurt that I'd been feeling for weeks and let loose. "I did it for you!" I pointed directly at his chest. "God, I was so dumb to think this could work. You're an overbearing man-child and I'm a freaking superstar," I said in air quotes. "Shit like this never works out." I spun on my heel and stomped to the front door. "I will see you in court and just so you know? I'm not taking a penny of your damn money. That was idiotic."

"You just cursed at me," he said in disbelief and I almost laughed at the absurdity of the statement. That was what he picked up on in my tirade?

"What does it matter, Cole?" All the anger was leaching out of me and I felt nothing but numb. "I can hear it in your voice that you've made up your mind. Hell, I can tell by the boxes all packed up. We should just end this before we kill each other."

"I was stupid enough to think if you saw me again you wouldn't want the divorce. That I could win you over, but I guess I was wrong."

That stopped me in my tracks. Wasn't that what I wanted? Wasn't that what I'd hoped he'd say? But, my hand lifted to the door knob. I had no idea what caused me to open it and walk out—pride or stubborn anger, it didn't really matter. "Goodbye Cole."

I was in a fog as I walked back to my room. It was such a stupid fight. He never even mentioned the fact that what I did pushed him out into the spotlight, something, Jake had told me that Cole never wanted.

Their father was a playboy and Jake was a rock star, but Cole he just wanted to live his life in peace. After his service in the military, he worked hard and helped his father build his empire and was totally happy with that until he met me. In a month, I turned his life upside down and thrust him into a life he never wanted, which was probably why he was leaving to run a new hotel, probably going somewhere far away from me and all the drama that followed.

Opening the door to my room, I heard my phone ringing from the coffee table. *Is it Cole?* I looked at the caller ID and hit the little green button.

"You were wrong, Jake. He's leaving. Did you know that? His suite is filled with boxes and he's just waiting for the movers. It's over." A single tear traced down my cheek, and I swiped it away angrily.

"What did that big dumb idiot do? He won't answer his phone, and I tried to stop that stupid press conference, but he hung up on me."

"I don't know, Jake. We just had the stupidest fight in the history of mankind and I don't know how to fix it. I don't know if I want to fix it or if it's even possible. He's leaving."

"Yeah, that's news to me. I wonder where he's going."

"I don't know," I sighed and flopped onto the couch. "He wouldn't tell me."

"Huh, that's weird. I wonder why he didn't tell me, either."

"Probably because he knows we're friends and he doesn't want me to know where he's going."

"That's bullshit, Riss. Cole's weird. He always has a plan, and good luck trying to get anything out of him before he's ready. I will guarantee you one thing though. I bet you I can find out. There are two people that I know of who I may be able to get the information from."

"It's fine, Jake. Really." Laying there on the sofa, my body felt like it weighed a thousand pounds. Every decision, every hurt—those I gave and those I'd received—were weighing me down, and I no longer had the energy to fight. "We're just going to get the divorce and go our separate ways." I really didn't want to look into why that comment hurt so much. The idea of never seeing Cole again was carving my heart out of my chest. I had no idea how to fix it, so I just let it go. Who knew, maybe we would see each other again and get past all the stupid mistakes we made. It was the best

I could hope for.

COLE

She ruined everything. All my carefully laid out plans were completely blown to pieces. How on earth could she think that she had anything to prove to me? How could she release the marriage certificate to the press? I was pacing my suite thinking about everything when my phone rang. "Eric, I asked you to distract her."

"Well, I wanted to stop you from being an idiot and ruining everything," he countered.

"Too late." I sat down with one hand over my eyes.

"What happened?"

"I blew it and got angry with her when I figured out what she did. She never should have played with her life like that."

"You ass," Eric admonished me. "You threw away the girl who jeopardized her life to show you that you were important to her? You really are an idiot."

He was right, but through my anger I still couldn't see it. "That's the point, she didn't have to do that. I'm so pissed that she would sit there and throw away everything over me."

"Cole? Listen to yourself, man. Weren't you doing the same thing with your grand plan? Not telling her that you are moving to LA, when in fact you're doing it to be closer to her? Giving her the divorce she wanted and the space she wanted… even though it killed you?"

"No, I *did* have something to prove. I'm the one who kept the truth from her. I'm the one who lied. I needed to prove to her that I would do anything for her. Even if it meant staying away from her."

"Yeah, but I don't think she sees it that way. I think she was taught from a young age to bottle things up and not show her emotions, and when she found out about Jake and that you lied to her, she said things she didn't mean so that she wouldn't break down in front of us. Don't forget that I was in that room too. It wasn't anger. It was hurt. I saw a girl who had been mistreated and was looking for a reason to believe that you were the same way and you know what? You gave her exactly what she needed to hate you. The thing is, she doesn't hate you. She went out of her way to show you and all the world that she cares, and you went off and got pissed. Granted, what she did was certifiable and was bound to blow up in her face, but she did it for *you* and you pushed her away. Why? Because she ruined your plan to get her back? Stop being such an idiot and man up!"

When he was finally done with his rant—which I had never in all my years with him heard him talk that much at once—I huffed out a breath. "Shit, what am I going to do now? She cursed at me. Did I tell you that? How am I supposed to get her back when I made her so mad she actually swore?" I laughed without humor.

"Figure it out, man. LA is going to be a lonely place for you if you don't fix this. You know you can't go through with this divorce now, right?"

"Yeah, I know. But, how do I do this without pissing her off even more?"

"I don't know, but you better figure it out quickly."

I looked down at the laptop that was still set out on the table.

TMZ was showing a video of the press conference. Rissa stormed in and the look on my face would have been comical if my head wasn't so fucked up. Reaching over, I turned up the volume and heard the complete chaos that was in the background. At the time, I only had eyes for Riss, but I heard them all now and they were asking insanely personal questions. I growled completely forgetting that Eric was still on speakerphone.

"What's that?"

"I'm watching that shit show of a press conference."

Honey Davies had this to say in a statement released by her publicist late this afternoon. "Cole is a victim here and doesn't deserve your treatment. Leave him be. I know you want answers and here they are: I did something stupid. I was young and hurt. My boyfriend cheated on me, so I picked up and went to Vegas. I got really drunk and don't remember what happened, other than waking up and the next morning realizing I was married. Up until three weeks ago, I didn't even know who Cole was. We hit it off when I fled to Vegas after being cheated on a second time. I didn't know he was Jake's brother at the time, but we are all moving past this. Jake has been a real friend to me since the news broke, and I would appreciate it if the press and the public respect all of our privacy as we figure out where to go from here."

It sounds to me like she has real feelings for Mr. Hillard. I guess time will tell. Will the divorce be finalized? Or, will Honey Davies, America's it girl remain married to the heir of the Hillard hotel fortune? We'll keep you all updated as more news comes in.

"Cole? Cole!" Eric was yelling at me through the phone. "What the hell was that I heard?"

"They just read the statement that Riss put out to the press," I sighed and rubbed my stubbled jaw. Things like shaving hadn't seemed as important to me lately. The five o'clock shadow I was sporting had the makings of a full-on beard.

"Hold on, I'm looking it up right now," he said briskly. It sounded like he was on the move. A few minutes later he grunted into the phone. "Shit man, what are you gonna do now?"

"Whatever it takes."

RISSA

I was sitting in the hotel room feeling sorry for myself and wondering what the heck I was going to do now, when there was a knock on the door. I checked the time on my phone. Cliff had said he was on the next flight over, but there was no way he could be there already. Stepping up to the door I opened it slowly and saw Marco on the other side.

"Miss Taylor, you forgot this the last time you stayed with us. I thought you might like to have it for your reservation tonight," he said as I opened the door all the way to let him in.

"Marco, thank you but I don't have a reservation tonight," I replied confused, shutting the door behind us.

"You don't? Mr. Hillard said you had a table at the steakhouse tonight and needed the dress."

"Hmm, he did, did he? What time did he say I had a reservation for?" I grabbed the garment bag he held out for me, and grabbed a few dollars out of my bag sitting on the side table by the door.

"It's at eight, miss," he confirmed.

Slipping him the cash in his hand, I opened the door for him. "Thanks so much Marco. I appreciate you bringing this to me."

"You're welcome, and thank you."

Shutting the door without a second thought, I looked down at the bag and smiled. What he was planning now? I grabbed my phone and dialed Jake, who was currently on speed dial. "Hey, how's it going, babe."

"Ugh, Jake don't call me that; it's just weird now." I half laughed.

"Sorry, but you know, we didn't speak this much when we were actually together," he chuckled. "What can I do for you?"

Studiously avoiding that comment, I asked, "Are you in Vegas? Even though I told you not to come?"

"You got me, and yes, the plane just touched down. Why? What's up?"

"Cole's up to something," I replied tapping my finger on my lips. "I don't know what."

"Quit analyzing everything, Riss, and go get ready for dinner," he said and hung up on me.

Huh... I hadn't told Jake about dinner, yet he obviously had been speaking with Cole. I was gonna kick his butt when I saw him later. Make that two butts I was going to kick.

A half an hour later, I was getting out of the shower when there was another knock on the door. I wrapped the towel securely around me and opened to the door to the most beautiful Calla lilies I had ever seen. The bouquet was so huge, it was hiding the delivery person. Opening the door farther to allow entrance, I gasped, "Cliff!"

After depositing the flowers on the table in the foyer, and with no other greeting, he instructed me, "Read the card, babe."

Quickly giving him a hug, I winked at him and teased, "They aren't from you?" Looking through the massive arrangement I didn't see a card, but what I did see made me stop cold.

A platinum heart pendant, hanging in the middle of the brightly colored lilies, was beautiful. It was simple, yet elegant with a cluster of diamonds in the shape of a flower on it, and sure enough, stuffed into the flowers beneath it was a card. Grabbing them both I looked up at Cliff and shook my head. I always hated when guys tried to buy my affection. "I can't…"

"Hush, and read the damn card," Cliff reprimanded me.

I tore open the card, which was really more like a note. Scanning the words, I nearly started crying right there on the spot.

Riss,

I'm sorry. Please wear the necklace tonight? I know I screwed up. I know that we both did things that we shouldn't have. It doesn't change the fact that I want to be with you. I want to be around you. I want to revel in your accomplishments, and be there to catch you when you fall. Please give me, no… give us… another chance?

Love,

Cole

"No tears, you'll be all blotchy for dinner." Cliff pointed at my dress. "Now, go get dressed."

I laughed at my eccentric friend and moved towards the bedroom still clutching the note and pendant in my hand. *What is he doing?* I realized then that it didn't matter what he was doing. I was completely and totally in love with him. My knees buckled, and I barely made it before I collapsed on the bed from his beautiful words, and the way my heart felt, finally stitched back together. Like my mother, the meaning of love had escaped me, until Cole. It didn't take much for me to see that I wasn't really mad about the lie. I had been scared of letting myself fall, when in reality I had already fallen and there was nothing I could do but hope to God that I never hit the ground. That Cole would be there to catch me.

COLE

Waiting in the restaurant for Riss went against every instinct that I possessed. I wanted to pick her up at her door, to be with her as much as possible. My palms were sweating and my body was rigid when the hostess popped her head in and winked at me with a smile. Or, she might have been flirting with Jake who simply smirked at her over his glass of brandy. *Huh, that was highly unusual, my brother not giving the cute hostess the time of day. Maybe he really was turning a new leaf.*

"She's here. They are bringing her back now," she whispered to us before she left.

Jake stood up and clapped me on the back. "Stop stressing out. She loves you. She never even cried a tear over me, bro. You're it. Tell her about the move. Tell her everything. It's all you can do and hope she doesn't let her fear win over."

He walked over to the door and gave me a genuine smile, then turned to Rissa. "Hey doll, you look beautiful. Don't let the over grown ape push you around. Come on, Cliff, let's go get a drink while these two talk."

"That sounds like a fabulous idea." Cliff gave her a final hug before taking off with Jake.

I barely noticed the exchange. My eyes were glued to her. She looked amazing in that green sequined dress with the pendant hanging from her neck looking perfect, just like I knew it would. She smiled shyly as I stepped towards her and kissed her cheek. "You look incredible," I said, my voice rough. I moved to back away but she clutched my shirt in her hands.

"Cole, I'm sorry. I never should have run. I was scared of what I felt for you. I never should have leaked the marriage license, but I just felt..."

"What do you feel for me, Riss?" I whispered staring into those gorgeous violet eyes.

"I never knew what love was until I met you, Cole. It's insane and I don't know how or why it happened so fast, but when I found out about Jake, I was terrified that you were just like him, and the fact you lied, just proved my point, but it doesn't matter because I love you so much, Cole. I didn't realize how much until I got your note today. I don't want to be without you."

Pulling her close, I crushed my lips to hers forcefully. The weight in my chest lifted and I felt better than I had in weeks, hell *years.* She was mine and there wasn't a damn thing anyone could do or say to change that. The kiss turned possessive and I growled when her body melded to mine. It seemed like the blink of an eye before she broke the kiss. She was smiling bright and we were both out of breath. "We still have to talk, and I'm hungry."

"Yes," I agreed because I would agree to anything if it meant keeping her. Never taking my hand off of her waist, I led her over to the table and pulled her chair out for her. She smiled at me and sat down as I made my way to sit across from her.

"I still think we should go through with the divorce," she rushed out and I flinched. I opened my mouth to speak but she cut me off. "No, no, hear me out. We don't have to be married to stay together and that way the press will leave you alone. They won't have any reason to follow you around anymore." She picked up the glass of water and took a sip, never taking her eyes off mine.

"I don't care about any of that. I could care less if they follow me around for the rest of my damn life. All I care about is you, but I think you're right. I think the divorce is the right thing to do because when we get married for real I want it to be a day you will never forget."

"How is this going to work, though?" Her face fell at some sudden realization. "You're leaving. I don't even know where you're going."

I laughed then, I couldn't help it. She was completely and utterly clueless. She shot me a disgruntled glare and I laughed even harder. "I'm sorry, you look so cute when you pout. Babe, the new hotel is in LA. I was going to surprise you."

"Wh-what? You mean?"

"Yup, I'm moving to LA as soon as the divorce proceedings are over." I don't think I had ever seen anyone move so fast in my life until she flew into my arms and nearly toppled the chair I was in. I had never been happier than I was in that one blissful moment when she kissed me hard and I knew that what we had was going to last forever.

"So, we're really gonna do this?" I asked between kisses.

"Yes, this is all I ever want to do, now shut up and kiss me."

"Yes ma'am," I chuckled and did just that.

RISSA

Five months later...

The trendy upscale restaurant was packed to capacity when I got there. Cole said he had to work late at the hotel and he would meet me. It wasn't really our type of place, but I had heard the sushi was great. Walking up to the hostess, I felt like I had eyes on me, which was nothing new. People recognized me everywhere I went.

The Golden Globe announcement for nominees the week before seemed to skyrocket my fame even more. I was nominated for two by myself and the show was nominated for two more. The episode where Maria's character got killed off had broken all kinds of ratings records. I laughed when my producers told me that. People were just glad to see her gone.

The hostess smiled warmly at me and led me to a private room in the back. I should have known Cole would do that. He was always doing little things to ensure our privacy. We just wanted to be like any normal couple and go on dates, but since we were outed not long ago and dubbed the hottest couple in Hollywood, it had gotten more and more difficult to find any type of privacy. The hostess opened the door to the private room and winked at me. "Have a wonderful evening," she said in a dreamy sing-song voice as she walked away.

I looked at her in confusion and walked through the door. The entire room was filled with brightly colored lilies. The table was set with a crisp white table cloth and the whole room was lit by candlelight. None of that was what had my attention though. The only thing I saw was Cole, kneeling on the ground. I nearly melted until I saw the apprehension in his eyes.

"Cole? Baby, what are you doing?" I asked in a shaky voice.

"Rissa." His voice was rough and he cleared his throat and attempted to start again. "Riss, we haven't had the most conventional love story. It was actually pretty rocky there for a bit, but I have known since that first night in Vegas five years ago that we were meant to be together forever. Would you do me the honor of becoming my wife... again?" I nodded wildly, tears streaming down my face. I had no words to tell him my answer but he got to his feet, ring in hand, and closed the distance between us. Picking up my left hand, he slid the ring down and whispered, "I love you Rissa," before giving me a searing kiss.

Before I let it get to heated, I looked down and nearly laughed. "Where did you get this?"

"I found it when we were packing your stuff to move into the hotel, and I kept it. I figured you could wear it on our wedding day as something old. That ring is what brought us together, and it seems only fitting that it be the symbol of our love."

"But Cole, its huge," I said, looking at my original wedding ring. Before he could respond, I heard the door open.

"You're too quiet, Riss. I couldn't even hear if you said yes or not." Cassie said as she stomped through the door with a wide smile. She was absolutely glowing and I had to take a second look. "You know you have to wait at least a year so I can get all this baby weight off and be your maid of honor, right?" Holy crap, was my first thought. The woman just walked in after being away for six months and hello! She just sauntered in pregnant.

And if by the cute little mound growing she looked six-months pregnant. I shot Cole a worried look right before Eric strolled in the room with Jake and Cliff. I watched the smirk Cassie gave him then he stopped dead in his tracks and looked her up and down. The murderous look on his face was unlike anything I had ever seen cross Eric's handsome features, and damn if it didn't wipe that smirk right off her face as he tore from the room. Looks like my friend had gotten herself involved with a man that was way more than she bargained for. And if I knew anything after becoming good friends with Eric over these past months, Cassie was about to learn some serious lessons.

I took a step forward but Jake shook his head and took off after him. "Come here, darling. You did say yes, didn't you? Because if you won't I certainly will." Cliff winked at Cole who laughed good naturedly.

"Of course I said yes. I would never deny him anything." I smiled and looked into his eyes. Even with the tension between Cassie and Eric, this was still the happiest day of my life.

THERE'S SOMETHING ABOUT VEGAS

Author Note

Thank you so much to all of you amazing readers for reading There's Something About Vegas! I appreciate every single one of you. I always love hearing from readers so if you ever want to connect with me, just drop me a line on any of the stalker links I listed below!

If you enjoyed There's Something About Vegas then stay tuned because Vegas, Baby, the second book in the Las Vegas Nights series is coming soon. I'm sure you can't wait to find out what happens with Eric and Cassie!

26148073R00168

Made in the USA
San Bernardino, CA
16 February 2019